Hearts On Fire
ᴬ Tiger Lily's Café® Mystery
By Kathleen Thompson

Kathleen Thompson

Hearts On Fire

Volume 10

A Tiger Lily's Café® Mystery

By Kathleen Thompson

ISBN-13: 978-0-9984023-9-0

ISBN-10: 0-9984023-9-7

© Registration # TX 8-533-446

Library of Congress Control Number: 2018901562

The verses at the end of chapter 32 are from "They Call The Wind Maria," by Alan J. Lerner and Frederick Loewe, from the Broadway musical, *Paint Your Wagon,* 1951.

Kathleen Thompson

A List of Tiger Lily's Café® Mystery Series Books:

This cozy mystery series has everything you seek: an eclectic cast of characters, a mystery or two, and diligent detectives on duty. The detectives just happen to be feline.

Tiger Lily's Café is set in a Midwestern town nestled into the coast of a Great Lake. The setting itself acts as a character, bringing the reader into the sights, sounds and smells of the small resort community of Chelsea.

Read the series in order, or read any book alone. While characters grown and change, each volume stands alone with a clear beginning and a clear end.

- Turtle Soup (2014)
- Boo! (2015)
- Phishing (2015)
- Holiday (2016)
- A Rock And A Hard Place (2016)
- Splash (2016)
- Chasing A Butterfly (2017)
- Pumpkin Squash (2017)
- Snowblind (2017)
- Hearts On Fire (2018)
- Morel Of The Story (2018)
- Dragon Fire (2019)
- Beach Bunnies (2020)
- Shipwreck (2020)

Kathleen Thompson

Cast of Characters

Humans

Annie Mack, with the help of her "kids" and a talented staff, owns and manages a bed and breakfast, a cafe and other businesses on the south side of The Avenue. She has lived in Chelsea for only a few years, but her ancestral roots to the town date to the Civil War era.

Annie's SASHET Rainbow: (sa SHAY) a model that assigns color to each core feeling. **S**adness is blue; **A**nger red; **S**care green; **H**appiness yellow; **E**xcitement orange; and **T**enderness purple.

For more information, visit Liberation Psychotherapy: www.libpsych.com/articles/sashet/sashet.html.

Austin and Angela live in another state. They are the parents of Chris and have not been supportive of his career in the Coast Guard or his choice of a woman. Annie.

Ben and JoJo are college students. They work part-time all over town, including most of Annie's businesses.

Boone is the person to call if you need anything: mowing, snow removal, landscaping, maintenance, preventative maintenance, and just about anything else. He is married to **Harriet (Hilly),** who provides business cleaning services. His sons **Daryl** and **Donny** work for him. Their roots are in rural Appalachia, and they are so much more than people think.

Candice is the head waitress at Mo's Tap. A native of Chelsea, her long, thick, dark hair is the envy of most women who meet her. She is married to George.

Carlos is the manager and baker at Mr. Bean's Confectionary. He is a citizen of the US but was originally from Mexico. He supports his mother and younger sisters, who still live there. He is married to Isabel.

Cheryl inherited The Marina from her parents. It's a small deep water marina with basic amenities. Cheryl is married to Ray. She has known Annie since they were children.

Chris is Annie's special friend. They have committed to a permanent relationship that doesn't necessarily include marriage. He is the Officer in Charge of the Coast Guard Station. His stress relieving hobby is art. His watercolors and sketches – in charcoal, pencil and pastel – are sold for charity.

Clara owns the flower and gift shop, Bloomin' Crazy. She is a citizen of the US, originally from Haiti, and has an ebullient personality. She keeps The Avenue decorated with fresh and silk flowers year-round.

Daniela is a former professional baker from Mexico. She has been a mother figure to Isabel, who is married to Carlos. She and her adult daughters, **Rosa** and **Valeria**, now live in Chelsea

Diana is the chief instructor at L'Socks' Virasana (Veer AHS ana). She is Mem's daughter. Diana left home right after high school and did not speak to her mother until her return ten years later. Their relationship, while tenuous, continues to grow stronger.

Felicity is the chef at Tiger Lily's Café. She is young, perky and extremely talented in the kitchen. She manages the Café, the upstairs catering facility and outside catering operations.

Frank owns an antique shop, Antiques On Main. He and Mem are in a relationship.

Gema owns Gema's Creations. She makes and sells unique jewelry pieces from a space in the front corner of Antiques On Main.

George is the bartender and manager of Mo's Tap. He is a top-notch bartender and can be counted on to keep confidences. He is a volunteer with the local Coast Guard and is married to Candice.

Georgia manages the kitchen at the Bon Vivant Grille on weekends, coordinates catering for the Café, and cooks part-time at Mo's Tap. Her father, **Fred Calendar**, comes to town on occasion to see her and her daughter Frederica **(Little Fred)**.

Geraldine was the leader of the "it" crowd in high school, and somehow, life didn't turn out quite as she expected. Everything Annie isn't – perfectly dressed, perfectly coiffed, and perfectly awful – Geraldine is more than a thorn in Annie's side. **Everett** is her on-again-off-again husband.

Ginger is the daughter of Pete, the Chief of Police, and Janet. She works part-time at L'Socks' Virasana. Because she moved to town as a teen (when her father retired from the Marine Corps), and because she is one of the few African American teens in town, she sometimes feels like an outsider.

Greg is a progressive realtor in Chelsea. His goal is to get the right property to the right owner, always moving Chelsea forward.

Gwen is Annie's accountant. A motherly figure, her financial acumen is hidden from all but those lucky enough to have her in their corner.

Hank is a former member of the Town Council. He opposes Annie in every way.

Harry is the regular driver for the rental company used almost exclusively by folks on The Avenue.

Henrie manages the KaliKo Inn in an elegant manner. He does not invite confidences and speaks little about himself. Always formal in tone, people have difficulty pegging his accent. Is it French? Cameroon? Rwandan?

Holly and Jolly, twins, own DoubleGood, an electronics and hardware store. Holly lives in a wheelchair. Natives of Chelsea, they used to hate the names given them by their parents. Now, they enjoy the novelty of it.

Ian is a childhood friend of George. He coordinates local sporting and community events. He is light-hearted and fancy-free.

Isabel is married to Carlos. She is attending classes to become a citizen. She works with Carlos in the bakery and at Bon Vivant as the hostess.

Janet is Pete's wife. She spent twenty years as a Marine officer's wife. She traveled the world and is now living in Chelsea. She is an outsider, not having grown up here like Pete. She is the ultimate community volunteer.

Jennifer and Marie, sisters and nurse practitioners, own The Drug Store and The Clinic. Folks call the sisters before calling nine-one-one. Chelsea natives, they know everyone. And their secrets.

Jenny is an attorney who focuses on family law. She enjoys taking on cases that will right an injustice. She is always ready to engage in battle with those who don't believe a woman, much less a woman of color, can dance with the big boys.

Jerry learned how to make candy in a minimum security federal prison. He was not an employee. Jerry works hard to overcome his shyness, particularly around women.

Jet is from Puerto Rico. He moved in with Holly and Jolly, taking up residence with Holly. He works at Sassy P's Wine & Cheese.

Jerry is the candy maker at Mr. Bean's Confectionary. He learned how to make candy in a minimum security federal prison. He was not an employee.

Jesus manages Sassy P's Wine & Cheese and also selects the wines. His family, famous vintners in the Napa Valley, owned, farmed and made wine for generations before California became a part of the United States.

Joan is a member of the Town Council. She opposes Hank in every way. Clara's pet name for her is "Joan of Chelsea."

Juanita is a reporter for the local newspaper. As every reporter on every small town paper, she also sells ads, develops and places the ads, does photography and…reports.

Justin is a former bully boy who now works for Boone. Justin is making a break from his former bad partners and misplaced energy. He attends community college part-time.

Laila owns Babar Foods. A traditional Pakistani, she is raising her children without the assistance of a husband. Her children are **James**, **Ava** and **Carl**, who lives with Autism.

Marco is a police officer in Chelsea. He is "second in command" because he was the only officer that didn't go off-kilter during a hostage situation. Marco prides himself on being one-hundred-percent-Italian-American.

Martha used to own a bed and breakfast. The cottage was renovated to add an apartment suite, now occupied by Georgia and Little Fred. Martha is retired and enjoys spending time at the Inn.

Mem owns the health food store and cyber café, CyberHealth. Her wisdom is reassuring to everyone, including her daughter, Diana. She teaches the safe use of social media to all ages and has equipment and technology that is helpful to the small-town police department.

Minnie chooses perfect cheeses to accompany the rotating wine selections at Sassy P's Wine & Cheese. She comes from several generations of cheese makers in Wisconsin.

Nancy and Sam are Annie's mother and step-father. They have been married since Annie was a child. They come for extended visits in Chelsea and have learned to call this town their second home.

Pete is a native of Chelsea. He retired from the Marine Corps and is now the Chief of Police. Like Annie, his ancestors arrived in the Civil War era. His, however, came up via the Underground Railroad. He and his wife Janet have three children, the eldest of whom is Ginger. Clarice and Tamara are in high school and junior high.

Ramon is Clara's boyfriend. A Jamaican by ancestry, he plays saxophone with a jazz fusion band called Bergamasco (after the breed of his dog). He and Clara work hard to maintain their mostly long-distance relationship.

Ray owns and operates The Escape, a yacht fashioned into a cruiser for fishing, diving and pleasure. He is married to Cheryl; Chris is his best friend.

Teresa is a newcomer to the area. She came to this community to serve. She pastors a small church, Soul's Harbor, and pastors the community through her outreach.

Terrence & Jerald Timmer-Schmidt have just moved to town. Terrence is a heart surgeon; Jerald is a psychiatrist. They have opened a medical office building in town.

Trudie is the barista at Tiger Lily's Café. She is from Jamaica and ended up in Chelsea when a former boyfriend dumped her at the campground. Felicity saved her, and they have been the best of friends ever since.

WQVX Channel Two. "The Lake Region's good news station" is anchored by **Charles Veritone**. The "ace onsite reporter" is **Dan Tapper**. **Felix** does weather.

Annie's Cats

Annie has seven cats. Most people would call them "rescue kitties." From Annie's perspective, each of them rescued her.

Tiger Lily is a beautiful tabby cat with soft green eyes. She is the titular manager of Tiger Lily's Café, the main gathering place for Chelsea. She is generally calm and logical.

Little Socks is a bright-eyed black cat with white socks. She has a commanding personality and is small and sneaky enough to serve as a cat burglar. She spends time at the yoga studio, L'Socks' Virasana (Veer AHS ana).

Kali, Ko and Mo are litter mates. They shared a secret language as kittens; Kali and Ko now speak "cat," but Mo still speaks "secret." Kali and Ko can be found at the KaliKo Inn, a lakeside bed and breakfast. Mo spends time at Mo's Tap, an upscale blues bar.

Sassy Pants is aptly named; it's difficult to keep this little girl's attention. She is overly sensitive and will react out of emotion instead of reason. She entertains at Sassy P's Wine & Cheese.

Mr. Bean is the baby of the family and is mostly gray with traces of tiger. He has two speeds: fast and love me.

Other Companions

Brown Mousie lives in the long building and roams from the Café to the Wine & Cheese shop. He stays primarily at Sassy P's.

Claire is a blue point Himalayan cat whose human is Frank. She's beautiful and loves people. She is stand-offish with other cats.

Cyril is an English setter whose human is Pete, the Chief of Police. Cyril is friendly and calm. He is an excellent hunter.

Daryll is a multi-colored tabby cat with an air of perpetual confusion. His original human was the manager of the state park. Following his untimely death, Daryll was rescued by Tiger Lily and eventually went to live with Martha.

Fiamma is a Bergamasco. Dreadlocks cover her face. In fact, her entire body is covered with a combination of long dreadlocks and mats of hair. She is an outrageous flirt. Her human is Ramon.

Honey Bear is a large, golden, long-haired mutt of a cat who believes it is his perfect right to be anywhere. Other cats hate him. His human is Annie's mother, Nancy.

Jock is a Portuguese water dog whose human is Ray, the captain of The Escape. Jock is spirited and affectionate; he loves children.

Oscar McMurphy was a stray, named Scaredy Cat by Annie's cats. Despite the name, she is a girl who now lives with Holly and Jolly. She claims Holly as her very own. She is often in and out of the Inn and other places on The Avenue with her brother, Simon Finnegan.

Simon Finnegan was a stray, named Fat Cat by Annie's cats, who now lives with Holly and Jolly. He claims Jolly to be his mom. He is often in and out of the Inn and other places on The Avenue with his sister, Oscar McMurphy.

Sis is a dark gray giant schnauzer. Tiger Lily rescued her during a snow storm. Together, the kids introduced her to Chris, who is now her human.

Speckles is a tortoise shell cat, named for her orange speckles. She belongs to Georgia and is Little Fred's chief nanny.

Tillie came to live on The Avenue with her dreadful family from England. She is a Jack Russell Terrier and now lives with Carlos and Isabel above the Confectionary. She has free run of The Avenue, including the Inn. She is small enough to squeeze in and out of the cat doors.

Guests at the Inn

Brian & Janet Thomas are the new owners of the Chateau Simon Winery, set to open in the spring. They are staying in the carriage house. Simon, their cat, is a tuxedo with a pointy strip of white on his face.

Hearts On Fire

All of the guests in the main house are members of the computer-based lonely hearts club, Hearts On Fire. The group is meeting in Chelsea for several days spanning the weekend before Valentine's Day through the day itself.

Elena is a second generation Russian whose father has ties to the Russian mafia. This information is conveniently missing from her information form. She loves to tell people her name means "torch."

Farah is an exotic-looking beauty with an accent that no one has placed. It sounds faintly like Henrie's accent, a fact that is not lost on her. She is looking for a good time, not marriage.

Liz is a leggy blond. She is running out of family money and has signed up for Hearts On Fire to find a man to keep her in the style in which she is accustomed. This is her first group meeting.

Peggy is a fresh-faced and freckled redhead. This is her fifth group outing. She is bubbly on the outside and venomous on the inside.

Tiffany is short, curvy and dark-skinned. This is her second group meeting, but she has hooked up with a couple of men since signing up. She is becoming discouraged with her lack of success with the group.

Others In Town

Dan and Jenny Evans are investors in the winery. They live in Marsh Haven and are unknown in Chelsea.

Several members of Hearts On Fire stay in other bed and breakfasts or motels in town.

Women:

- **Charlie** has always lost the battle with her weight and has, for now, given up. She wants to find a man who accepts her as she is. This is her first outing.
- **Tonya** is a leggy blond and from the back looks like Liz. When she turns around, however, the first thing people see is a whip-like scar from the corner of her right eye to the middle of her chin.

Men:

- **Bob** is fit and well-put-together. His information form neglects to mention two prior marriages or that his money comes from a settlement from wife number one. He's always looking for someone to enhance his portfolio.
- **Brent** has just received a promotion and is making money that he never imagined. He is not looking for a soulmate at this event. He is trying to learn how to behave in circles where money is prominent.
- **Dorian** dresses and acts like a millionaire. His information sheet says he manages the family fortune, and that he is looking for someone who cares for him, not his money.

- **Fritz** has built a persona for himself. He introduces himself as being employed for a company that cannot be named. Is he, or isn't he?

- **Jim** is middle-aged and dumpy. His information form says he owns a multi-million dollar business but does not state the nature of the business. This is his first group outing.

- **John** is approaching elderly. He is looking for someone to replace his dear, departed wife. This is his fourth outing with the group.

- **Mike** is one of the younger men of the group. This is his first experience in the group setting, and he is unsure of himself.

- **Nick** is a very large man. His bank account is the same. His temper, unfortunately, matches both.

- **Paul** may be the only man genuinely looking for someone to love.

- **Thad** is middle aged, widowed, and lonely. Everything about him is middle-of-the-road. Mid-income, mid-height and weight, mid-looking. He's an accountant in a small town.

- **Tom** has stated his desire for commitment, leading to marriage. He has a taste for the exotic.

- **Travis** is in his late twenties and is the founder of Hearts On Fire. He is a whiz at computer programming. Not so much at human relationships.

Kathleen Thompson

1

Henrie gazed out the kitchen window at the still-nearly-dark February morning. The weather forecast called for a balmy day – just under freezing – with snow and icy rain. Lovely. And here he was, operating on about two hours of sleep. That would be the last time he would stay out late when guests were present.

He opened the oven door. Yes. The strata was nearly ready. He heard the front door open and stood to listen. It was Nancy. She said something in low tones. Judging by the sudden sound of growls and hisses from the dining room, he presumed she was speaking to her cat, Honey Bear.

Henrie could imagine a carrier door opening to reveal the large, orange and white, long-haired and haughty boy. And he could imagine a slow and regal march from a cat carrier to the dining room as the growls and hisses increased.

Anxiety in the dining room had reached a fever pitch, but Nancy, oblivious, walked past and into the kitchen.

"Good morning, Henrie. Breakfast smells heavenly."

Henrie knew Nancy would not hear the carnage as Honey Bear moved into a pile of seven household cats, displacing one, then another, until he found the best place to sit.

Not because she was deaf. Nancy was approaching what one would call elderly, but she heard everything she had a mind to hear. She did not have a mind to hear the angst caused by her precious Honey Bear.

Henrie set a cup of coffee in front of Nancy on the table. She took a deep breath. "I smell bacon. What did you make?"

"It is a strata, and it is nearly ready to come out of the oven."

"And what's in it besides bacon? And eggs, I presume."

"Spinach, Gruyère cheese, Greek yogurt. I soaked the strata overnight. The bread has fully absorbed the egg mixture. If I calculated correctly, the strata will be crisp on top and creamy on the inside."

"Henrie, you have never calculated incorrectly."

He smiled and turned to complete preparations for breakfast.

Henrie was the chief cook, bottle washer and toilet bowl cleaner of the KaliKo Inn, the largest and most highly-regarded bed and breakfast in the tourist town of Chelsea. It was a grand house from the post-Civil War era: three stories with a wrap-around porch in front and a white sand beach in back.

The Inn and the town were nestled into the sunset side of a Great Lake, surrounded on two sides by a wooded state park. The town almost seemed to be cut off from the rest of the world, and the Inn was a world unto itself.

Managed by the soft spoken, mind-reading, coffee-colored and faintly French-accented Henrie, the Inn offered an elegant, yet casual respite for tourists.

Nancy was not quite a tourist, but she was a guest. She and her husband arrived the night before to stay on the ground level of the carriage house. This was their home-away-from-home. While their friends owned or rented homes in warmer climates, escaping from Midwest winters for several months each year, Sam and Nancy rented the honeymoon suite for a few weeks several times throughout the year.

It was a good arrangement for them. They could visit friends and enjoy resort amenities during every season. It was a good arrangement for the Inn. The couple paid a lesser rate, but then, they didn't get the daily attention that other guests received. And a paying guest is a paying guest, after all.

Henrie said, "I trust you found everything to your liking? I apologize for being unavailable when you arrived."

"Everything is fine, Henrie. Annie made sure we got settled. I hate getting here as late as we did, but, well, it couldn't be helped. Where were you? I asked Annie, but she just said you had the night off."

Henrie pretended he had not heard the question and changed the subject. "Do you like the new colors?"

"I think they're perfect. I got the new quilt out of the bag, but I wanted to wait until today to put it on. I want to throw the blinds open and look in the natural light. Do you want to come over and help? You can see the quilt for yourself."

"I would be delighted. We should wait until our guests are gone, but then, you must tour the other rooms with me."

A few months before, Nancy made five quilts in record time, each with a different color combination and each featuring a species of bird. Henrie and Annie waited until the slow month of January and redecorated each of the rooms. All that remained was to hang plaques on the doors for the newly-named rooms.

On this trip, Nancy brought a quilt for the honeymoon suite – the suite in which she now stayed – and several for the second floor of the carriage house.

Nancy chattered on as Henrie pushed forward with breakfast. He arranged breakfast breads – white, wheat, rye, pumpernickel and oat, three kinds of bagels, wheat and white English muffins and freshly baked Danish, some cheese and some apricot – as she told him about Sam's most recent workshop projects, the rainbow-colored quilts for the second floor of the carriage house, and Honey Bear's latest – and terminally cute – exploits.

As she talked about Honey Bear, the cats, underneath a table in the dining room, began a new round of howling and hissing. Henrie glanced at Nancy. Not a glimmer that anything at all was happening in the next room.

The cats were quiet by the time Annie got to the kitchen. Annie, Nancy's daughter, inherited the Inn and other businesses from her father, Nancy's first husband. A casual woman with straight, graying hair, she enjoyed life on the lake and her family of seven rescue cats.

Annie was quick to say her cats did the rescuing. Each and every one rescued her.

Annie's high cheekbones hinted at an American Indian ancestry, an ancestry that Nancy had recently revealed to be true. Annie's natural father was a member of the Cherokee nation. The family tree was a bit tangled in places.

On this Friday morning, Henrie thought Annie looked sleepy. She perked up as she inhaled. "Do I smell the strata? The one you made yesterday?"

"Yes. It is nearly ready."

"You made more than one, right?"

"I did. With a full house and carriage house, I hope that two will suffice."

"I'll just have a bite."

Henrie was facing the stove. He was certain she could not see his smile. "I may allow you to smell it. Touch it, no. Not until the guests have eaten."

He heard Annie sniff, then say, "How are you this morning, Mom? Did you and Sam sleep well?"

"After a fashion. Henrie, Sam sends his regrets not to see you first thing this morning. He's meeting Frank for breakfast at the Café."

"So there, Henrie. I can have Sam's portion."

"Perhaps."

Nancy asked, "Who is upstairs, Henrie? In the carriage house?"

Henrie finished plating breakfast meats: bacon, ham, whole hog sausage and chicken sausage links. As he turned to take the strata and the French toast casserole out of the oven, he answered.

"The owners of a new vineyard, called Chateau Simon. It is scheduled to open in the spring."

Annie added, "Their house sold, and they moved in two weeks ago while they look for a home here."

"Do they have a dog?"

Annie answered. "A cat. Simon. A tuxedo. Looks a lot like Little Socks, but with a wicked white slash from her nose to almost her eyes."

"That must be the problem."

"Is there a problem?"

"Honey Bear roamed the suite all night, and I kept hearing thuds from upstairs. It must have been that cat."

"I hate to say it…boy, do I hate to say it…but do you want to leave Honey Bear here? Until they get used to one another?"

"Oh, honey, he'd love it. He just loves to play with your cats."

Henrie turned back to the stove to hide his smile.

Nancy said, "You have a full house here, too?"

Henrie answered as he spooned brown sugar, cranberries and walnuts into the oat groats. "It is a club of some type."

"A club?"

"They have taken over the town. Our five rooms were reserved by five women. I believe we can count ourselves lucky in that women called to make their reservations first. I shudder to think what would happen if both men and women had reserved rooms."

"Why?"

"It is a computer-based lonely hearts club, called Hearts On Fire."

"You're kidding. What are they doing in Chelsea?"

Annie said, "The coordinator – some computer guy from Chicago – thinks having get-togethers in smaller towns will lead to, um, bigger commitments."

"Does anyone know anyone else?"

"I don't know. Henrie, did the women say anything when they arrived?"

"No. They arrived at different times, from late morning through mid-afternoon. I believe they left at approximately the same time shortly before I left the house."

"Lots of club members were at the winery last night. They wear a thing that identifies them to others. The women wear a cloisonné brooch. It's shaped like a heart with a black background. Most of the heart is covered with orange and red flames. The men wear red hearts on a stick pin."

"I trust the jewelry will serve two purposes."

"Two?"

"Yes. One is to identify themselves to one another. The second is to say to anyone else in town, 'hands off.'"

"Henrie!"

He turned to look at her. "Not that you would be tempted. Some in town, however, may have other ideas."

"Like who?"

"Ian comes to mind. He enjoys meeting single women."

"You're right. This could be an interesting week. Oh. Come to think about it, Geraldine was there last night. I'm trying to think…um…yeah. She was talking to a couple of the men."

"An interesting week indeed. Were our guests there?"

"I kept my distance. It's possible they were, but I'm not sure. Clara and I stayed at the bar and talked to Jet. He kept us current on who was doing what with whom. Anyway, did our guests tell you what time they'd be up?"

"Each indicated a preference of eight o'clock. We should see them soon. By the way, I Googled the club this morning. One of our guests is the featured woman for January."

"This is February."

"The coordinator has probably been too busy putting this event together to update the page. Would you care to see?"

"Sure. Is this something like Playmate of the month?"

"I believe they call it the Monthly Flame."

"Gag me with a spoon."

"I would rather not." Henrie sat at the computer and found Hearts On Fire. In the top right corner was the photograph of a tall, blond, Nordic-looking woman. The caption read, "Elena, nicknamed 'Torch' by those who know her, is an artist from the Midwest. She is looking to set someone's heart afire."

"I saw her last night. She's even prettier in person."

"I agree. Did you see the man?"

On the bottom left corner was a picture of a handsome man in a silk suit. The caption read, "Dorian will take time from managing the family fortune to woo the woman of his dreams."

"Egad. Do people believe this crap?"

"Apparently. I gather this is a marketing ploy to pull people to the club."

"You'd think they would see through it. Anyway, to answer your question, yes, I did see him. He spent time with a lady lonely heart and Geraldine."

Peggy looked at the view from her deck. Her room at the Inn faced the state park. It was winter, and the trees were at their worst. But between the Inn and the trees was an open space, probably used as a town or private park. She could see the lake, and a marina was in the distance.

She would not do this again. This was her fifth attempt to find a man. At least it was her fifth group outing. She could no longer afford to do this. Her credit cards were maxed out, she had not made a house payment in two months, and the electric company threatened to turn off her power if payment was not made by next week.

She brooded. It was her pride, and that vindictive side that she couldn't control. She wondered if she would miss playing with Travis. That part had been fun. However, she had almost blown it the night before.

After her argument with Travis, she slammed two wine coolers and said more to that guy Fritz than she had intended. But it turned out okay. Better than okay.

Peggy reached into her purse and pulled out the wad of cash Fritz had given her. It was enough to bring her mortgage and utilities up to date. If she could get what he needed, she would have enough to pay her credit cards down to a manageable level.

And buy something nice for herself. She would limit herself to two hundred dollars.

By eight thirty, Annie decided it was time to go, guests or no guests. She walked to the dining room, lifted a corner of the table cloth and poked her head in. Eight cats looked back at her. One was insolent. Seven were angry.

Annie held her ground and looked at the seven angry ones. The sign on top of the table read "Nine Cats Detective Agency." It originally read "Seven," but after a heroic adventure, two of their neighborhood friends had been added.

The cats were sensitive, intelligent and, truth be told, better detectives than most humans that were paid to do the job. The trouble was, they had difficulty telling the humans what they needed to know. They had yet to meet a human who had mastered the art of speaking "cat."

Annie was smart. But she wasn't smart enough. Henrie was very smart. He wasn't smart enough, either.

Tiger Lily, glaring at Annie, finally roused herself. *"Come on. It's time to go to work."*

Six cats stood slowly. Honey Bear yawned, stretched, and kicked two cats in the process. Growling, they walked out from under the table and followed Tiger Lily.

Two large dilute calicos walked to the library, tails high in the air, back ends moving back and forth, on their way to a nap on the dining room windowsill. They were Kali and Ko, for whom the KaliKo Inn was named. They would spend their day napping, helping Henrie with the food – which meant they would pick up what fell on the floor – and visiting with guests when appropriate.

Kali was already in high dudgeon. She loved men. Not. One. Single. Man was in residence, if you didn't count the male half of the couple in the carriage house. She rarely went to the carriage house, so he didn't count. The cat, though, might need additional investigating. His name was Simon. It sounded like he would be moving to town.

Tiger Lily and the rest gathered in the foyer, waiting for Mommy to walk them to work. Eventually, she finished saying goodbye to Grandmommy and joined them in the foyer. "Ready?"

Five cats looked up, expectant. Annie reached down to pick up Mo, who loved to be carried on her shoulder. "Let's go."

As they walked to the porch and down the steps, Annie said, "I hate to tell you this, but your Uncle Honey Bear will be staying at the Inn for a while. Apparently he isn't getting along with Simon."

Tiger Lily gave a low hiss and trotted forward swiftly, not looking back.

Annie and the other cats hit the sidewalk and hung a right. They walked up Sunset Avenue, known as The Avenue by locals, and headed for the next building, a long, two-story post-Civil War era building. It held five storefronts, all belonging to Annie. All named for her cats.

At Sassy P's Wine & Cheese, the first business they reached, Annie slowed. Sassy Pants, a multi-colored, sometimes blank-eyed little tabby, looked up and spun off. She ran through the cat door, a staple in all of Annie's interior and exterior doors, to start her day.

The next place was Mr. Bean's Confectionary. The young gray cat, strong and with two speeds – fast and love me – peeled away with a swish of his tail. No one could tell if the outstanding baking and chocolate-making drew in hundreds from the region, or if Mr. Bean's antics in the window brought them in. It was probably both.

Annie put Mo on the ground as they reached Mo's Tap, a blues bar known for its artisan beers. Mo rushed through the cat door, long gray hair flowing in the breeze. He hated to be outside more than absolutely necessary. He was made for loving. Mo would take a nap and ready himself for the first female customers, who would arrive in a couple of hours.

At L'Socks' Virasana, Annie's yoga studio, the tuxedo cat with bright green eyes, Little Socks, walked in quickly. She jumped to the windowsill and was making a black cushion comfortable before Annie got past the storefront.

When Annie reached Tiger Lily's Café, she was by herself. Tiger Lily had not slowed. She sat at her post, on top of the hostess stand, in a huff. When Annie walked in, she turned her back and cleaned her claws.

Annie rolled her eyes, something learned from her mother, and shook her head. She waved good morning to Trudie, the barista and only Jamaican in town, and walked to the kitchen.

Felicity had a really big knife in her hand and was buried in prep work. Normally perky, this morning, she looked anything but.

"Hey, Felicity. What's up?"

"We seem to be having a Friday the thirteenth, and it's only Friday the ninth."

"What's wrong?"

"Well, it doesn't help that I got in really late last night. I'm working with about two hours of sleep. And then that Flaming Hearts group..."

"Hearts On Fire..."

"Yeah, them. They're supposed to start their fabulous weekend here tonight, but Bon Vivant has a problem."

The Bon Vivant Grille was Annie's foray into fine dining. The Café was eclectic and chic and was the gathering place for most of Chelsea, residents and tourists alike. It was open from early in the morning until mid-afternoon six days a week.

One of the cooks at Mo's Tap desired a challenge, and the Café was available nights. Annie and her staff rose to the occasion and hosted Bon Vivant at the Café on Friday and Saturday nights. Throw linen tablecloths and napkins on the tables, add a bright floral piece, and viola! A fine dining restaurant was born every weekend. Maybe.

"What's the problem?"

"Cookie. He called this morning and quit."

"Quit?!"

"Quit. Something about his mother or grandmother or maybe a cousin. Someone is sick, and he's moving home. Back to Minnesota."

"Today?"

"Today."

"Oh, no! How bad is it? Well, I know it's bad. Forget that. What do you need from me?"

"I don't know yet. I put out a text SOS to everyone. Georgia said she can run the kitchen, and she's pretty sure she knows how to make everything. Isabel is coming in early to make sure the dining room is set up. She's going to call Rosa and Valeria to see if they can help out in the kitchen. I'm doing some prep work, based on his menus for the weekend."

Felicity pointed with her really big knife to a pile of fresh fruits and vegetables in her secondary kitchen. "When I'm not keeping my own kitchen open, that is."

"Can I call someone else in to help?"

"Already done. I texted Ben and JoJo. JoJo has a free day today, and she'll be here soon. She's going to take over the prep work, and get with Georgia to see what else she can do."

"I should never worry. You always have everything under control. You're priceless, Felicity."

Felicity looked up, a bit of perk back in her eyes.

"Not priceless. I can be bought."

"Name it."

"I have a date. Bon Vivant is supposed to be open Wednesday, for Valentine's Day, and my next call was going to be to this guy I met…to tell him I had to cancel."

"No problem. We just need someone to step up and get things ready, right?"

"Right. Which means George would have to let Georgia off from Mo's Tap Wednesday. And Cookie had promised to cover me on Thursday morning before opening up at Mo's."

"You don't have anyone?"

"Not a soul. I had already asked and accepted no as an answer from all of my part-timers."

"Have you talked to George?"

"I haven't. I don't want to tell him why I need the help."

Annie sighed. "Do you want me to ask George?"

"Could you? Maybe tell him I had something that I couldn't miss? A funeral or something?"

"A funeral that's already scheduled for Valentine's Day."

"Or something. I don't want George to, you know, get a head start on teasing me."

"No problem. I'll think of something. Who's the guy?"

"Not telling."

"Where ya goin'?"

"Not telling."

Annie left the kitchen and made the rounds in the dining room, saying hello to her guests and giving her step-father a hug.

Travis sat at the desk in his hotel room. Nothing was going right. His headaches were getting worse. Sometimes he had trouble seeing or walking.

His computer wasn't operating like it should. There were unusual popups. At times, everything slowed to a crawl. Then, without warning, it would go back to normal.

Last night had been a nightmare. That witch-with-a-b, Peggy, had cornered him at the winery and called him all kinds of vile names. Later, he saw her in the corner talking with Fritz for several minutes.

That reminded him, he wanted to look at Fritz's information again.

He entered the password, opened the Hearts On Fire folder, and navigated to Fritz's file. What was it that had caught his eye?

For profession, Fritz had entered "United States Government Top Secret." Was that how they identified themselves? If you worked for the government, didn't you have a cover story, like a made-up occupation?

To be fair, no one's private information – information that could lead to identification by persistent suiters – was in this particular database.

The public database contained a "face sheet" that could be viewed and printed by any member. The information contained in the face sheet was general in nature. Members could view and print photographs as well.

This database also contained information that only Travis could access, information that could help him as he connected men and women. Some private information was contained here, but nothing that could identify the member. For example, a member might have given a specific reason for joining the club or might have expounded on preferences or non-starters.

Things like the actual name of the employer, town and state of residence, date of birth, even last names, were in a separate, private database that was not connected to the internet. That computer was in the bottom dresser drawer. Under his socks.

He opened Charlie's file for what was probably the one hundredth time. All of her pictures were adorable. She carried a significant amount of extra weight, and she was cute. Fresh face, open eyes. He had fallen in love as soon as he saw her photograph. Last night at the winery, though, he couldn't make himself approach her. He tried to do it several times. Each time, he returned to his table in the corner and sipped a bit on his sparkling grape juice.

The pain in his head throbbed again. He closed his eyes, pressed his hands into his forehead and doubled over on the bed.

2

Sam and Frank sat at a table on the wall of windows. Sam gazed at the darkish, dampish clouds and said, "You know, my friends, a lot of them, are sitting someplace warm and sunny now. Texas, Florida, Alabama, Arizona. And yet, here I am."

"Are you ready to ditch the arrangement? Get a home somewhere out there for the winter?"

"Oh, no. No, the ole gal and I are just fine with the change in seasons, and how many old folks have an innkeeper for a daughter? We'd be foolish not to take advantage."

Frank, Sam's best friend in Chelsea, was a relative newcomer. He moved to town to open an antique store – his life's ambition – and now enjoyed a mature relationship with a business owner on The Avenue, Mem. He enjoyed another partnership. Gema, a jewelry designer, rented space in the front of his store.

Frank looked around the room. "Hey, look, there's Greg. He's sitting by himself. Maybe he'd want to join us."

Sam turned and waved. Greg waved back and walked over. Sam asked, "Want to join us?"

"Sorry. I'm waiting on a client. It's good to see you, Sam. How long will you be here?"

"At least until the end of the month. We haven't been here since Thanksgiving."

"I thought it had been a while. Hey, this client I'm meeting, he's opening a new winery this spring. It's going to be really nice."

"It's amazing how many of those places can open and they all do well. And Sassy P's never seems to lose business."

"Well, Sassy P's is different. They purchase from all the local and regional wineries. Their hours are different and they serve food."

"Annie keeps telling me that, but it's hard for me to wrap that around my old head."

"Yeah. Old like a fox. Oh, here's my guy. Frank, it's good to see you. Sam, let's get together soon."

A server delivered breakfast. Over lemon-strawberry pancakes covered in honey and fresh berries, Frank told Sam everything he knew about the people in town for the week. The Hearts On Fire club.

Brian put his coat on and turned to Janet before leaving. "I'm serious. You've been working too hard. Take the day off."

"No. I want to finish painting the tasting room. Once I see the colors on the wall, it will be easier to shop for fixtures."

"You won't do any shopping for fixtures if we don't get these investors on board."

"Do you want me to be with you when you talk to them? I could go to the winery a little later."

"I won't be seeing them until noon."

"Noon? I thought you were going to see them this morning."

"I tried to get with them this morning. Actually, we were going to meet for breakfast, but they remembered something else they had to do. Greg had already told me he could be there, so I'll go ahead and meet him. Maybe he has news about a house. I'll hang out until noon to meet them."

"I don't mind. I prefer painting without you around. You distract me."

"Are you going to take Simon with you?"

"I was going to, but I'm pretty disgusted with him. He kept me awake all night. He would get on the counter, then jump down. Then get on the dresser and jump down. Then get on the back of the sofa and jump down. Then back to the counter. All night long. I almost put him in his carrier, but he would have screamed all night."

"Wonder what's up with him?"

"I saw some folks go into the downstairs room last night after you went to bed. It looked like they had a cat carrier. But that shouldn't be a problem. Simon likes cats."

"Maybe it was a ferret. Or a small dog. Did you hear barking?"

"No. I didn't hear anything, but I'll tell you one thing. In my next life, I want to come back as someone who can sleep like you."

Tiger Lily came out of her funk long enough to greet her Grandpoppy, Sam. She trotted to his table and jumped to greet him.

Lest the reader believe she was gauche enough to jump to a table top in the Café – which she does on occasion, but not often – Annie had fitted all of the tables with ledges on each side.

They were large enough for her to be seated, low enough for an easy hop, and high enough that she could reach to the table to suggest a menu item.

This happened most often with tourists. The menu warned them – Tiger Lily's interpretation was that the menu told them they might receive the honor – and nine times out of ten, they accepted her suggestions.

Frank and Sam had nearly finished their pancakes. She sat on a ledge and accepted her due. Full body pets with one hand as Grandpoppy finished breakfast with the other.

Once the petting stopped, she climbed to the table and lay in between their plates, slapping her tail every now and then. This was a favorite way to pick up gossip.

Frank said, "Gema is hoping to make a lot of money this week. She made several new pieces of jewelry in all of her metals: gold, silver, platinum. She used most of the gems she had in stock, too. Matter of fact, she asked if I would be able to drive to Marsh Haven to pick up more. I can't get away, though."

"When did she want you to go?"

"Today. The only free time I have, I'm using up with you. Even if I'd cancelled, that wouldn't give me enough time to do what she wanted."

"I can go. I don't have a single plan today. Maybe Nancy would enjoy the ride."

"That would be great. Come over with me when we're finished. Anyway, I hope she did the right thing. I did a little snooping on this group. They've gone to a few towns with these group meet-ups, and it's been a mixed bag."

"Mixed for who? Them? Or the town?"

"A little of both. Apparently, sometimes a real connection is made, and someone goes off to live happily ever after. Mostly, that doesn't happen. For the town, again, it's a mixed bag."

"How so?"

"Well, take Gema as an example. A newly in-love couple will come in, place an order for a beautiful one-of-a-kind piece, and of course it has to be different than her display piece. They want silver instead of gold, or an emerald instead of a ruby. She asks for a deposit, and then, what do you know? The couple doesn't stay together. The order is cancelled, she's made a piece that she now has to sell, and she has to give part of the deposit back."

"So what can she do?"

"She's going to ask for payment upfront, and it will not be refundable."

"What else? What about your shop, or Annie's places?"

"I'll have a little of the same, mostly with the larger furniture pieces. Everything else, people mostly walk out of the store with that in hand. The furniture has to be delivered, and sometimes, acceptance will be denied. At least, that's what I heard."

"How do you protect that?"

"Well, I'll have the money for the furniture, and I'll charge them up front for the delivery. Here's the deal. I won't actually deliver the furniture until a seven-day cooling off period elapses. They'll sign something about that. After seven days, I'll call, and if they still want it, I'll deliver. If not, I refund the money. Neither of us will lose."

"But the Café, the bar, the Winery, they should do well, right?"

"They will. A fight or two might break out, but other than that…"

Tiger Lily grew bored with the conversation. She moved to Greg's table. He was usually good for accidently dropping food in front of her.

When Tiger Lily jumped up, Greg asked, "Brian, have you met Tiger Lily?"

"Sure. I've seen her here and at the Inn. I haven't introduced her to Simon yet."

"You'll have to do that. They'll get along fine."

Greg accidently dropped some pieces of crumbled bacon in front of Tiger Lily. She helped by cleaning it up.

"Let's set up a tour this weekend. The family is moving at the end of the month. They're ready to sell, and I think it's just what you've been looking for."

"Great. Tomorrow or Sunday? Set it up, and we'll be there."

"Alright. So tell me about those investors. I know several people in Marsh Haven."

"Dan and Jenny Evans. They stopped by one day to take a look around, liked what they saw. They asked about the possibility of investing, and, hey, if they have money and are willing to sign a contract…. We haven't found anyone else willing to help financially."

"Never heard of them. I showed that property to another couple from Marsh Haven. This was before you were interested, of course. The deal fell through."

"Did they have experience? Did they see something…I mean…you're my realtor, but…did I make a mistake?"

"No, nothing like that. They couldn't get a loan. Yours went right through, but they couldn't qualify for a loan that size. They tried to get the former owners to come down on the price."

"I don't see how they could have. The building needed a lot of work, but the land is prime."

"You've done a good job renovating. And that deck and terrace? Wow!"

"Thanks, Greg. But, um, these people, do they want to invest? We could always use more than one investor."

"They were interested in owning their own place and being hands-on. I think they had a certain amount of money to purchase something, but they aren't flush."

Tiger Lily sighed. No more bacon. No gossip worth reporting. This was going to be a very boring day.

3

By noon, the Café was at full throttle. Annie helped, as always, wherever she was needed. She made and delivered coffee. She bussed tables. She greeted and seated guests. She stayed as far from the kitchen as possible. Almost everyone in town knew Annie was a disaster in the kitchen.

She seated Geraldine, one of her least favorite persons, at one of her best tables. This was part of her continuing smother-her-with-kindness campaign. As she handed over a menu and prepared to relate the specials, she said, "Geraldine, what a lovely dress. Do you want to hear the specials?"

Geraldine was everything Annie was not. Perfectly dressed, perfectly coiffed, perfectly made up, perfectly shod in three inch stilettos, and perfectly horrid.

She sniffed. "I am so tired of your compliments. Can't you just stop?" She drew the word "so" into two syllables.

"I'm sorry, no. I confess I'm a fan of everything Geraldine."

Annie felt as if her smile would crack her face. Unless she choked on her own words first.

"I'll wait to order when my guest arrives."

"Would you like coffee in the meantime?"

"Oh, alright. What are your specials?"

"Our specials, in honor of Valentine's Day, are Chocolate Kiss, Chocolate Cherry, and Rose."

"What's the Rose?"

"It's Turkish coffee with cardamom and saffron."

"That sounds dreadful."

Annie closed her eyes so Geraldine would not see them roll.

"Just give me coffee with skim milk and some of that fake sugar."

"Coming right up."

Annie stopped at the hostess stand on her way to the coffee bar. She leaned into Tiger Lily and asked, "Did you give her a hiss when she came in?"

Tiger Lily purred.

"Good. All rules about customer service go out the window where she is concerned."

At the bar, Annie asked for regular coffee, skim milk and fake sugar. Trudie, in the middle of making several specials, and with her back to the dining room, said, "Let me guess. Geraldine."

"Yep. Hey, who's Felicity dating?" Annie moved behind the bar. It would be better for all concerned if she poured Geraldine's coffee on her own.

"I don't know. She won't even tell me. She's going out of town to see him, though."

"Do you think it's someone we know, and she just wants to keep it a secret?"

"I thought about that, but I've run through everyone I know that's single, and nobody seems to fit."

"We need to keep our eyes open."

Tiger Lily heard and thought that she should do the same.

Annie seated five women, all wearing the cloisonné pin, and listened to their chatter as she walked them to a table in the middle of the room. Suddenly, she realized they were not following. She turned. They stood, staring at Geraldine's table.

A man wearing an expensive-looking suit with a heart stick pin had joined her. Annie had seen the man at Sassy P's the night before, and his picture was on the website. He had been talking to…Annie turned to look at the women. The blond. He'd been talking to the blond. And he left with the blond.

The women, almost as one, began walking again, nearly running Annie over.

"Oh. Pardon me. Here you are. Someone will be right over to take your drink orders."

As she turned, she nearly tripped over Tiger Lily, trotting to the table to, Annie supposed, do her duty as Café hostess.

Tiger Lily had other things on her mind.

Mo's Tap was not too busy for a Friday, but George wasn't fooled. The day was heating up to be wicked. Cookie had resigned, leaving a gap in his Friday cooking staff and putting pressure on Georgia, his second lead cook. She had to leave early to get ready for Bon Vivant's weekend activities.

With the lonely hearts club in town, this was not a weekend to be a cook short. He had long ago augmented his weekend staff because of Bon Vivant, but the absences still put a crimp in his style, so to speak.

Most of his noon crowd consisted of men from the Hearts On Fire club. He could tell because of the stick pins scattered around the room.

George looked at Mo. It was rare that no women were at the Tap. Mo decided that if he were to find one, he would need to stick close to George. He lay in a lush position close to the clean glasses, his long, fluffy tail curving around stems and slapping rims.

George smiled to himself. He loved the boy.

One man, a red stick pin on his collar, had seated himself at the bar. He wasn't necessarily following club rules, which strongly recommended he introduce himself only to fellow club members. He said something to Candice that caused her to waggle a wedding-ringed finger under his nose. She then pointed to George as the other half of her life and moved on.

Now he moved to sit next to a local woman who worked at the bank. George knew her as a co-worker of his best friend Ian. He wandered to that end of the bar to say hello.

"Hey, Kelly. Are you here for a to-go order?"

"Um, yeah, George. It should be ready by now."

"I thought I noticed Ian's burger." George turned to the window between the bar and the kitchen, saw the package going up and reached for it. As he took her money, he said, "Make sure you tell him I said hello."

George made eye contact with the man. He knew Ian and Kelly weren't dating, but he wanted to give her a little cover to get away.

Kelly gave him a grateful smile and slid off the stool.

Alone with the man, George asked, "Can I get you another drink?"

"No." He sighed. "I just don't seem to have any luck with girls. Looks like you're doing okay." The man motioned with his head toward Candice.

George noticed that Mo had followed. Mo lay on the bar in front of the man, long tail tapping into the bowl of Hershey's Kisses. The man reached a hand automatically and began to stroke the long, gray-haired body.

"I got lucky. Looks like you're a member of that club. Aren't there mixers and other ways to get together with women?"

"Yeah. I tried to introduce myself a few times last night, but...nothing doing."

"Why not? I mean, you look okay. I'm close enough to you to know you smell okay, at least to a guy. Do you have a hard time talking to women?"

"I didn't when I was younger. Maybe I give off a vibe. Maybe I'm too desperate. And you know, I'm not as rich as most of the other guys. Girls like men with money."

Mo curled his front paws around the man's lower left arm, pressing against his wrist in a slow, rhythmic beat.

"Well, if what I've seen is any indication, you appear to be younger than most of the other guys. Maybe that's why you aren't as rich. You haven't had time. And how would they know, anyway?"

"We get information sheets on all the people here. Most of the men include their net worth."

"That's a little, um, let's go with strange. Is all of the information accurate?"

"Well, probably not."

Mo moved closer and curled his tail around the man's upper left arm.

"Come on. You can tell me. What did you lie about?"

"Well, I said I was thirty-five."

"You aren't a day over twenty-eight."

"Twenty-seven."

"Why'd you do that?"

"I want girls to think I'm more mature, you know, settled."

George sighed. He should keep his mouth shut…just keep it shut…just shut up. But he couldn't help himself. "By the way, I'm George."

"Pleased to meet you. I'm Mike."

"Mike, you haven't asked for my advice…"

"Please! I'd love some!"

"First thing? You are meeting women. Women, not girls."

"I know that."

"Then change your language."

"What?"

"You're calling them girls. I noticed you say 'men' instead of 'boys,' but you're stuck on 'girls.' Think before you talk."

"Why's that even important? Woman. Girl. Both the same."

Mo gave a low hiss, grabbing the attention of both Mike and George.

George continued. "If you call a pre-teen a girl, you're okay. If you call a teenager a girl, you're flirting with disaster. If you call an adult a girl, you've passed disaster and you're on the way to oblivion."

"Well...I can't see that it means anything, but if you say so. I'll try to pay attention."

Mo sighed and slapped Mike's shoulder with his tail, once again pressing his paws in rhythmic time against his wrist.

Mike said, "What else?"

"Don't act desperate. Maybe you come on too strong. You've had one drink, and you've hit on two women that I've seen. Maybe more, before I was paying attention."

"I want to get in there before someone else has a chance."

"Play hard to get. At least a little."

"How do I do that?"

"Hold onto that thought, Mike. I have a customer. Don't talk to a woman until I come back."

Mo watched as George moved to the front corner of the bar. Then he looked into the face of the young man. He thought he would be most useful sticking with this guy for a while. If anyone knew about love, it was Mo.

George greeted another young man. He didn't have the signature red heart stick pin. He had a larger one, a heart with a flame superimposed. "Help ya?"

"Yes. I'm looking for Cookie?"

"Cookie quit. He doesn't work here anymore."

The man's eyes grew large and his face turned gray. It looked to George as if the man had stopped breathing. Finally, he blurted, "Quit? How? When?" He grabbed a stool as if to sit, but continued to stand. "What am I gonna do?"

"Uh…I don't know? Who are you?"

"I'm…I'm…uh…Travis? I'm in charge of the…uh…stuff this week?"

"Oh. I see. Well, I probably should have tried to reach someone, but I didn't have any information."

"I was…uh…pretty much working with him. Oh, this is a disaster."

"Not necessarily. We're pushing ahead with the restaurant activities, and, well, there are a couple other things going on, right? There's a buffet tomorrow and a dinner Wednesday night…"

"Yeah…"

"Well, we'll have the food. Do you need anything else?"

"Well, yeah! Everything is scripted! Especially tonight! Down to the last detail! Who sits with whom, who gets special treatment, what happens when a couple hooks up… It's scripted!"

"Was Cookie involved with that?"

"Yeah! He has all the notes!"

"Just a sec." George moved to the serving window. "Hey, Georgia, got a minute?"

Georgia was cleaning up, turning her cooking duties over to other staff. She walked to the window and leaned in. "What's up?"

"Do you know anything about scripting stuff? Who sits with whom, what happens for special people or hook-ups?"

"Oh. I forgot all about that. Cookie said something about that, but he didn't share any of the details."

"Did he keep notes?"

"I'll look. I'll tell you what, George, I can't handle that on top of taking over for him."

"I won't ask you to. Look for notes, and then get out of here. I'll think of something."

George stood at the window, giving Travis a 'just a minute' sign with his hand. Travis played with a bowl of Hershey's Kisses, touching them, picking them up, squeezing them into odd shapes. George sighed. Another bowl that would have to hit the trash.

He looked through the window and watched as Georgia rifled through a filing cabinet. She pulled out a file and looked through it. On her way out of the kitchen, she handed the file to George, keeping several sheets of paper in her own hands.

"He had some notes not related to the food. I'm taking the menus and recipes."

"Okay. I'll handle it. Or something."

George walked back to the end of the bar slowly, reading through the notes as he went.

"I think these are all things we can handle, but I'm going to have to have someone else take care of it. Can you come back or give me a call in about half an hour?"

"Half an hour? This is a disaster! I'll just sit right here. Give me a drink."

"Sure. What'll it be?"

"Virgin Mary. Extra hot and heavy on the olives. And bring me something to soak it up. Crackers, maybe."

George tried not to laugh as he moved away to make the drink. After he put it on the bar, he went to the other end, pulled out his cell phone and called Mr. Bean's.

"Carlos, George. Is Isabel in?"

"Getting ready to leave. She's doing extra duty getting ready for tonight."

"She might be doing more. Have her stop here before going to the Café."

4

While Mike waited for George, he enjoyed the luxurious long hair that was Mo. From his head to his tail, the cat was one sexy little piece of work.

He sighed. He really wasn't cut out for this meeting women stuff. He wasn't cut out for anything. He had yet to find the perfect job, his niche in the world.

He turned to look at the men in the bar. He had seen several of them the night before. They seemed confident enough, but if he were making decisions, he would have introduced them to women to which they weren't drawn.

Like the one that was looking for true love. He needed to get with the redhead. And the accountant. He would be happy with someone like...was her name Charlie?

Oh, well. He wasn't a matchmaker. He couldn't even figure it out for himself.

At Mr. Bean's Confectionary, Carlos, the manager and head baker, watched a tiff taking place. He didn't know what was being said, but he saw the bopping and nipping and heard hissing and snarling.

Mr. Bean bopped Tillie on the nose and said, *"It was my turn to dance. You got all the last people."*

Tillie, a Jack Russell Terrier who called Carlos her human, nipped Mr. Bean's tail and said, *"I did not. It was my turn. You're being selfish."*

Bop. *"Am not."*

Nip. *"Are too."*

Two pawed bop. *"Not!"*

Suddenly, two large feet, connected to two long, thick legs, and a torso that seemed to reach to the moon stood in between them. Carlos said, "Children, if you can't behave, you will have to go home."

He returned to the counter and filled the muffin bin with selections of fresh-out-of-the-oven muffins. Coconut mango, spiced pear, peach and spiced tea, and lemon sesame.

Mr. Bean ran to a table and lay down underneath it, his back to the counter and the window. Tillie, surprised that he had ceded his place, ran to the window to dance for customers.

Isabel called from the kitchen. "Carlos, are there only two desserts for Bon Vivant?"

"Yes, dear. Cookie and I decided to pare down the menu to something more manageable. We'll have to take care of special diets by prior request only. It was…well…too much."

"I'm glad. Well, I'll be going over in a few minutes. I'll crate these up. What are they called?"

"The little pots are salted caramel pots du crème, and the tarts are chocolate-on-chocolate maple almond."

"I'm going to gain ten pounds a year just being married to you."

Isabel was recently married to Carlos. He had lived in Chelsea for several years and had become a citizen, sponsored by Annie's father. Isabel was from his hometown in the central part of Mexico. She and his family members were in the process of becoming citizens.

Isabel worked at Mr. Bean's and also served as hostess for Bon Vivant on weekends. This weekend, pressed into extra duty because of Cookie, she called her two sisters-in-law, Rosa and Valeria, and asked them to help Georgia cook.

In Chelsea generally, and in Annie's businesses particularly, disasters were handled by family. One did not have to be related to be blessed with the occurrence.

Carlos smiled, trying to imagine his darling Isabel getting larger and larger over the years. That would not be a bad thing. She would still be Isabel.

He looked up. Brian, the owner of the new winery, came into the door with two people who looked vaguely familiar.

"Brian, it's good to see you. Have you found a house yet?"

"Maybe. We're going to look at one this weekend. It will be great to have our own furniture. The carriage house is nice, but...we're still living out of suitcases."

"I know the feeling. Are you here for lunch?"

"Yes. I'm going to have that honey grilled chicken and swiss and a cup of Texas chili. Dan, Jenny? Lunch is on me. What will it be?"

Carlos tucked the names away. They were not the names he expected to hear, but he couldn't put his finger on it. They didn't seem to recognize him, so he paid no more attention.

"We're light eaters. We'll split that Cajun turkey melt, and we'll each have a cup of baked potato soup."

Carlos pointed them to the few tables and said, "Light business today. You have your pick of tables."

They happened to pick the table under which sat a sulking Mr. Bean.

Mr. Bean moved to the side of the table that didn't have feet. He curled up, ready to stay in his sulk, until he heard the beginnings of the conversation.

"If I listen hard, I'll have something to tell Tiger Lily," he thought.

Once seated, Brian asked if they were happy with what they had seen to date.

Dan answered. "We've been very pleased. It's looking very nice. Very nice indeed."

Jenny added, "I think the inside is going to be beautiful. Has Janet finished painting yet?"

Brian answered, "Hopefully today." He then laid out their plans for the winery. He wanted them to be excited, then he would ask for a specific amount. He and Janet had calculated it to the last detail, including payback.

"We signed off on the construction documents – you know, the renovations – right after that winter storm in December. Since then, we've been working on the interior. We've finished everything but the tasting room, and…"

Dan interrupted. "So you've got insurance now, right? You have occupancy?"

"Yes. We're progressing on schedule…"

Dan interrupted again. "What about the wine making itself?"

"The fermentation and storage tanks are in, and we'll plant this spring. Several acres are planted from the former winery, but we'll change out some of those grapes and add to them. For the first year, and maybe into the next few, we'll have to rely on purchased grapes, but we have enough land to handle almost all our needs. We'll develop our..."

Jenny broke in. "Tell me about the décor."

"We're going for an upscale look. You've walked around on the inside. Everything is polished walnut and teak, a combination of recessed and pendant lighting, and every wall to the outside has a large percentage of..."

Dan didn't let him finish. "How much work is left to finish that terrace?"

"The concrete was poured before it got cold. There are entries from both the first and second..."

Dan interrupted again. "I hear you've got quite a bit of competition in the region."

"Yes. There are several wineries in the area. The winery with the best reputation is the Blue Bottle, and it's just..."

Jenny couldn't wait for him to finish. "That can be a problem."

"Research has shown that it is more of a benefit..."

Dan, again. "I like a good moscato. You gonna make moscato?"

"Yes, that's one..."

Isabel delivered their lunches. "Excuse me. Here are your meals."

Jenny looked up with a smile. "I'll think we'll take this to go. Do you have a container for the soup?"

Annie stopped at the hostess stand. "Lily, I have to talk to George on the way home. Do you want to go with me, or go on to the Inn? It's drizzling. Rain and sleet."

Tiger Lily answered by jumping down and trotting out the door before Annie had her coat buttoned. She stood at the window of the yoga studio and patted the window with her paw.

As Annie left the Café, she saw Little Socks join Tiger Lily. They made their way to the Inn, stopping at each place – with the exception of Mo's – and gathering the rest of the cats.

Annie stepped into Mo's. George was at the other end of the bar, leaning in and talking earnestly to a young man. For some reason, Mo was there as well, stretched out onto the bar and curled around the man's left arm.

George saw her and stood. She waited at the end of the bar. "Everything okay?" he asked.

"Sure. How's everything here, now that you're a cook short?"

"I put a blast on social media, Word travels fast when there's an opening."

"I need to talk to you about next week."

"Bon Vivant is open on Valentine's Day."

"Yes. We'll need Georgia Wednesday, and we'll need her Thursday morning."

George put his elbows on the bar and his head in his hands. This was a classic thinking pose. "Okay. I'll call Ben. He's great as a fill-in cook and can generally come in afternoons and evenings. But what's up with Thursday morning?"

"Cookie had promised to cover Felicity before coming over here to open up. Georgia is the perfect person to ask. It's not taking anything away from you on that day, but she's going to end up with some sweet overtime that week."

"What about JoJo?"

"She's filling in for Henrie at the Inn."

"Henrie's off?"

"Short break. Wednesday afternoon to Thursday afternoon. I only need to cover one breakfast, and it's a light day. The lonely hearts people leave that day. Anyway, JoJo isn't available."

"And you're sure Felicity can't change her plans."

"Nope. They're cast in stone."

"Plans can't be cast in stone unless they involve a wedding or a funeral…wait, is someone getting married?"

"Not that I know of."

"Then what?"

"Well…maybe it's a funeral."

"On Valentine's Day. Six days from now. Pre-scheduled. Annie, come on."

"Well, I promised her I wouldn't tell…"

"She has a date, doesn't she? Why doesn't she want me to know?"

"I think it has something to do with teasing?"

"Me? Tease? I'd never!"

"You do. You have to promise me not to say anything. I told her I would give you an excuse that would give her some cover."

George laughed. "I can't wait to tell Candice."

"George!"

But he was walking away, back to the customer who apparently needed his earnest attention.

Annie called to Mo. "Come on. I'll carry you if you come right now."

Mo didn't even say good-bye. He was up and trotting down the bar toward Annie before the man could protest.

5

As Annie entered the foyer, she looked at several puddles of water on the floor. The cats had shaken dry and now sat, wet butts on upholstered or wooden furniture, licking their paws dry.

She sighed. Tiger Lily looked at her with a "What?" expression and returned to the business at hand.

Nancy came to the foyer with a cup of hot chocolate. "Henrie made this for you. There's a shot of coffee in it."

"Wonderful." Annie put Mo on a dry spot and took the cup. "What do you want to do this afternoon, Mom?"

"I have no plans. Sam left on a mission of mercy for Gema, something about picking up jewels in Marsh Haven, and I've been puttering around with Henrie and Hilly, putting out the last of the quilts."

"Oh, I want to see. I wonder if Brian and Janet are still out."

"I think so. I was disappointed not to see Simon. He was either with them at the winery or hiding somewhere."

As they walked across the yard to the carriage house, Annie said, "I made a reservation for Bon Vivant tonight, for Chris and me, you and Sam, and Frank and Mem. We'll have the only table that isn't reserved for the lonely hearts club. We closed the restaurant for private parties this weekend."

"I do enjoy Cookie's delightful meals. I can't wait."

"Except it won't be Cookie. He quit."

"When?"

"Today."

Annie didn't have time to expound. They were in the Honeymoon suite. She stopped to look at the quilt. It was a masterpiece.

"So this is the classic wedding ring design?"

"Yes. Do you like the colors?"

"I love it. I love everything about it. I was afraid that it would be, well, a distraction to folks renting the room that weren't married or on their honeymoon, but this is lovely. It will work for everyone."

The quilt, made to fit a king-sized bed, had an ivory background and large, entwined circles, looping together across the quilt and forming scalloped edges. Annie looked at the rings, made with floral fabrics in every color of the rainbow.

In preparation for the quilt, and using pieces of fabric shared by Nancy, the suite had been repainted. Two walls, one long and one short, were light taupe; the other two were light slate blue. Trim around the windows and doors was dark slate blue. The colors blended in a surprisingly gentle fashion.

"It's beautiful, and perfect. Thank you, Mom. Let's look upstairs."

Annie knocked before using her pass key, in case Brian or Janet had slipped in. They had not.

This room had windows on only two sides. The long back wall, which had several windows at one time, had been walled in to make the patio with hot tub a private area for the honeymoon suite. To assure the room didn't go dark, that wall and the wall where the kitchen nook stood were eggshell. The two accent walls were muted peach and the trim coral.

The quilts were a riot of color. This was now known as the Rainbow Room.

Each of the queen beds had quilts with triangles. The one in the middle used triangles to form squares, one in the center, a larger one surrounding it, and on and on. The beds on either side were variations of one pattern: triangles of bright colors in rows interspersed with gray on one quilt and white on the other. The quilts not only used the same pattern variety, alternating rows of blue, red, green, yellow, orange and purple, but they mirrored one another. One quilt seemed to point up and to the right; the other pointed up and to the left.

The lower bunk had a simple quilt of thick stripes that ran from side to side. The upper quilt had a three dimensional loom effect. It reminded Annie of the toy she had as a child that allowed her to make loomed hot pads.

Nancy pointed to the sofa. "The quilts thrown on the sofa are for those roll away beds you have, Annie."

One had a three dimensional effect of boxes stacked together; the other looked like a traditional pattern of squares attached with more decorative squares, but again, using alternating rainbow colors.

Simon lay on the sofa. He had pulled down the box quilt and had rearranged it until it was perfect for a catnap. He looked at Annie and Nancy with a "don't bother me, I'm supposed to be sleeping" look, closed his eyes and sighed himself asleep.

"So that's Simon," said Nancy. "He and Honey Bear will get along fine, once they get to know one another."

Annie didn't respond.

On the way back to the main house, Nancy said, "The rooms are just lovely, Annie. I think you need to add nameplates to the doors, even at the carriage house, with the names of the rooms."

"That's next on the list. Henrie's looking at samples now. Something that will meet his criteria of 'elegant yet casual'."

"Good luck with that."

In the foyer, they met the five women Annie had seated at the Café.

"Oh, hello. I'd hoped to meet you at breakfast. I guess I met you at the Café, but I didn't introduce myself. I'm Annie. This is my mother, Nancy. She and her husband are staying at the carriage house."

The tall blond took Annie in. Coolly, she said, "How involved are you in the Hearts On Fire events?"

Annie, taken aback by the tone, said, "Well, we're hosting you as guests, and some, well…probably most of the venues will be held at my establishments, but I'm not a decision maker. Just lucky to be in the middle of things, I guess."

"Don't mind her," said a bubbly, fresh-faced redhead. "She's just, well, she's having a bad day. I'm Peggy. I'm an old hand at this. This is my fifth one. This is the first time for Liz."

Liz turned out to be the leggy blond.

Henrie entered the foyer. "Good afternoon, ladies. I have prepared tea and scones in the dining room."

"Tea and scones. How elegant." This was said by an exotic beauty with some kind of an accent. Annie couldn't place it, but it sounded faintly like Henrie's. Hmmm. The woman seemed to bat her eyes at him also. She threw an accusing glance at Annie – Annie wasn't sure what she was being accused of doing – and led the way to the dining room.

"Mom, let's have tea."

"By all means, dear."

"Let me check on the kids first."

Henrie said, "They have had an afternoon snack, and I believe they have settled with their delightful Uncle Honey Bear in the library."

Nancy said, "They love him. They really do," and she followed Henrie into the dining room.

Henrie had used three of their elegant tea services. He explained, "The rosebud pattern has black tea, chocolate, blended with pink rosebuds. The floral pattern contains oolong blended with orange. The last set, the oriental design, has an herbal tea, flavored with cinnamon and vanilla."

The exotic beauty batted her eyes and simpered. "Which do you prefer, Henrie?"

He smiled. "The herbal tea is my favorite, but for the season, one should at least try the chocolate."

Henrie turned on his heel and went to the kitchen. The exotic beauty started to follow but turned to look at Annie. Annie gave a slight shake of the head. The kitchen was one room that was off limit to guests.

The beauty looked at Nancy. "She was in the kitchen today."

Nancy was nothing if not intelligent. She played a bubble-headed ninny when Honey Bear was concerned or when the situation required. She apparently decided the situation required. "I'm not a guest, dear. I suppose you could consider me Henrie's mother-in-law."

Annie hid her laugh, turning to pick up a plate. "Scone, anyone?"

The women found seats for themselves, the exotic beauty the seat closest to the kitchen door, and Annie walked around, placing scones on plates. They were heart-shaped, almond with a Grand Marnier glaze.

Peggy, the five-time-grand-dame of the lonely hearts club, claimed the right of hostess. "Annie, Nancy, let me introduce you to our members. I'm Peggy. I said that already. This is my fifth time with a group get-together. I guess you can say that I'm experienced."

The leggy blond, Liz, said, "Or inept. By now, I think you would have found someone."

"Oh, don't be harsh. Let me continue. This one? The one that just spoke? She's Liz. I think I said that earlier, too. Anyway, this is her first time."

"Yes. My first. Hopefully my last."

Peggy pointed to the exotic beauty at the end of the table. "And of course, I should introduce you to Farah. We talked a bit last night."

She turned to Farah. "This is your first time, too."

"Yes. And unlike many of the others, I am looking only for a good time. Not a life partner. But if you are the mother-in-law?"

Nancy said, "You could say that. But I'm not, really. It's a pleasure to meet you, Farah."

"I'm sure."

Peggy, who, Annie noticed, was very good at this hosting stuff, pointed to the Nordic-looking woman from the site's home page. "This is Elena."

"Charmed," said Elena. She spoke with a Cyrillic trill. "Elena Long. My name, in my parents' home country, means 'torch.' I have come to light my own, hoping to find some excitement. Something I cannot find in the place my parents chose to live."

"Where do you live?" asked Peggy.

"Omaha. No torch bearers there."

Peggy said, "I looked through your information, Elena – oh, don't worry, I look through all of them – and it doesn't say where your parents are from."

"I did not realize we were required to say."

"Oh, we're not. I'm just, interested. Your accent is so unique."

Elena said, "Thank you," and ignored the question.

Peggy, a little flustered now, introduced the last woman. "This is, um, Tiffany. This is, what, your second time?"

"Yes, my second." She sighed. She was dark skinned, short, and very curvy. "I met a couple of guys at the last one, and we got together afterwards, but…I need to change something that I do. I keep picking the wrong men."

"Wrong, how?" asked Annie.

"One turned out to be 'divorcing.' Did you catch that word? Not 'divorced.' 'Divorcing.' Big difference. The second one had three kids from three different women. His money goes to child support and he can't seem to coordinate visitation. He was always cancelling because he had to do this or he had to do that or why don't you join us…and that was always with his daughter. It was like the man was terrified to be alone with his six-year-old daughter."

"What does he need with a lonely hearts club?"

"I think he got kicked out. He had forgotten to mention a few things when he signed up."

"There are rules?"

The women nodded and said various forms of yes, then they started to chatter. And laugh. Annie had a hard time keeping up. From time to time she glanced at Nancy, who seemed to take an extraordinary interest in the rules on dating.

Peggy said, "First of all, there are always more men than women. I don't know if that's a rule, but that's what happens at a club outing. And the men have to put things into their information sheets that women don't. It's kind of sexist that way."

Tiffany said, "Kind of? Extremely!"

Liz responded, "Well, most of us are looking for money, anyway."

Farah said, "I'm looking for a good time."

Tiffany said, "I'm looking for a soul mate."

Liz put some finality to it. "I want that money, honey, and a ring would be nice."

Annie asked, "What kind of information goes on the form?"

"Not enough to identify us. They have more, but the files we can see don't have last names, the names of our employers, where we live, our ages. But we see enough that we can tell if the men are OHOT or OHOC."

"What's that?"

"They have to submit several pictures – well, we do, too – sitting and facing the camera, standing and facing…"

"Standing to the side and looking back at the camera…"

"Standing next to our car, or if we don't have one, whatever public transportation we use…"

"And in front of our home…"

"And in the kitchen, living room, dining room…"

"Even the bedroom…"

"And however many it takes, with all the equipment we use for sports or exercise."

"And then we have to say if we own or rent our homes, own or lease our cars…"

"And what we do for a living, if we work…"

"And if we don't work, what we do for money…"

"And the men have to give an estimate of their portfolio. Something we don't have to do."

"Oh. Marriages. How many, how long, how long ago, and kids, ages and if they live with us."

"But how does that tell you the "oh hot" stuff?"

"OHOT is 'own hair, own teeth,' which you can kinda figure out with all the pictures."

"And OHOC is 'own house, own car,' which you can figure out, too."

"If he's honest."

"Were you honest?"

"Mostly…"

"If the lie is anything important, like you forgot to mention three kids from three different women, you get booted…"

"Some things they just make you fix, like if you used someone else's car…"

"Not house. They'll boot you in a second if you lie about your living conditions."

"Who's 'they,' and how do they find out if someone lied?"

The room grew quiet, then Elena answered. "Actually, it's a little nerd named Travis. He has the computer program."

"Someone needs to fix his lonely heart."

"His heart isn't lonely. It's just locked up in those programs and stuff. He's really not very good at this."

Peggy said, "He likes the little chubby woman, Charlie."

Liz said, "That wasn't very polite. Anyway, how do you know that?"

"I was just saying. He's not very good at this."

"Which is why he came up with the group idea. He can do something…"

"Algorithms."

"Yeah, that, and figure out groups of people that might get along. But for some reason, he hasn't been able to figure out the single stuff."

"His stats were terrible. Until the groups started. Now his stats are going bonkers."

"What stats?"

"Hook-ups, engagements and marriages."

"He keeps statistics on that stuff?"

"Sure. How else would you know if you were working with a legitimate company?"

"I don't know…Better Business Bureau? Online reviews?"

"Well, yeah. You can check that stuff, but what I look for is hard data."

Annie sat back in her seat. If someone could fabricate a house or a car, certainly the computer nerd could fabricate statistics. But what did she know?

"Okay. But how does he find out if someone lies?"

"He won't, not always. He sends a follow-up questionnaire after each group meeting, and then another one about a month later. There's a place for people to say if they found something out that wasn't right."

"I filled it out on the guy with three kids. It took a while, and I don't know what Travis did with the information, but eventually, his site came up as 'deleted.'"

"'Deleted' as opposed to…"

"Retired means you left the program of your own free will. A wedding bell icon can either mean 'engaged' or 'married,'…"

"Or some other form of long-term commitment. You like to see more bells than anything else."

"So 'deleted' is booted out."

"Yes. And you won't see why, because the site is taken down. Nothing else is ever said."

"Have you ever wanted to report something, but you didn't?"

"I did. I found out one guy, who said he was a millionaire, was on his last dime."

"Why didn't you say anything?"

"I figured he'd run out of money to keep up with the charade."

"Did he?"

"No. This is the fourth time I've seen him here. I steer clear and try to tell others the same."

"Who is he?"

"Can you point him out?"

"What's his name?"

Peggy seemed to look everywhere but into the eyes of the other women. "He was the Monthly Flame for January, and his picture is still up. He dresses like a million bucks, and he has the charm to go with it."

Everyone else looked at Liz, whose face had lost all elasticity. She stared at Peggy. "You introduced him to me last night. When were you going to tell me?"

"I would have. I was keeping an eye on it."

"We left together. We…hooked up."

"I didn't know that! He came back without you and left with someone else, that local woman."

Liz said, "He left with her? When were you going to tell me?"

"I didn't know it was so important…"

Liz slapped her hand on the table to stop Peggy's excuse.

She said, "We barely know one another, and it's not like you have to protect me from a wolf or anything. But everyone in that room thought he was rich. Everyone wanted him. Everyone except you, Peggy. You should have told us."

"I never try to discourage people on the first night…"

"Oh, stop it! You were having a great laugh on our behalf. You could have told me before I… before I… for goodness sakes! I hooked up with him! And he's poor!"

Liz looked like she had eaten a lemon. "Ick!"

The room grew quiet. Nancy finally reached for the pot of herbal tea and asked, "Can I pour for anyone?"

No one said a word. Nancy put down the pot, not pouring, even for herself. Eventually, Farah asked, "Annie, are you and Henrie…ah…in a relationship?"

Annie laughed. "No. Henrie and I both live here, but we live quite separate lives."

"He lives here? And you do, too?"

"Yes. And my seven cats."

"Pardon me for asking, but is he gay? Or something?"

Annie's eyes went wide. "Excuse me?"

"Well, he's so handsome…"

"So well dressed…"

"And he takes care of our every need…"

"I swear he reads minds…"

"And he hasn't flirted with any of us. Not once."

Annie finally got a word in edgewise. "That doesn't mean a thing."

"But is he?"

"I won't answer that question."

"He is."

"I knew it."

"Such a shame."

Farah looked at Annie and said nothing.

Nancy jumped up. "Oh, Annie, you must come help me unpack. Sam's gone, and two of those bags are too heavy." Nancy pulled Annie by the arm, and they walked quickly from the room.

In the foyer, Annie hissed, "What got into you?"

"Just getting you out of the way before you became angry, dear. I know you and how you hate for people to ask about Henrie."

"Do you really need my help?"

"Of course not!"

"Then let's go around to the kitchen door. We can stay out of sight until they leave."

6

Tiger Lily sat on the windowsill in the library. Her siblings had saved her the best place on the cushions. She would join them shortly. She loved to watch icicles form. It was so pretty, and so magical.

To be honest, she wasn't actually watching them form. She measured the change in width and depth from the morning. This had been a good icicle day. They had grown in size and number. None had fallen.

She jumped down to the cushions and yawned, stretching herself as long and tall as she could. If all the cats did this, Honey Bear would have to sleep somewhere else. Too late. He was already here, pushing himself in between everyone, going for the best place.

Darn it! That was her place! She wasn't going to give it up.

When Honey Bear reached her, she hissed and bopped him on the nose. Unlike her usual bops to the noses of her siblings, her claws were not retracted.

Honey Bear, not about to be taken by a girl, swiped back, and soon, it seemed as if everyone was fighting with everyone. Where was Mommy? She generally intervened about now.

Eventually, Tiger Lily relented, gave up her space, and stalked to the other side of the library. One by one, her siblings joined her, laying around her on a rug, while Uncle Honey Bear had the cushions to himself.

Tiger Lily sighed. *"Well, we should at least report in. What's happening around town?"*

Mr. Bean said, *"That guy from the carriage house, Brian, met with some people today. It was really strange. They met to talk about something, but they never let him say anything. They asked questions and didn't let him answer. And he paid for the meal, but they didn't even eat it. They got containers and left with it."*

"That was rude."

"Dat's impolite, an yeah. Rude."

"Did you pick up on anything?"

"Yeah. After they left, Isabel left, to go to the Café, and Carlos came out to sit with Brian. He seemed to know something was wrong. He asked what was up, and Brian said he had hoped to get an investment…what's that?"

Tiger Lily said, *"I think it's money or something. Someone gives money, and when they get it back it's grown somehow."*

"How?"

"I don't know. Magic, I guess. Anyway, what did he say about it?"

"He said he was counting on these folks, but it looked like they weren't interested."

"What does that mean?"

"Carlos asked him that, and Brian said he didn't know if they'd be able to pull it off."

Sassy Pants, having some difficulty following along, asked, *"Whats dey pull off, and whats it come off of?"*

Little Socks bopped her in the nose. Sassy Pants, embarrassed, hid her head under her paws. Little Socks said, *"They don't know if they can pull off the winery, get the winery up and going, without the money."*

"Oh, no!"

Kali and Ko said together, *"They're nice people." "I'd hate for that to happen."*

Comments flew around the rug from everyone. *"Maybe Mommy can help." "I bet Chris needs a winery." "Trill!" "What about that kitty?"*

At that comment, everyone stopped. Eventually, they all looked to Tiger Lily. She said, *"I know his name is Simon, but I haven't met him. Kali, Ko, have you met him yet?"*

The girls answered at the same time, *"They keep the cat door locked." "They take him to the car in the carrier sometimes."*

"Huh. We'll have to keep our eyes and ears open."

"Is anything else happening?"

Mo said, *"Trill, trill, purr, trill."*

Mo had never progressed beyond speaking kitten. His litter mates, Kali and Ko, understood him and could easily translate.

Sassy Pants, who had the most tenuous grasp on the English language, had, for some reason unknown to any of them, learned to read minds. She could also translate.

Smarting from her rebuke from Little Socks, she kept her head under her paws. Kali translated. *"He said George is trying to help some idiot learn how to talk to women."*

"Trill, purr, trill."

Ko added, *"And the guy that runs the lonely hearts is upset. Cookie quit."*

"Cookie quit?" "What?" "When?"

Tiger Lily said, *"He quit today. We'll get to that in a bit. Why is the guy upset about that?"*

"Trill, trill."

Kali said, *"Apparently there is stuff Cookie was supposed to do that was more than just cook. Starting tonight."*

Ko turned to Tiger Lily. *"Tell us about Cookie!"*

"Apparently someone in his family is sick, and he left today to go home. Everybody has to work harder to get it done. But that's not the most important thing. Felicity has a date!"

"With who?"

"She's not telling."

"When?"

"Valentine's Day."

"Where?"

"She's not saying."

"Can you ask Trudie?"

"Trudie doesn't know anything, but she's taking Wednesday afternoon and Thursday off to see him."

Mo said, *"Trill!"*

Sassy Pants sat up straight. *"No!"*

Several cats asked versions of *"What?"*

Sassy Pants said, *"Henrie's taking off dose same days."*

They went silent. Little Socks looked at Tiger Lily. *"Do you think they're going together?"*

Tiger Lily shook her head and sighed. *"We'd better watch that one."*

The cats were silent for several moments, thinking private thoughts.

Tiger Lily finally said, "There's one more thing, but I don't really understand it. The women that are staying here were talking about a man named Dorian. Apparently he's 'dating outside the box,' whatever that means, and he's doing it with Geraldine."

"Geraldine! Well whatever it means, it has to be bad."

"Did she leave her husband again?"

"Why does that witch-with-a-b always have to be in the middle of things?"

Conversation stopped abruptly when Annie stuck her head in the library. She looked toward the cushions, saw only Honey Bear, and looked around the room. Finding her cats on a rug in the back of the room, she shook her head.

"Come on, kids. Time for supper. You, too, Honey Bear. You're staying here for the next few days."

Tiger Lily sighed.

Fritz looked at the text message. Russia suspected but not confirmed. Last name Long. Omaha.

It was a long shot, but the nickname "torch" had drawn the attention of his bosses. Anything was worth a try.

He forwarded the text to an untraceable number.

Annie fed the cats and dressed for dinner. She went downstairs to wait for Chris, her special friend. Her commitment. Her not-quite-fiancé-because-they-didn't-plan-to-marry. Her boyfriend. Her manfriend. She had not yet hit upon the proper term.

As she walked down the stairs, she ran through possible words.

Paramour. Too French.

Suitor. Not suited.

Admirer. That sounded as if he admired her, but she didn't necessarily admire him.

Beloved. Ick.

Escort. Too risqué.

Flame. No.

Inamorato. Too Italian.

Lover. Leads people to the bedroom in their minds.

Steady. Too high-school.

Swain. Now there was a word you didn't hear often. And for good cause.

Sweetheart. Ick.

Gentleman Friend. Too nineteen fifties.

Gentleman Caller. Ick.

True Love. For goodness sakes.

Honey. Hmmm. Honey. She tried phrases out loud as she walked into the kitchen. "Meet my honey." "This is my honey." "You're my honey, bunny."

Henrie looked up from his breakfast preparation – tomorrow he would serve what he called a Country Breakfast Benedict – to stare.

Annie stopped in her tracks. "Just trying the word on for size, Henrie."

"I do not want to know."

He turned back to his Benedict.

"Henrie, did you hear the conversation in the dining room?"

"The tea and scones conversation?"

"Yes."

"I did."

"All of it?"

"Yes."

"Do you want me to say anything?"

"About me? To them?"

"Yes."

"No."

"You're sure?"

Henrie turned to look at her again. "Annie, I have never been...what is the term I seek..."

"Hit on?"

"Yes. Hit on. I have never been hit on by a guest in this establishment. If they believe I am homosexual, that may prevent Miss Hot To Trot from attempting to snare my affection."

Annie laughed. "Miss Hot To Trot?"

"Yes."

"Okay, then. You're looking a little tired, Henrie. What time did you get home last night?"

"You mean, what time did I get home this morning."

"Oh, my. Felicity seemed to be suffering from the same thing. Plus she had another problem."

"Oh?"

"Cookie quit today."

Henrie, if possible, looked shocked.

"This is the first you've heard?"

"Yes. Apparently I have been outside the circle today."

"Loop."

"Pardon me?"

"Loop. You've been outside the loop."

"Yes. That. Was he not responsible for additional activities for the club?"

"He was. Isabel is handling some of that for the weekend, and I think Felicity has Wednesday night covered."

Henrie turned back to his work. "She does? Well, obviously, she will have to handle Cookie's duties on Wednesday."

"No, I promised her the night off."

"You did?"

"Yeah. She said she has a date, and she didn't want to cancel."

"Hmmm."

Annie turned away from Henrie. She thought about it.

Both Henrie and Felicity were out until early this morning. No one knew with whom or where.

Both Henrie and Felicity requested the night off Wednesday and had covered their Thursday morning duties with other staff.

Was it possible their plans involved one another?

Surely she was jumping to conclusions.

7

The Bon Vivant Grille had a special night planned. There would be only one seating, at seven o'clock. Only one table was given to someone other than Hearts On Fire club members. Entrance – with the exception of Annie's table – was by display of the official club pins.

Annie and Chris left the Inn early. She wanted to be available for issues that might come up. They walked slowly up The Avenue, a large umbrella shielding them from the light sleet.

Annie said, "It's going to be an icy walk home tonight. Maybe you can help Mom."

"I'll hold onto her. You hold onto Sam."

"It's a plan."

Annie had to admit they looked good together. Only because he looked good. She believed he made up for anything in the way of looks that she lacked. She was a medium everything. Height, weight, looks. He was a ten. Tall and slender with the bearing of a sailor, he had a full head of prematurely white hair and nicely trimmed beard and mustache.

He loved her. He was committed to her. What else could a woman ask?

Chris walked her to the door, opened it and said, "I'm going to have a beer at the Tap. I'll be back in time for dinner."

Annie found Isabel at the hostess stand, looking at a seating chart. Annie asked, "What's that?"

"This is supposed to be a kind of scripted mixer. I have no idea how it will work out. Most of the members came into town yesterday and have been meeting one another already. But…Cookie had this chart, and…"

A young man with a large heart stick pin embossed with a flame rushed in. "Is it set up? Ready to go?"

"Yes, Travis. We're ready. Do you want to check the place markers on the tables?"

"As long as you have it set up the way it looks there. I sent Cookie the list of who to put at each table. Where's mine?"

"You're here, closest to the hostess stand, so you can stand up to speak if you need to."

"And did you put, um, Charlie at my table?"

"She's sitting to your left."

"Oh no! I mean, um, my right side's the best. Can you switch her?"

"Certainly."

Annie looked at the table with place markers for Travis, Charlie, apparently a woman, Bob and Tonya. She traded Charlie's place for Tonya's. She walked through the room, looking at the place markers. Most tables had markers for two women and two men. Some tables had markers for one woman and three men.

When she returned to the hostess stand Isabel was asking about that very issue. "But what are they going to think, when three men are sitting with one woman?"

"I couldn't very well tell men they couldn't come, not when they paid their money."

"Did you tell them up front that more men than women would be here?"

"No, I didn't. But I guess it just makes for more competition."

"Does your competition stay friendly?"

"Usually, but then, this is the first time we've been this lopsided."

"Are all of your members signed up for tonight's dinner?"

"Not all. A few of the men aren't able to come until tomorrow."

"Our tables are set for forty-four. I didn't realize there were so many in town. I counted twenty-six men to eighteen women. That appears to be sixty/forty. At least for tonight. How many more men will be here tomorrow?"

"Five or six."

"Have you done this before?"

"Well, sure."

"And how successful has it been in the past?"

"Truthfully? It could use some work. I'm not real good with women, and, well, it always seems like such a good idea, but…it never really gels."

"And how often have you seated yourself with a woman?"

Travis looked away and blushed. Looking at his feet, he mumbled, "I gotta get my paperwork together. Is there a place I can sit and work?"

Annie pointed to the back dining room. "You can go back there. Just switch the light on, to the right as you go in."

"Thanks. I'll be out as soon as folks start coming in."

Annie looked at Isabel. Isabel asked, "So what do you think? Is this his first date with the group, or has he been doing it for a while?"

"I think he's been doing it for a while."

"With Charlie?"

"I don't know. Charlie is the name that came up in conversation."

"This should be fun."

"Or not."

Janet finished painting behind the tasting bar and stood back to survey her work. She thought it would look good when it dried. She took a slow walk around the room, looking up and down, underneath bars and over cabinets. She didn't see any places she had missed.

Brian came up behind her, two plates in hand.

"Are you done?"

"Yes. Done. What do we have?"

"I got small plates from Sassy P's, and a bottle of red is breathing on the table by the window."

Brian went to the table and poured the wine while Janet cleaned the last of the paint off her hands. When she sat down, they smiled at one another. Janet's smile was sad, tired and wistful. She thought Brian's mirrored hers.

They had sold everything they owned to move here. They were lucky not to have a mortgage, because the home they sold had been in the family for generations. Leaving a home that had been in the family so long had been hard enough.

They were the only ones left. Both sets of parents were gone. Both were only children. They had no children of their own. Only Simon.

Only Simon. Ha! Simon was their love child. He was spoiled. He would be the perfect winery cat. He would bask in the attention of their guests, pick the best table based on the placement of the sun, find the perfect spot on the balcony or the rail.

Simon could charm the oil off a snake.

Janet looked out on the rolling hills that belonged to them. At least for the moment.

"It's too dark to see. Everything's a shadow."

"I was thinking of some photovoltaic lights at the edge of the deck and into the parking lot. For nights we're here late."

"That's a good idea."

They sat, eating and drinking in silence, looking over the dark vineyard.

Janet didn't look up as she said, "What do we do now?"

Brian sighed. He didn't answer.

"Have we gone through everyone that could possibly invest?"

"Everyone that I know of."

"We can't give up. Not now. Why don't we give ourselves a deadline?"

"And then what? We get this place in tiptop shape, and then we have to put it on the market?"

"Would Greg be able to help us?"

"Funny you should bring him up. He showed the property to a couple and they couldn't get the loan. I've thought about that a few times this afternoon. Maybe he could introduce us. Maybe they'd be willing to invest, make a profit, and buy their own place in a few years."

"It's worth a shot. Why don't we ask him tomorrow? What time are we looking at the house?"

"Ten. I tell you what, though. If we don't get investors, I don't see how we'll be able to buy a house."

"One step at a time, Brian. One step at a time. Let's go home. I'll bet Simon is pretty angry about being left alone for so long."

Nancy dropped her cell phone into her purse. As she put on her coat, she said, "Henrie said Annie already fed the little dear. Are you ready to go?"

Sam yawned and took his feet off the ottoman. "I've been ready for an hour. I've already had a nap."

"That's nice, dear. I'm sure you'll be able to stay up until all hours."

Nancy caught the smile that Sam tried to hide. She smiled herself. One of her favorite pastimes was providing entertainment for him. It helped with the boredom of retirement.

As they walked out the door, a young couple trudged up the walk. Nancy smiled, "You must be Brian and Janet. It looks like you've had a very long day."

"Yes, ma'am," said Brian.

Janet asked, "How long are you staying?"

"Oh, we stay for a few weeks. We never know exactly how long. I'm Nancy, this is Sam. Annie's our daughter."

Janet brightened. "She's so nice. And Henrie. And, well, everyone in town. We're looking forward to living here."

"And we're looking forward to seeing your winery. Well, Sam has already reminded me we're late, so…"

They turned and walked up the street, umbrellas ready for the next spit of rain or sleet or whatever would fall.

The cats were happy to see Sis. She was a dark gray giant schnauzer and a new friend. The cats rescued her from a fierce snowstorm before Christmas. She had escaped from her human, who had turned bad. When she needed a fur-ever home, Chris said yes.

The cats were especially pleased. They now had a branch detective office at the local Coast Guard Station.

As they gathered on the cushions in the dining room, they heard a call from downstairs. Sassy Pants ran to the apartment's cat door.

"Come on ups, Tillie! Sis can't get through the door so we's up here!"

Tillie ran up the stairs and through the door. Being a small dog, she almost fit without squeezing. Almost, but not quite.

She nearly ran into Mr. Bean. They had not reconciled from their earlier fight. Mr. Bean, trying to learn to be more mature, like Tiger Lily, said, *"I'm sorry, Tillie. I shouldn't have hit you."*

"I'm sorry, too. Next time, let's just flip a coin or something."

"We don't have thumbs."

"It's just an expression. We'll have to find a way to make decisions."

Sis asked, *"Why do you need to make a decision?"*

Little Socks said, *"They fight sometimes about dancing in the window at the bakery. It's silly."*

"Is not. We're supposed to take turns, but sometimes we forget. It's not silly."

Tiger Lily said, *"It's okay, Mr. Bean. Sometimes we get caught up and forget."* She turned to Sis. *"Tell us about the Coast Guard Station. Have you been going out on the boats?"*

"Not yet. It's been so cold. Chris said I can't go on the water until I learn how to swim. He said I can't start training until the water warms up."

"What do you do when Chris goes out?"

"I stay in his office, but he usually leaves the door open. If I have to go outside, lots of people are good to take me and get me in."

"Do you hear any gossip?"

"I do, but I haven't heard anything that would interest you yet. I mean, nothing for the detective agency."

Little Socks asked, *"Have you trained Chris yet?"*

"In several things. He doesn't argue with me about sleeping in the bed anymore. And he feeds me only what I like."

"What about talking? Have you tried to teach him to talk to you?"

"He showed me the yes/no."

"Cyril's yes/no?"

Cyril was their friend, an English setter whose human was Pete, the Chief of Police. Pete taught Cyril how to respond to simple yes/no questions by bumping his right or left fist. Now, all of the cats and dogs used it to train their humans. Turn about is always fair play to cats and dogs.

"Yes. It works pretty well. And then I taught him how to know when I need things, like food, water, or going out."

"What do you do?"

"If I need food, I bump him with my head. If I need to go out, I stand by the door. If he doesn't notice, I knock against the door."

Tiger Lily said, *"And I bet you bump harder and harder until he notices."*

"Yes. How did you know?"

"That's what I do with Mommy."

Henrie relaxed in his apartment. He had just confirmed reservations for two at a fine dining restaurant in Heyworth. Heyworth was about twice the size of Marsh Haven, which Chelsea residents typically frequented when they went "out of town."

It was also two hours in the other direction.

Henrie preferred to conduct his personal life behind closed doors.

He confirmed the one-night reservation in one of the better hotels in town, took a sip of single malt whiskey poured over one ice cube, and sent a text message.

"Reservations confirmed. See you there."

He watched until the message left and deleted his text history.

At the Café, Sam and Nancy pushed through the crowd at the door and made their way to a table in the back. Annie and Chris sat with Mem and Frank. Someone had ordered a carafe of aperitifs. It sat on the table in a chiller.

Chris said, "I thought we might get a late start on dinner, so...let me pour you a small glass."

"What is it?"

"We had a choice of jalapeno-infused or prickly pear margaritas. I got the prickly pear."

"Interesting." Nancy took a sip. "Almost like watermelon." Nancy was seated facing the hostess stand. "Say, isn't the crowd at the door getting a little loud?"

Isabel was surrounded by several men; most of them seemed angry. Nancy looked around the room. Tables of four – two men and two women – seemed to be getting to know one another, sipping aperitifs. At several tables, women sat alone, most of them appearing ill-at-ease.

Annie excused herself and walked to the hostess stand to help Isabel. Chris put his head in his hands.

"What, Chris?"

"Look who just walked in."

Nancy looked. She didn't see it. Mem did. "Geraldine. What's she doing here?"

Nancy looked at Mem. "I guess she's out to dinner, like the rest of us."

"No, not like the rest of us. Bon Vivant is closed to everyone except the lonely hearts club members. Our table was the only one allowed in, and that's because they had room for us. They can't hardly tell the owner she can't eat here."

Nancy turned to look. Geraldine looked around the room until she saw a man who waved and invited her over. He stood and appeared to be looking around for another chair.

Isabel, who had been occupied when Geraldine entered, walked toward the table.

Nancy watched as Isabel, the man and Geraldine appeared to argue. Isabel held her manner in such a way as to call her portion of the conversation a "discussion," but the others, not so much. Soon, Nancy could hear the words. She heard Geraldine first, then the man.

"I was invited. Dorian invited me."

Dorian, voice raised so the entire room could hear, said, "This is a singles weekend. I'm single. She's single. I wasn't told I couldn't bring a date."

Nancy couldn't hear Isabel, but she heard Dorian's answer. "I paid enough for the week that certainly you can squeeze one more dinner out of it!"

Isabel turned to look for someone. Annie? No, she looked right past Annie and stared at a young man. Annie walked toward the same man. He managed to look everywhere but at the argument in the middle of the room. Nancy looked back at Isabel, whose attention had returned to Geraldine and the man. She still could not hear Isabel.

Annie had taken the man by the arm and was leading him to the confrontation. Nancy couldn't hear him, either. He looked at the floor as he talked. Dorian said, "You didn't say we couldn't invite a guest."

Mumble, mumble, mumble.

Geraldine rose to her full height, which was already enhanced by three-inch stilettos. "I will not join your little club for only one meal. Come on, Dorian."

Her dramatic exit was quickly deflated. Nancy pulled the menu card to her face to cover her laugh as she heard the man say, "Well, Geraldine, I'm sorry. I thought you would enjoy the meal, but I've been seated with Liz, and, well, maybe I could see you later?"

"Well! I never!"

Geraldine turned on her heel and walked out of the restaurant. Isabel returned to the hostess stand, where she, Annie and the young, mumbling man did what they could to mollify their agitated customers.

Eventually, and at least half an hour past the stated meal hour, servers came around to deliver menu cards. Annie had not yet returned. She seemed to be in conference with the mumbling man.

The Bon Vivant Grille served a limited menu, something different each weekend, and guests paid one price for a several-course meal. Guests merely chose what they wanted and turned in the card at the beginning of the meal.

Generally, drinks before, during and after dinner were extra. Tonight, Hearts On Fire had paid an exorbitant price to include everything. Annie and Chris, hosting her parents and their best friends, paid the price of the full ticket.

Nancy turned to her menu card. "I'm glad you got the drinks early, Chris. What do you suggest we order?"

"The Grille has pared their options down to only two items per course. I'll order one of each for Annie and I; we'll share."

"That's a great idea. Sam, why don't we do that?"

Nancy took care of marking their tickets and asked, "What about people who can't eat what's being served?"

"People who choose to eat vegan or vegetarian, or who have food allergies, are encouraged to say something when they make their reservations. If they don't, the cooks will do what they can to accommodate."

As Annie returned to the table, people in the room turned almost as one. A police car from across the street started up, and a siren blared to life. The car careened out of the parking space and headed out of town. Fire trucks could be heard starting up and heading away.

Charlie noticed that Travis was seated at her table. The night before, it seemed like he was headed her way a couple of times, but when she looked again, he had gone back to his corner.

Maybe it was wishful thinking. Or maybe she should have listened to Peggy.

Peggy said he pitied her. Peggy said he was not nearly as nice as he seemed. Peggy said he had the heart of a snake.

She looked at her reflection in the window. Yes, she was overweight. Quite a lot. Her face was okay. She had a good job and could afford to buy nice clothes, as long as she didn't pay for things like this anymore.

This was her first time, and it would be her last. If she didn't meet someone this time, she would try something else. Maybe she would just give up on men and fill her life with female friends. She had a lot of those. She should cultivate them more.

The other people at her table were Tonya and Bob. She had met both briefly the night before. They were probably well-matched. Tonya was beautiful. She acted like that scar didn't even exist. Maybe she could learn a thing or two from Tonya.

Bob smiled to himself as he walked to the table. Two women were seated. A dumpling and a scarred tomato. He would go for the scarred tomato. Chances were, she'd been in a disfiguring accident and she was now rolling in dough.

Bob's first wife left him in good financial shape, but his second wife had emptied all his accounts. He needed a solid financial success with wife number three.

The dumpling was on her own tonight.

Liz considered her strategy. Last night, she thought she had met the man of her dreams. Today, she learned he was a stuffed silk suit. Frankly, she hoped this local woman would get her hooks into him and take him away from her.

As the argument went on between the woman, Dorian and the hostess, Liz, sipped her aperitif and looked around the room, trying to appear as if this had nothing to do with her. She tried to concentrate on her list.

After the conversation at the Inn this afternoon, she had gone back to her room to read through the information forms on all of the men. She made a list of the possibilities. The other man at her table, his name tag said "Jim," looked too dumpy to be rich. He looked like a flesh-colored pumpkin. But wasn't that one of her names? The "Jim" in the information sheets was better looking and thinner. Much thinner. But no. This was the same man. Someone had touched up his photos.

Liz was rich. Well, she used to be rich. She grew up on Daddy's money. Then Daddy died, leaving it all to her. She had blown through almost all of it and was facing financial ruin.

She would have to move out of her high rise apartment within three months. She might have to get a job! She had no idea what she could do. She had done nothing throughout her life but spend money.

Oh. Here came that nerd, Travis. Liz pulled a mirror out of her purse and pretended to check her make-up. This was a finely honed technique. She could move her head around, picking up conversations around her without appearing to notice.

She didn't need that ruse to hear what Dorian was saying. He had invited this woman to come. He intended to have the two of them sitting side by side, so he could, what? Compare them?

Gross. Well, he had no idea that she wanted nothing more to do with him. She could make that work for her. She could dangle his interest in front of men that interested her. Play hard to get. Maybe that was the element she had been lacking in the past.

She had tried to pick men up at country clubs or A-list parties, places where men of means could be found. A relationship never bloomed. Liz was beginning to believe there was something wrong with her. She was attractive enough. Witty. She had style. But she rarely got beyond the first date. Perhaps she was perceived as too needy.

She made this investment – that's what she considered the payment for this week to be – as a last gasp effort to find a man worthy of her. Rich enough. Passable enough to be seen with. Well, maybe that was her problem. Maybe she put too much stock into a man's looks.

She heard the little nerd say that Dorian would be able to pursue his interest in this woman in any venue that was not a pre-paid Hearts On Fire event. Good. Maybe she would succeed in getting her hooks into him.

The woman was leaving. Liz took a deep breath. This was life or death for her. She had to rise above the incident. She turned to Jim and said, "Now that we can hear ourselves think, let me introduce myself. I'm Liz."

Dorian stewed in his own juices through dinner. He needed a rich one. This time he had to get a rich one. He hoped he had not completely blown it with Liz, but it didn't look good.

He hoped he hadn't blown it with the local woman, either, but she seemed more desperate for company. He had taken her home the night before. She lived in an area of town filled with expensive homes. Hers was, well, it probably was the oldest home in the neighborhood, but that only meant she came from more than one generation of money, didn't it?

He had finally blown past the point of no return. His money was gone, and he was in hock to a real shark. The kind that broke legs if you didn't pay up.

He had begged for his legs. Well, for whatever body part they were going to hurt. He promised that after this week, once he scored, he would be able to pay them everything he owed.

Maybe he could borrow a little more…he'd need a little more to reel in whichever fish he caught. Then he could live off her money.

Felicity felt the buzz of an arriving text message. She reached into her apron pocket, read the message, smiled, and deleted it from her history.

8

Travis sat down and nodded to Isabel. Let's get this show on the road. Servers streamed out of the kitchen. They delivered chilled or room temperature bottles of wine and picked up menu cards.

He turned to Charlie to resume their conversation. "I'm really glad you could come. Are you having fun?"

"Yes…but if I don't meet someone, well, I can't afford to do this again."

"What are you looking for? In a man, I mean."

Charlie looked down at her lap. Without looking up, she said, "Someone who accepts me. All of me. I can't lose the weight. People think I'm a blimp."

"You're beautiful."

"I wish men would see me that way."

Under his breath, Travis said, "I'm a man."

Charlie said, "Did you say something?"

"Um, no."

Servers delivered the appetizers as ordered. Caprese skewers were made with cherry tomatoes and fresh mozzarella drizzled with balsamic vinegar and basil. The goat cheese salad contained mixed greens, goat cheese, walnuts, fresh figs and dried cherries, It was topped with sundried tomato vinaigrette dressing.

Charlie picked at her salad, moving a walnut next to a fig. Timidly, she said, "Peggy said you aren't supposed to, um, meet women at these groups."

"What?"

"Peggy. She said you put my name next to yours to be kind. You know. So other men wouldn't make fun of me."

"She said that?" Travis darted a look at Peggy, who happened to be looking in their direction. He glared at her. She smiled and waved.

"So I want to thank you for being a dinner companion, but I'll take it from here after the meal."

"I...I like you. I had you sit beside me because you intrigued me. I read everyone's profile. I liked what I saw."

"Then why didn't you say so?"

Travis looked at his plate. "I'm an idiot when it comes to women."

"So you really do like me?"

"I do." Travis felt as if his face would break. His smile was that big. "I've been looking forward to getting to know you."

Charlie smiled, picked up her fork and ate with relish.

And then she thought about it.

She dropped her fork on her plate, turned to look Travis straight in the eye, and said. "I'm not made of money. I sacrificed a lot to come to this event. You could have 'met' me as a single. Your site does that, too. If this was your way of 'getting to know' me, then let me just say you owe me for this. I'll expect a check by Wednesday night."

She picked her fork up again.

"Oh, and by the way, I'm going to enjoy myself, knowing it's on you."

In a daze, or maybe it was a haze, Travis finished his appetizer. And then, because he needed to listen to something, he listened to the conversation between Bob and Tonya.

They seemed to click. They had moved into a zone of their own before he was taken away to referee that stupid fight.

Tonya was saying, "I get it. People are put off by my scar. From the back, I'm a knock-out. I can't tell you how often last night people would come up to me from behind and call me 'Liz,' then get this look on their face…"

Bob almost purred his response, "You're a knock-out from every angle. And while the scar shouldn't be a problem for you, I hope you sued the guy that did it."

"I did. Drunk driver. I got a good settlement."

Bob reached across the table and put his hand on hers. "Good for you. It takes courage to make a stand."

Peggy smiled at the server as the soup and breads were placed on the table. She had the red onion and red wine soup, garnished with tarragon and heart-shaped croutons. She had wanted the lobster bisque, but it would have gone straight to her hips. She passed the bread to Mike, sitting on her right. He was very young. He was nervous. He took a lavender scone and dropped it on the floor.

Peggy smiled on the outside. On the inside, she was screaming. That nerd, Travis, had done this to her on purpose. On purpose!

She and Travis had hooked up during her first outing with the group. From the first night, when he seated her next to him. They spent the rest of the week together, and she left, thinking he would call. Or write. Or email.

She didn't hear from him.

She emailed him. He didn't respond.

She emailed him again. This time he did respond. Essentially, he said his schedule would not allow him to see her until their next outing.

She thought perhaps he would pay her way. He did not.

Once again, she found her place marker next to his on the first evening's dinner table. Once again, they spent the week together.

Once again, no contact afterward.

She vowed to get revenge.

Tonight, she sat with a young goofball who couldn't talk to women, an old guy that had been here four times and couldn't stop talking about his wife, and a new guy who had an intense look. He had trained that look on her and on others around the room.

Well, he was the most likely prospect for her, after all. "You said your name is Paul?"

"Yes."

Silence.

"Can you tell me something about yourself?"

"Um, well, really, I'm not ready to share. How about you, John? Tell us about yourself."

The older man took a sip of bisque and answered. "I was married for a long time. Thirty years. My dear wife died, and, well, I'm so lonely. I get so sad...I just want someone to replace her."

Mike, nervous around women, apparently had no such issues with men. "That's a sweet story."

"Sweet?"

"Yeah. Sweet. She must have been a wonderful woman. You know, wonderful women like that can't be replaced."

"What do you mean?"

"You can't replace her. You remind me of my dad. He and my mom were special together. They had nearly forty years together when she passed. He went through a period of mourning, then he started looking for someone who was just like her. He went through one woman after another, and finally, I told him to stop. Stop trying to find Mom. There would never be another woman like her, but there were women that he would enjoy being around."

"What happened?"

"He thought about that for a while, then he asked out this woman he'd known for a long time. Liked her, but, you know, she wasn't anything like Mom. They went out once, then twice, then they went on a cruise and came back married."

John looked at Mike. "You don't say. Maybe I'll give that some thought."

Great, thought Peggy. I'm sitting here with a group of losers, but one of them may go home and get lucky. Movement out of the corner of her eye made her look up. The little nerd was getting up to speak.

"Hello. Most of you know me. A few, maybe not. I'm Travis. Thank you for being here this week. Let me address some of the details of the week."

He looked down and shuffled some papers and cleared his throat. "Here we go. Well, tonight, you're here, so you know about tonight. This is what we call a scripted mixer. You're seated with people that you may or may not have met before tonight, and the computer generated with whom you would be seated."

From the middle of the room came a loud voice. "That's why I'm sittin' with two guys and one gal?"

Peggy looked. It was Nick. This was his third time with the group. He was big, rich, and he had a temper. She could tell Travis was getting more nervous. Good for Nick.

Travis continued, "Well, um, Nick, unfortunately, there were more men than women…"

Nick said, "We've been through this before. I'm tellin' ya, this is the end of it for me. I just hope I can find someone to hook up with before the week is over."

"And then, the week would have been a success for you. I hope that for everyone here."

"But only for some of us men."

"I'm sorry, I really am. I hoped more women would sign up…"

"Let's move on. We've heard it all before."

"Well." Travis cleared his throat and began again. "Some of you have been to a mixer before, but others are here for the first time. Please introduce yourself to as many people as you can throughout the week. We have several things planned."

He looked down again and shuffled his papers once more. "Here's the schedule. After dinner tonight, you're invited to meet at the bar next door or the winery just down the street. Actually, you can go anywhere, it's just that we encourage our members to stick to just a few places, so you can, you know, meet one another. And, let's see…oh, yes. Tomorrow is mostly free time. If you don't make plans to meet someone elsewhere, eat lunch here on Sunset Avenue. There are several great lunch options here, at the Café, at the bar, the bakery, the winery, and across the street there's a tea shop. If we keep our venues to just a few numbers, you'll always run into someone from Hearts On Fire."

Once again, Nick spoke up. "We got it! Stay on this street! Move on!"

Peggy laughed, but only to herself.

Travis wiped a bit of sweat from his brow and moved on. "Tomorrow evening, we'll have a buffet dinner on the second floor of this Café. There will be a cash bar, and a DJ will spin some tunes."

Peggy laughed inwardly again. She hadn't heard that term in a while.

"Sunday is free time. We're hoping that those of you who have found one another will take the opportunity to get to know one another better. For everyone else, well, you're really on your own. Except for church on Sunday morning, things on Sunset Avenue are closed. I have a list of places in town that are open and some options in nearby towns."

He used a napkin to wipe first his forehead, then his nose. "Monday, join us at a mixer at the winery in the evening. Tuesday is our final mixer. It's Fat Tuesday, so there will be a real New Orleans style get-together at Mo's Tap."

Peggy looked around the room. Most of the club members had continued to eat, barely looking at Travis, with the exception of Nick and a few other angry men.

Travis continued. "Of course, Wednesday night is the big night. You'll need to make reservations here at the Café, or with me, by no later than Wednesday noon. This will be a lover's only meal. Well, um, you don't actually have to be lovers, um have to have, um, well, it's a couples only thing. This will be the candlelight dinner. The soft music dinner. The please tell me that you love me dinner. The one you all aspire to reach with that one and only person of your dreams."

Peggy noticed several people trying not to laugh. A motion at the kitchen door caught her eye. Servers were standing, waiting, trying not to look impatient. Their next course was getting cold.

Travis started to sit down, but he ran back to the podium. "One final thing. Everyone here has registered and paid for the privilege of being here. The evening events are, um, reserved for club members. If you should find someone in town that you want to spend time with, we applaud you, but ask that you not do it during these events. Thankyouverymuch."

The last words were said so quickly, Peggy had to roll them around in her mind a couple of times to translate.

Paul thought, "If flies on the wall could talk, there would be a cacophony in this room tonight." This had been, without a doubt, one of his most expensive mistakes to date.

Why hadn't he listened to his sister? He would be better off finding volunteer opportunities or joining clubs, doing things he enjoyed doing. He would meet women doing those things. If only he were patient.

He believed his life was frittering away. He would never meet a woman, never marry, never have children, if he couldn't speed up this process somehow.

He had not pictured his evening sitting here. With these people. The woman was cute, but she had an edge to her.

Maybe, if he could get her alone later, he could get to know another side. Heck, with these guys, he probably looked like he had an edge, too.

Tonya wondered if this could be "the one." He said nothing about her scar. Well, not in so many words. He hoped she had received a fair settlement.

That was nice.

She thought that was nice.

Wasn't that nice?

Bob was good looking. He was attentive. He didn't do what so many men did, keep an eye roving for someone who did not have the face of a monster.

From the back, she was beautiful. From the right side, she was beautiful. From the left, though, not so much.

A drunk driver caused it. She had been out of work for months, had gotten behind in her bills. She had as much cosmetic surgery as her doctors would allow.

She had answered Bob's question honestly. She had received a nice settlement, one that pulled her even financially and that covered all of her medical expenses. The rest had gone to her attorney. Now, she was back on her career track with a disability. Not too many realtors had a face like hers. She made up for it with style and chutzpa. But she didn't have a financial safety net.

Elena and Farah locked eyes across the table. Elena believed they had many things in common. Elena was a first generation American. Farah had to be first or second. Elena spoke with a Russian accent. Farah's accent was more elusive to peg.

Elena's family had ties to the Russian mafia. She believed Farah's past would not stand up to scrutiny, but she wasn't sure of the reason. Both were exotic beauties, especially in this group.

And they had one other thing in common. Well, two. Tom and Thad. A more compelling reason for leaving this group in the dust could not be had.

Tom had decided, apparently, that Farah was the one for him. While they ate their vegetable and starch course – Elena enjoyed a carrot mole with toasted pumpkin seeds and tomato basil risotto – he was telling the commitment-phobic Farah that all he wanted was marriage to "the right one." A lifetime of bliss. A white picket fence. With her, apparently. Because he didn't hear, didn't pick up any of the body signals, didn't see her incredulous face. He was in his own little zone.

And she was stuck with Thad.

Elena enjoyed telling people the meaning of her name. Torch. She was going to set the world on fire. But not with this middle-aged, shortish, less-than-good-looking accountant from somewhere-worse-than-Omaha.

As Tom and Thad droned on, Elena and Farah looked at one another, picked up their wine glasses and drained them. Again.

The entrée was served to great fanfare. Tiffany was having a great time. Not.

She was used to being slighted. She was a woman. She was brown. Two strikes. Add to that, she was curvy. She wasn't what most would consider overweight, but she wasn't willowy.

Her lack of success with this group weighed heavy on her mind. She would choose the wrong man again, almost certainly,

She entered Bon Vivant feeling discouraged. Then she saw her name on the table. Her name, and the name of three men. Maybe this wouldn't be such a bad evening after all.

Then she got to know the three men.

Over pan-Asian glazed shrimp, she listened as Nick, Fritz and Brent talked about themselves.

Nick was a fat lout. He was angry; he didn't have a polite or positive thing to say about anyone. He made sure a three table radius knew the name and address of his financial manager, who could attest to his solid standing. He slipped in, more often than necessary, that his town didn't have "people of color."

I get it, she thought. You don't have to say it again.

Fritz was selling himself as some big super spy. "I work for an agency that can't be named." "When I was in the Middle East…." "Paraguay is the biggest drug stronghold." "They teach us to kill with a single finger. A little finger." "The President usually asks for me to do the job."

Yeah. Right.

Brent, every now and then, would try to include her in the conversation. Once, during a rare period of silence from Nick and Fritz, he leaned forward and said, "I'm interested in learning more about you…"

Nick interrupted with a comment about "the fat girl sitting with Travis." From then on, Brent spent the evening looking around the room.

At one point, she wondered why Nick, who was so adamant about being able to meet women, wouldn't give her the time of day. Oh, right. No "women of color" in his home town.

She sighed, finished her shrimp, and emptied another glass of wine.

Tom blinked. He was certain the algorithms had worked their magic this week. Which of these beautiful women was he to spend his evening with?

The literature had said this evening would be a scripted pairing. Four individuals, matched by algorithm, would be able to get to know one another over a several-course meal. An expensive several-course meal. With drinks included.

The literature stated the algorithms would provide ample opportunity for everyone in the group to meet their potential soul mate.

And here he was. One of these women would be it. His soul mate.

An outside observer would remind him to re-insert the word "potential." His inner child would not.

Brent was pleased to be sitting at Tiffany's table. He had noticed her the night before. Since his promotion, and his catapult into "the big time," as his boss liked to say, he had been to several corporate parties.

He was unsure of himself. He didn't know what to do, or how he was supposed to act. All of the women were young – much younger than their husbands – tall, svelte, and immaculately dressed and made-up. He supposed he was now making enough money to dress a girlfriend in that style, but he had to find the right woman.

His partners, his bosses, and his supposed friends had tried to introduce him to women who would be perfect for him. They were beautiful. They were well-off, or carried themselves as if they were. They talked in lilting tones about their trainer, their favorite dress shops, that "darling little jewelry store that has only the most unique pieces." He could barely make it through an evening with them.

This woman, Tiffany, was different. She had curves in all the right places. She wanted to talk about things of substance, if she could get a word in edgewise. She held up to the relentless badgering of Nick about "people of color."

Yes. He would like to get to know her. Not tonight, though. She had just belted down her third glass of wine. Who could blame her?

Thad was so excited to be in the company of two exotic beauties that he couldn't stop talking. He went on and on and on. While he talked about his work as a tax accountant – his clients included the mayor – and his home town of Doylestown, Pennsylvania – could he have made it sound any more boring? – and his hobbies – bowling in the winter and fishing in the summer – it sounded stodgy even to him.

But he couldn't stop.

Heaven help him, he couldn't stop.

By the time the dessert course arrived, Annie met Isabel's eyes. They had both kept an eye on the room and an ear to the conversations they could hear.

This evening could not end soon enough.

9

Annie went downstairs early on Saturday morning. She thought, perhaps, she could be helpful. She also thought, perhaps, Henrie would be chatty.

The chances of both were slim.

Today would be much warmer than yesterday. It would soar to one degree over freezing. Then it would drop to almost single digits. They might get lucky and see a sliver of sunshine. If they kept their eyes to the sky and never looked away.

Henrie was putting the finishing touches on his country breakfast Benedict, pouring hollandaise on the French bread, egg, chicken and bacon creation. He turned as she entered the kitchen. "Good morning. How was the Hearts On Fire dinner last night?"

Seven cats wandered around the kitchen, wrapping themselves around Henrie's legs and standing up to smell the bacon.

"Nearly a disaster, but, in a way, fun to watch. Chris and I continued people-watching for a while. We started at the Tap, then went to Sassy P's. We noticed only one couple sticking together following the dreadful match-ups for dinner."

"How did our guests fare?"

Henrie listened as he pulled seven little dishes from the refrigerator. Each had a few crumbles of bacon. They were placed on the floor for the cats. He noticed Honey Bear in the doorway and prepared another dish.

"Well, let's see. Liz, who made a play for Dorian, who made a play for Geraldine, and Peggy outed him for a fraud…this is all kind of circular. Anyway, Liz was paired with Dorian and another couple. I don't remember the names. Anyway, the second guy at the table wasn't the most handsome man in the room, which, I assume, is important to Liz. More important is the status of his wallet. Liz made a play for him, and spent the rest of the evening with him."

"That frees Dorian for Geraldine."

"Oh, that's the rest of it. He invited Geraldine to dinner, and she's not a member, so her meal was not paid. And it wasn't in the script, so to speak. She was thrown out!"

"I hope you did not do the throwing."

"I was nowhere near it. The head heart, Travis, tossed her."

"That must have been interesting."

"It was. Trust me. And then, Miss Hot To Trot, Farah, and her friend Elena were paired with two men who could not have been more obviously wrong. For them, at least. At least they were at the same table."

"I fear neither will find what they seek this week, from what I've heard."

"I fear you are correct. And last, but not least, it appears our sweet-looking Peggy has a rack of knives at her disposal. It seems she and the head heart do not like one another. He put her with three of the most contemptible men of the group. No, that's not right. Two of them were contemptible. The other seemed nice. Intense, but nice."

"It is a wonder this group has made it so far. This is their fifth outing?"

"Fifth or sixth. Certainly it will be the last. The head heart himself went down in flames."

"He was paired with someone?"

"Someone that he's had his eye on for a while, and instead of making a play, he made her pay to come. She made a big play for a few men after dinner last night. I think, if nothing else, she's come out of her shell."

"Perhaps there will be a happy ending for someone."

"Perhaps. Hey, have you heard what the police and fire departments were doing last night?"

Engrossed in conversation, neither heard people entering the foyer, then the dining room. They were shocked to hear Brian, from the doorway, say, "There was a fire at Chateau Simon."

Chris and Sis went out the back way, through the all-season porch, for a run on the beach. Mid-way through their run, they ran into Ray, owner of the yacht-for-hire, The Escape, and his constant companion, Jock.

The dogs greeted one another and sprinted away together. Chris and Ray stopped to take a breath.

"It's hard on them to run slow, when they're with us."

"It is." Ray was breathing hard. "How was dinner last night?"

"Dinner was great. The Hearts On Fire club had a few rough spots."

"How rough?"

"I'd say if you want to be entertained, come to The Avenue almost anytime between now and Valentine's Day for some outstanding people-watching."

"Sounds good. Why don't I call Pete and Janet, Maybe we can do it tonight."

"Great. I'll call Clara. I think Ramon is in town this week. We can either take all of the dogs with us or leave them at the Inn."

"With all the people in town, let's leave them at the Inn."

Henrie asked, "Annie, could you please bring the Benedict?" In the dining room, he poured coffee for Brian and Janet.

"Please tell us what happened." He sat. Henrie rarely sat in the dining room. His concerned tone had the desired effect. Brian and Janet talked.

While they talked, Annie served small portions of Benedict, sausage and oatmeal to the couple. Finally, she poured coffee for Henrie and herself and sat as well.

Tears ran down Janet's face while Brian talked. "The fire started in the tasting room, behind the bar. There wasn't a lot of damage, mostly water and smoke. It was small enough, it couldn't be seen from the road. Someone called it in from a phone they haven't been able to trace."

Janet sniffed and added. "They said I left a fan plugged in, and a faulty cord sparked turpentine. I didn't even use turpentine. I used latex paint."

Annie asked, "What did they say? The police, fire department?"

Brian answered. "The Chief of Police came out. He looked at the doors and windows, tried to figure out how someone could have gotten in. He said he had some ideas about that. And they did what they could do to take, you know, evidence."

"Do you have any idea who would have done it?"

Brian and Janet looked at one another. Brian looked down at his plate, then up at Annie and Henrie. "Greg said a couple from Marsh Haven wanted to buy it, but they couldn't afford it. We've put a lot of work into it, and now, if we can't get it going, the price will go down. Even though we've put tens of thousands into it."

"Did you tell Pete about this? The Chief of Police?"

"We didn't think about it last night. We're going to call him this morning."

"You could ask him to come here, if that would help. He's a friend."

"I'll just call him. We have an appointment pretty soon. Greg is going to show us a house. I sure hope we can still buy one."

Annie asked, "Surely your insurance will cover…"

"It's not that. Our investors seemed to back out yesterday. We're about on our last dime."

"That couple you talked about? They backed out?"

"They appear not to be interested. I met with them yesterday, and they, well, they left before I reached the pitch."

"They're from Marsh Haven, too, aren't they?"

"Yes, they are."

"It wouldn't hurt if Pete had that information as well. He likes to know everything."

"Okay. We'll tell him."

Underneath the detective table, Mr. Bean said, *"I told you something was wrong with those people. I bet they did it."*

By ten o'clock, Henrie put breakfast away, having fed no one but Brian and Janet. Annie left to spend the morning with Sam and Nancy. It was Saturday, but the cats had gone to work. Henrie didn't know why. He guessed they felt a need to "detect."

He sat down to put together a grocery and menu list for the following week, giving a great deal of attention to Thursday. JoJo had worked in the kitchen before, but he wanted to make sure he covered all possible contingencies.

Hilly typically took Saturdays off, so Henrie went through the rooms in the main house, to make sure they were clean and to replace used towels with fresh.

He did not need to tend to the carriage house. Brian and Janet had a special rate, as did Sam and Nancy. Their rooms were cleaned once a week. They had a supply of clean towels and linens, which would be replaced on Monday.

He partially cooked the butternut squash for Sunday's breakfast dish – a winter wheat and berry bowl – and retired to his apartment. There, he double checked his suit for Valentine's Day and the gift he had procured from Gema. Nestled into a gift box was a floating diamond solitaire pendant in platinum. He checked and put aside the clothes he would pack for travel.

Once again, he sent a text message. "Cannot wait for our special night." He watched it go and deleted his text history.

Annie sat with Nancy and Sam in their room. As they talked about the week ahead, Annie shared Brian and Janet's story. She also shared a private concern.

"I'm thinking Bon Vivant has run its course. With Cookie gone, I don't know, it seems like I'm asking too much of everybody."

"How hard would it be to close?"

"The thing is, it's very popular. There isn't another fine dining place in Chelsea. We're full both nights, every weekend."

"Have you talked to anyone else about it? Felicity? George? Henrie? Chris?"

"No. I'm just now putting my thoughts into words. I don't know what to do."

"Well, dear, take your time. Talk to your people. Figure it out. You're good at that."

Mo sat next to the clean glasses again. The Tap was busy. His eyes had grown accustomed to the brooches and stickpins. Before listening in to conversations, he watched for the telltale jewelry.

George had opened today, and once again, the inept Mike had come for advice.

While putting a lunch menu and a beer on the bar, George asked, "How'd it go, Mike?"

"Not so well. I was seated at a table with two other men and one girl."

"Woman."

"Right. Woman. Anyway, she seemed to be a professional member."

"A pro? A hooker?"

"No! It seems like she attends all of these group things, and she knows everyone."

"What's her name? Is she in here now?"

Mike swiveled on the bar stool and scanned the tables. "No, I don't see her."

"What does she look like?"

"She's a redhead, with freckles."

"I've seen her. She talks to just about everyone, men and women. She seems to stir the pot a little."

"Yeah. That's her. Anyway, I thought about practicing talking to her, but she would probably just tell everyone how stupid I am. So I talked to the other guys at the table."

"That's okay. I didn't see you in here last night. Did you go to Sassy P's?"

"No, man, I went to bed. I'll try it again tonight. There's a buffet dinner and dance. Maybe I'll ask a couple of girls…"

"…women…"

"…women, thanks, to dance with me."

An older man took the stool next to Mike. "I looked for you after dinner. Didn't find you here or the winery."

"Oh, hi, John. Have you met George?"

"No. How do you do? Are you a friend of Mike?"

"We just met." George put a menu on the bar. "Can I get a drink for you?"

"I'll have whatever pale ale you have on tap."

George left to get the ale, but kept an ear open to the conversation. John said, "I've been thinking a lot about what you said last night. This morning, I called a woman that goes to my church. She's a widow; I knew her husband."

"Really? How'd it go?"

"Very well, very well. I'm leaving early. My car is packed. Tomorrow morning I'll meet her at church, and afterwards, we're going to go out for a bite to eat."

"I'm happy for you! I hope it turns out well."

"I do, too. Actually, I wanted to get your telephone number. I want to let you know how it goes."

"Sure. Here." George set the beer down as Mike pulled a business card from his pocket.

John turned to George. "I'd like this grilled crab cake sandwich with sweet potato fries. Mike, what will you have? Lunch is on me."

"You don't have to do that."

"I do. You are the one that should be in charge of this lonely hearts club. You're a natural. I want to show my appreciation."

"Thanks. I'll have the same."

George turned the order in and was ready to ask Mike about his skills, when Travis came in.

He staggered to the bar and sat, elbows up and head in his hands. "I need a hair of that dog that bit me."

George shook his head. "I made your drinks all night, Travis. Do you want the same?"

"Yeah. Extra hot and heavy on the olives."

George made another Virgin Mary and picked up some crackers on his way back. Putting them on the bar, he asked, "What happened last night? You sat in the back of the room and cried."

"You saw that?"

"Everybody saw that."

"Oh, no. They must think I'm a fool."

"No, everyone thought you were drunk. I didn't tell them what I was sending over. So, what happened?"

"I've been...well...I was attracted to this woman, and, well, instead of getting with her on my own, I recommended this group thing to her."

"And she had to pay for it."

"Yeah. And she's...well...she's..."

"Ticked."

"Yeah."

"How much does one of these group outings cost?"

George coughed when Travis gave him the amount. "And what else do they have to pay for?"

"Um...hotel, breakfast and lunch every day, everything on Sunday, transportation to and from town...um...some cash bar stuff...any extras...."

"That's pretty salty. Did you offer to pay her back?"

"Well…that's the thing. I didn't offer. She demanded repayment. Today, she sent a bill to my hotel. It includes transportation, hotel, meals she'll have to pay on her own, you name it."

"How much?"

George coughed again at the answer. "Do you have that much?"

"Barely."

"Well, sometimes mistakes are costly."

"Yep. I tell ya, when I get through thish week, I'm shuttin' it down."

Travis had started to slur his words, as if he were drunk. George asked, "Did you have anything to drink before you got here?"

"No. Doan drink."

George bent down and tried to look Travis in the eyes. Like a drunk, it was hard for him to keep his eyes open. He pulled his phone from his pocket and dialed The Clinic.

Jennifer answered.

"Hey. This is George. Have a crazy situation here. A guy is drinking a Virgin Mary, extra hot sauce and heavy on the olives. I swear he's acting drunk."

"I'll be right there."

Within minutes, an ambulance pulled up. Jennifer, a nurse practitioner and one of the local emergency responders, walked in with a medical bag in hand. She went straight to the bar and swiveled the stool, looking into his face and eyes.

"Hey, there. I'm Jennifer. What's your name?"

"Travish."

"Travis, do you know what day it is?"

"Shaturday."

"Date?"

"Um….Shaturday afore Valentine."

"Well, Travis, I can't tell if you're having an allergic reaction or if something else is going on." Jennifer turned to Greorge. "Has he done this before?"

"Last night he sat in the corner and put a few of these down. I thought he was crying, like he was upset or sad. Today, he came in asking for the hair of the dog, and acted like he had a headache. I just thought, you know, he was…"

"Odd."

"Yeah."

"Well, you made a good call today. Come on, Travis. I'm taking you to the hospital for a check-up."

Travis made a feable attempt to protest. "I have ta make sure it runs…"

George turned to look at Mike, then he looked back at Travis. "Tell you what. I'll get someone to take over for you, okay? Take care of yourself. I'll take care of you."

George thought about it. Before Jennifer moved him, he added, "Do you have files or something? Stuff about the group?"

Travis dug around in a pocket and brought out a key. "Ace Hotel. Room forty-eight. Eighty-four. Shomethin' like that. Pashword 'heartson123.' No cap."

George thought Travis had gone round the bend, until he realized all of the files must be on a computer. He grabbed a napkin and wrote it down.

10

Annie pulled her coat closer. The temperature had not yet reached its lofty goal of thirty four degrees. She left Nancy and Sam and went to the Café. Having the lonely hearts group in town would bring extra business. Plus it would be a great people-watching day.

She arrived to find Clara, owner of the flower and gift shop, Bloomin' Crazy, and her – I need to ask her what term she uses – male friend Ramon. Ramon's Bergamasco, a large dog whose fur was a variety of brown colors in mats and dreadlocks, lay behind the hostess stand. Tiger Lily was curled into her stomach, back against her hind legs. They appeared to be deep in conversation.

Clara was a Haitian beauty. She wore her dark hair pulled back. This time of year, the signature red flower worn behind her ear was silk. Ramon's dreadlocks, secured to the back of his head with a colorful band, mirrored those of his dog. When he was in town, on break from his jazz fusion band, he was the second Jamaican in town.

Annie ran through a few more words on her way to their table.

Buddy. Too much like a pal.

Cohort. Sounds scientific.

Comrade. Russian?

Helpmate. He doesn't help me with much.

Mate. Maybe on a ship.

Sidekick. Is he the Lone Ranger to my Tonto?

Companion. Maybe.

Annie waved away the server headed in her direction as she sat down. "I have a question."

"We already said yes."

"What?"

"We said yes when Chris called."

"Why did Chris call?"

"To invite us to get together tonight."

"Oh. He did? What are we doing?"

"Meeting at Sassy P's. People-watching."

"Oh. What time?"

"He said we'll start a little later, because the flaming hearts…"

"Hearts On Fire…"

"Yeah, them. They have a dance thingy first, so they'll get to the winery later."

"Good idea. What time?"

"Have you talked to your man today?"

"That's kind of my question. What term do the two of you use to refer to one another?"

"What?"

Ramon, who typically sat back until the conversation reached a point of stability, sat forward. "I call her Empress."

"Empress? Impressive."

"Not really. It's a common Rastafarian term for girlfriend."

"Still, it sounds very nice. What about you? What do you call Ramon?"

"I call him my kòkòt."

"What's that?"

"Sweetheart in Haitian."

"That's beautiful."

"What's up, Annie?"

"I'm trying to figure out what to call Chris. I've been through a lot of English words, but none of them seem right. I hate to borrow from Jamaica or Haiti."

Ramon asked, "What about Spanish?"

"I just hate to steal. American culture doesn't have a kòkòt or an Empress. Emperor. That sounds awful."

"Sugar?"

Annie tried it on. "Sugar. Sugar-Daddy. Sugar-Bun. Sugar-Darlin'. Sugar-Pie. Sugar-Plum."

Clara's next word summed it up. "Ick."

"I'll give it a rest for now."

They turned and watched as Geraldine walked in with lonely heart Dorian. While they watched, Annie asked, "So, are she and Everett separated again?"

Clara said, "I don't think so. He called in an order for flowers just yesterday."

"For her?"

"Yes. To be delivered on Valentine's Day."

Mike watched Travis leave for the hospital with a mixture of feelings. On the one hand, he felt bad for Travis. On the other, he wondered what would happen with the rest of the week if Travis was incapacitated.

John, whose exit was delayed by the mini-drama, said, "You know, Mike, you can take over for him tonight, if he doesn't come back."

"What?"

"I'm serious. You have a knack."

George approached them. "Don't leave, Mike. I have to make a couple of calls, but I have a proposition for you."

George moved away and dialed a couple of times. Mike assumed he was alerting people to the circumstances. This was a great group of people. They seemed to work well together, and if he wasn't mistaken, they shared staff on occasion.

John said, "Thanks again. I'll let you know how it works out." And he left.

George returned. "Okay. I took care of the details."

"What details?"

"Making sure food happens, drinks happen, music happens, you know, in case anyone was waiting to hear from Travis about anything."

"That's good."

"Now, all they need is an emcee. A coordinator. A gatherer."

"Where you gonna find someone to do that?"

"I'm lookin' at 'im."

"What?"

"What you did, for, was his name John? That was a piece of matchmaking magic."

Mike considered it. "John said the same thing. He said I could do it."

"You can. Isabel, the hostess from last night, is coming over to talk to you. Keep an open mind. You can do this. Here's a key to a room at the Ace Hotel. I called the manager. He'll get you to the right one. After you meet with Isabel, go there and get Travis's computer. Here's the password. Hope I got that right."

Isabel nearly ran into Greg as she hurried from Mr. Bean's. "Sorry, Greg. Hello, Brian, Janet. I'm so sorry to hear about the fire last night. I know it won't make everything better, but Carlos said if you came in today, lunch is on the house. I have to run. Again, I'm sorry."

Greg stood aside, holding the door, and eventually, they were in and taking a look at the menu board.

Mr. Bean reached as high as he could, tapping Greg's hip and asking for attention. Greg, being a Chelsea native fully in touch with his cat side, gave Mr. Bean the pet he craved. A full-head, getting him behind the ears pet.

Daniela, Carlos's mother, came to the counter. "Hello, Greg. It's so good to see you. And you're Brian, and Janet, yes? You order whatever you like. We pay. Everything. All three."

Brian said, "You don't need to…"

"Shush. You order. We have two grilled cheese sandwiches today. One with cheddar, bacon, chicken and apple slices, one with caramelized onion, mushroom and Swiss. You choose the bread. And we have a Reuben po' boy. I made chicken tortilla and butternut squash soup."

They ordered and sat at the table furthest from the door. Mr. Bean joined them, sitting on the fourth chair and – for the most part – keeping his paws off the table.

Janet said, "I think you know we love the house."

"It's perfect," added Brian. "And the yard is just right. Nicely landscaped, but small enough to be manageable."

"Yes. We won't have time for yardwork. Or cleaning. The house is a perfect size for that, too, and not a thing needs to be done to it."

Greg said, "If you buy it, Daniela will be your neighbor. She and her daughters live in the house across the street."

"That's a pretty one. It's a little bigger, with a bigger yard."

"Perfect for three adults. So, let's get to the 'but.' The two of you have been nothing but 'but' today."

"You know about the fire…"

"And I know you're covered by insurance."

"But there are deeper issues. Our investors seem to have evaporated. And the fire was probably arson."

"What?"

"Arson. And when we talked to the Chief of Police, he wanted to get the names of the people that were interested in buying it before us."

"Whatever for? Are they suspects?"

"As he said, everyone is a suspect until they're not. Including us, I assume."

"Surely not."

"We have a tiny window of time, in between when people saw us and when the fire had to start."

"Pete's a fair guy. And he seems to have a sixth sense."

Mr. Bean purred at that. He knew he was part of Pete's sixth sense.

"Well, let's talk about first things first. You like the house. We'll figure out how to make that happen. You lost your investors. That's big, and could be the killer for everything else. Brian, you asked if these buyers might be interested in investing. I can talk to them, but having them come under suspicion for a fire might put a damper on the conversation."

Brian sighed. "I don't know how that can be helped."

"It's all fairly depressing," added Janet.

"Let me give those folks a call." Greg browsed through his contacts list and found them. He pressed "dial" and waited for them to answer.

"Dave, this is Greg."

"Hey, Greg. Did you find a winery for us?"

"Well, after a fashion. I was wondering if you would be willing to consider investing in a winery."

"Investing? I don't think so. We want to own it. Run it. Say, I heard that one we looked at had a fire last night."

"You heard about that?"

"Yeah. It was on the news."

Greg's cell phone chirped. He glanced at the screen and saw a breaking news alert from the local television station, WQVX. "Fire Nearly Destroys Winery" flashed out in red letters.

Greg asked, "What station was that?"

"Oh, you know, the one that everyone watches. The one with the goofy roving reporter."

"WQVX?"

"Yeah. You haven't heard about it? I thought maybe those folks would want to, you know, sell?"

"No, they don't. But I didn't know about the fire. That might change things. If not, I take it you aren't interested in investing?"

"Nah. But if anything shakes loose on the one we saw, let me know."

"Okay. Thanks Dave. Say, what time was that news report on? I want to look for it online."

"It was the morning news. Nine o'clock or so."

Greg hung up, looked at the couple and said, "No, he isn't interested. But I just had an interesting conversation."

Annie walked toward Marco's table to deliver coffee. She was stopped in her tracks by Geraldine, who stood so quickly, Annie almost ran into her with the tray. Annie had the catlike reflexes of a seasoned server. Her arms, carrying the tray, went one way, and she sidestepped in another. Not a drop was spilled.

Marco was Pete's second-in-command with the Police Department. They didn't have a budget for a deputy chief, but Marco had been elevated to that status after he, because he was otherwise occupied, didn't participate in a Keystone Cop event.

When Annie did the server two-step, Marco leaned around to see what had happened.

Geraldine stood over the gaping Dorian. She slapped him in the face so hard that nearly all the Café's patrons turned to look.

"I will NOT be the patsy you use to connect with…with…that woman! I don't care how rich you are!"

She punctuated her comments by reaching to Annie's tray, picking up the first cup within her reach, and throwing the contents into his face.

She turned on her heel and stormed out, leaving him gasping at the surprise and at the heat of the liquid thrown. Annie put her tray down on Marco's table and grabbed for napkins to dab the hot water off his face.

He pushed her away and looked around, taking inventory of all who saw the event. Annie noticed several Hearts On Fire members staring back.

11

Tiger Lily sat on the windowsill of the library once again. And once again, she compared the icicles to her memory of them.

They were longer and fatter. Once again, none had fallen off.

The temperature had briefly reached the magical above-freezing number, and the sun made an appearance every now and then.

She rolled over. Honey Bear had already taken the best seat on the cushions. The other cats were slowly gathering. They looked at Honey Bear, then jumped to the windowsill. Soon, the sill was filled. Mr. Bean, who had jumped up next to Tiger Lily, said, *"I think Greg found out who set the fire."*

"What" "Huh?" "Greg?" "Trill!"

"Yeah. He had lunch with the winery people, and he called some other people, and they said some strange things, and then, when he hung up, he called Pete."

"Pete? Did you see Cyril?"

"Yeah. Cyril thinks those nice people are being scammed."

"Wot's scammed? Is dat when pitchers get took?"

Little Socks pressed her forehead into the cold window, hoping to escape the slow mind of her little sister.

Tiger Lily said, *"Scammed means some kind of crime, where someone tries to steal something."*

"Wot is it when pitchers get tooked?"

"I think that's scanned."

"Yeah. Scammed."

Little Socks sighed dramatically and exclaimed, *"They stole something!"*

"Wot dey steal?"

Tiger Lily glared at Little Socks and answered. *"I don't know. What did you hear, Mr. Bean?"*

"I didn't understand everything. There was this name and that name, and then it all sounded the same. And there was something about they heard it on the news before the news reported it."

Thoroughly confused, they decided it was time to nap.

Henrie heard his guests come into the house. They must have taken lunch together, or gone shopping. Sure enough, when he entered the foyer, he saw they carried bags from Bloomin' Crazy and CyberHealth.

Farah, who had been laughing, turned sultry when she saw him. "Henrie, I've been hoping to see you. I didn't want to invade your space."

"How can I help you?"

"I was hoping you had no plans tonight and would agree to spend it with me."

"I hate to disappoint, but allow me to make it up by offering refreshment. I prepared caprese tartlets, oyster shell canapes and virgin sangria.

"How do you make a virgin sangria?"

"Sliced lemon, lime, oranges and apples have been soaking in black tea, pomegranate juice and a touch of orange juice. Glasses will be topped with a spritz of ginger ale and each glass will have a cinnamon stick for stirring."

"Yum. I'll follow you anywhere."

"You need only follow me to the all-season porch."

Laughter trailed behind him as he led the way, Farah stepping up to take his arm. Graciously, he allowed her to take it, but once on the porch, he took her hand, removed it from his arm, gave a slight bow and left.

Isabel and Mike were on the second floor of the Café, the catering venue. He walked around, taking stock of the tables set for various foods, the space set aside for the DJ, and the tables for seating.

"So there aren't any place markers? People sit anywhere?"

"Yes. Hopefully men and women are meeting, getting to know one another."

"Doubtful. I don't think Travis had a clue how to choose companionable folks. I don't know what to do, how to make it better."

"It's not my place, but why not think about a mixer activity?"

"Like what?"

"I don't know. Let's Google some things."

Isabel took a tablet out of her purse and set it up on a table. She Googled, they read, she Googled again, and eventually they found something that looked as if it would work."

"See? If you do this, and use your natural skills with people…."

"Why are people saying that?"

"I saw what you did last night. You got the older man moving in the right direction."

"That was one thing, and he's a lot like my dad."

"I can tell. You know people."

"So what's the final head count?"

"Last night we had twenty-six men and eighteen women. Six additional men registered for tonight."

"Minus one. John left. Actually two. I'm taking myself out of the mix. Oops, three. Travis is gone.

"Well, that helps, but not a lot. Do you think some will decide not to come?"

"Probably not. Everyone's paid, and the food will be good."

Mike paused. "Okay. Let's assume we'll have twenty-nine men. We can't do a two-minute mix. It will have to be one minute."

Mike looked around the room. "How can we make it comfortable for people to stand for about a half hour?"

Isabel thought about it. "We have fifteen cocktail tables for dinner and drinks. That's enough for a couple to stand on either side. They can lean, or if someone can't stand, we can pull a bar stool over."

"That will work. Then we'll just leave the tables in the circle for dinner."

"So, drinks first for about a half hour, then invite people to join the mixer for about a half hour. And during the mixer, the food comes out."

"What about the appetizers?"

Isabel looked around the room. "We'll put that table out and decorate it, put it by the bar. Appetizers will go there."

"That's a plan."

Pete sat in his office. He looked at the two index cards. Two sets of names, two telephone numbers. The names were similar. The numbers were only two digits apart.

He looked for all four people on a variety of social media sites and came up empty-handed. That was unusual. It would not have been unusual for one couple to be out of the social media loop, but for both….

Once again, he Googled their names and came up empty. That, too, was unusual.

"Okay, Cyril. It's time for me to make the first call."

He looked at the cards again. One had the names of Dan and Jenny Evans, investors. The other, Dave and Jessica Emerson, purchasers. He put Dan and Jenny on top, so he wouldn't get confused, and called the number.

A woman answered.

"Mrs. Evans?"

"Yes, who is this?"

"This is the Chief of Police of Chelsea. I'm calling in regard to your interest in the Chateau Simon Winery."

"Well, yes. We were going to invest." She apparently turned from the phone. She called, "Dan! Dan, come in here." Speaking to Pete again, she said, "We heard about the fire on the news. Was anyone hurt?"

"No, ma'am. I'm just making as wide a circle as I can to interview everyone connected to the winery. I'm wondering if you can come in for an interview."

She had given the phone to Dan. "When would you want us to come in?"

"Today or tomorrow would be good."

"Well, we're busy today, and tomorrow's Sunday. Are you open?"

"We're always open. Would you be able to come in?"

"Well…would it be possible for you to come here?"

"Certainly. Give me your address, and tell me what time."

After making an appointment, Pete put the second card on top and called. It rang several times, finally going to voice mail. The voice was a canned recording. He left a message. He did not expect to hear from them. At least, not today.

Elena picked a caprese tartlet from the plate and said, "Farah, give it up. He's gay. Gay. Not your type."

"Oh, for one night, maybe he'll change. I told you, I'm not here for marriage. I'm here for a good time."

Liz said, "Why is that?"

Farah laughed. "I guess I can tell you. It's just us girls. I'm married."

"What?" "No!"

Elena stopped sipping on her sangria, She was stunned. She knew Farah had a secret, but this?

"So, why Hearts On Fire? Why not spend a weekend at a resort or something?"

Farah said, "I've done that. I've tried Paris, Monaco, the Caribbean, cruises. I've spent so much of his money traveling to have a good time that I lost track. Hundreds of thousands."

Liz got a wicked grin on her face. "Your form says you're filthy rich, doesn't it?"

"Yes. That seems to draw them. Somehow, this time, it hasn't worked."

"You know I hooked up with Dorian on the first night." She leaned in. "He's not bad, you know. I think, for tonight, if that's all you're looking for, go for him. And lead him down the primrose path. Let him think he's going to fall into big bucks."

"He hasn't seemed interested. I wondered if it was my, um, complexion."

"I don't know. But don't worry about it. Make a play."

Elena agreed. "She's right. Make a play for him. Make it hurt. But have a good time in the process. I'm wondering what to do myself. I'm afraid I'll go back to Omaha with nothing to show for it."

Liz said, "I think I'm going to make a play for Jim. He's not much to look at, but he's loaded."

Peggy asked, "What about you, Tiffany?"

"There's a guy named Brent that I'm going to try to go further with. He's nice. He seems kind of shy."

Peggy said, "I know about him. He's making mega bucks for the first time ever. He's not rich, yet, but he doesn't know how to act in what you would call high circles. He's keeping an eye on everything."

Elena gave Peggy a hard stare. "How do you know so much about everyone here?"

Peggy shut her mouth and looked at Elena. "I, um heard him telling someone."

"He actually told someone that story?"

"Well, yeah. He did."

Liz leaned in. "What are you doing, Peggy? Do you have some kind of inside track?"

"No, no, nothing like that. I heard him. I think he was talking to that bartender."

Elena wondered about that, but she got sidetracked. Peggy was saying, ""If you're only looking for fun, Elena, why don't you try Fritz? I'll bet he would show you a good time, if you can get past his line of crap."

"I might try that. I saw you talking to him the first night, Peggy. What's he like, really?"

Peggy gave a dismissive wave. "He'll sell himself as a super spy. But he's a hunk, isn't he?"

12

Annie swooped into the kitchen and grabbed an oyster canape. "Yum. This is really good, Henrie."

"Thank you. Are you going out tonight?"

"Yes. Chris made plans with Pete and Ray, and he called Clara and Ramon, too."

"Are you getting together here?"

"To start with, then we're going to Sassy P's. If the people-watching is good, we'll go on to Mo's Tap."

"People-watching. That should be an illuminating experience."

"Did you ever see our guests?"

"I did. I am apparently very gay."

"Good. Means we're truly open to everything."

"I suppose so."

"Did they say anything about the club?"

"From what I could hear, everyone is changing their battle plan. Two are going for fun."

"Let me see…Farah definitely, and Elena?"

"Very good. One has lowered her standards and is going for not-so-good-looking but wealthy."

"Liz. I saw that last night."

"Again, very good. One is looking for a relationship."

"Tiffany? Who did she settle on?"

"It appeared to be the least awful person at her table last night."

"That leaves Peggy. What's her story?"

"The only thing I picked up is that she seems to know more than anyone else about everyone else."

Annie said, "This is her fifth time out, but she knows more, apparently. She knows details about first-timers. I wonder if she and Travis are in this together."

"Or perhaps she has a back door into the information."

"Henrie, you are positively paranoid."

"Positively."

"Hey, did you hear about Travis?"

"Is that the computer genius? The one that can't seem to handle people?"

"That's him. George realized something wasn't right, and Jennifer took him to the hospital. It wasn't the allergic reaction she hoped it would be. Something is really wrong. I don't know what."

"How is the weekend going to progress without him?"

"George took care of that, too. He realized that this young man, Mike, I think, had a skill with people. After he sent Travis to the hospital, he got Mike to say yes."

"George has a way of getting things done."

"Yeah. Whenever we have a disaster, it's best if it happens in front of him."

"Sam shared an interesting conversation he had with Frank. He researched the experience other towns have had with this group."

"What did he find out?"

"He learned how businesses can protect themselves. For example, Gema makes specialty items that are often purchased as gifts for loved ones. She could put a substantial amount of money and time into a special piece that – given the whims of a heart – are no longer wanted."

"Oh. Good point. What else?"

"He learned that, on occasion, a brawl may break out. You want to be aware of this as you watch people tonight."

"Good thing Pete will be there!"

Mike looked up from Travis's laptop. He had been engrossed in the Hearts On Fire personal applications when he heard Isabel some in.

"Isabel, I think we won't do the mixer."

"Really?"

"Yeah. I think I'm going to try to find certain people and walk them to other people, you know, just introduce them. We'll go with an hour for cash bar and appetizers. Will there be enough?"

"We'll have enough food and drink. Are you positive about this?"

"Yeah. There are lots of people who will never find a match with this group, but I think a few may benefit, if they get in front of the right person."

"We'll do it your way."

Nancy knocked on the door of the Rainbow Room. Janet answered. "Good evening, dear. I know you're in the middle of several things, but Sam and I want to take you out to dinner. Are you available?"

Janet looked into the room, probably checking with Brian. "We really need to talk about our situation..."

"I know you do, dear. But honestly, you might be able to benefit from a night out. And with people who may be able to offer the perspective of age and maturity. Or, we can just have a great meal and fantastic wine."

Brian came to the door. "That sounds wonderful. Let me clean up."

"We'll get a table at Sassy P's. What wine can we order for you?"

Janet answered. "Ask Jesus to choose a dry red for us."

A bottle of dry red and a chilled bottle of dry white were on the table when Brian and Janet walked in. Sam had chosen a table just around the corner from the tasting room. For now, it was fairly private.

Nancy handed out menus. When Minnie came around, they ordered New Orleans cuisine to share: shrimp and chicken etouffe, dirty rice, red beans and rice, creole crab cakes.

While Sam poured wine, Nancy did what she did so well. She broke the ice with a sledge hammer.

"When you live here, and when your business is going, you'll understand that nothing stays a secret around here for long. We know about the fire, and about the suspected arson. We also know that you've lost your investors, so there is no need to go through all that."

Brian and Janet looked at one another.

Nancy continued. "It seems to me that you have a few mountains to climb. We might be able to help."

"How?"

"We don't have the money to invest, but we may know people who would be interested."

"Really? People here? In Chelsea?"

"Yes. Are you interested in meeting them?"

"Sure!"

"Are you willing to keep their identities a secret?"

Janet laughed. "I think you just told us that can't happen in this town. I mean, you don't even live here, but you know everything about us."

"This might be possible, as long as we are discreet."

"We'll be as discreet as possible. When can we meet them?"

"First of all, what do you need? Financially?"

"We think twenty-five thousand will be all that we need."

"Need. To do it right, is that enough?"

Brian and Janet looked at one another. Brian answered. "To do it right, we could use fifty."

"What arrangements do you plan to propose?"

Janet said, "For twenty-five thousand, we were willing to offer ten percent, compounded, with full payout at the end of five years. For fifty, we'll give fifteen percent, with full payout at the end of ten."

Sam said, "That's generous."

"We think we can do it. We have a prime piece of property, and the building is perfect for events, fundraisers, maybe even a weekend restaurant."

"Really? You'd open a restaurant? What kind?"

"We were thinking about fine dining."

"Only on the weekends?"

"Yes."

Sam and Nancy looked at one another. Perhaps they could kill two birds with one stone.

Sam made some notes on a napkin. Nancy, looking over his shoulder, saw $25K 10% 5yr on one line, and $50K 15% 10yr on another.

Minnie brought their food. "More wine?"

Nancy said, "Bring these young people another bottle, please, Minnie. And take these dirty napkins as you go."

"Sure."

"Thank you, dear."

Nancy looked at Janet and Brian. "Let's talk about something else. Where are you from? Why did you decide to open a winery?"

Nancy drew them out as only she was able. They talked, they ate, they drank, and before too long, Brian and Janet were laughing, something Nancy would have bet they didn't think possible.

As they finished their meal, Jesus came out. He stopped at the table and asked, "Did you enjoy your meals?"

Brian answered. "It was great, Jesus. Thanks."

"Can I get anything else for you?"

Sam said, "I don't think so. Thanks for a great meal, as always."

Jesus shook Sam's hand as he left. Nancy saw the napkin go into his pocket.

"Let's get together again. Soon. But now, it's late. We old folks have to go to bed."

Mike introduced himself to everyone during the cocktail hour. He had a good memory for faces, names and personal details. While he couldn't remember everything – he'd had little time to prepare – he could pull facts up if he breathed into it.

He approached couples who seemed to struggle getting to know one another. He could start a meaningful conversation by saying things like, "Jerry, I understand you're an accountant. Did you know Francine has a master's degree in business? She works for a similar firm, but, it's in the human resources division, right?"

Or, "Cheryl, I read about your love of water sports. Did you know Charlie has won water-skiing competitions?"

Bells would go off, lights would flash, and Mike would move on.

He considered his best pairing of the evening that between Charlie, who had let him know her intent to get all of her money back, and Thad, a middle-aged widowed accountant.

He approached women standing by themselves and, with a hand on an elbow, would lead them to men standing by themselves. He seemed to have the Midas touch. An introduction, a smile and a nod, and most were off to the races. So to speak.

In some instances, he said hello, smiled, nodded and moved on, adding a mental note to keep an eye on the situation. Such was the situation with Farah and Dorian, Tonya and Bob, Liz and Jim.

There were men, obviously, who would never get their foot into the game. One man put his foot into his mouth and his fist into a platter of stuffed mushrooms. Mike took a deep breath and waded in.

"Nick, I'm going to have to ask…"

"That son-of-a…"

"Don't say it. Mixed company."

"You know what I mean. He's hogging everyone. He got Liz. Then he got that local dame. Now he's got Farah. He ain't lettin' any of us make time with any of the hot ones."

"You aren't helping your situation."

"This is all a load of crap!"

"How about this. I will refund everything from tonight on. You just need to go. You'll get a check within the week."

Nick took a step back. "What?"

"I will refund your money, from tonight on. I just need you to leave. Now."

"You ain't got the right…"

"I do."

"You little…"

"I have the right, I've asked you to leave, I've promised you payment. You have witnesses to that. Now please leave, or I will have to summon local law enforcement."

"I'll deal with you tomorrow."

"That's fine, but it will have to be at something other than a Hearts On Fire event, because you are not welcome to return."

Mike stood firm, and in what seemed to him to be forever, but in actuality was about two minutes, Nick turned and left. As the door closed behind him, applause erupted around the room.

Brian and Janet lay in bed, Simon between them, and watched the evening news.

Janet said, "What do you think? Do they really know someone?"

"They do. And I think I know who."

"Who?"

"I think it's Jesus and Minnie."

"Why do you think that?"

"Nancy and Sam are just a sweet older couple who would have made it rich as matchmakers. We're going to be okay, Janet. It's all going to work out."

Isabel and Mike collapsed into chairs. Servers continued to work around them, cleaning up tables and closing out the cash bar.

"That was something else!" said Mike. "They didn't seem to mind that it was me and not Travis."

"I didn't see anyone last night that cared for him."

"So…let's be honest. It was a qualified success."

"You're right. But that's only because there are more men than women. From the women's perspective, I think most got what they wanted tonight."

"You're right. Some of the women are looking for…let's say a good time. And that's okay. I'm a little concerned about some of them, but…we have a couple more days to finish things up."

Isabel said, "You have a day of rest tomorrow. Then Monday is…"

"Sassy P's. Tuesday, Fat Tuesday, is Mo's."

"And then the big night. I won't be around to help you until Wednesday. You have my number. Call me if there's anything you think I can do to help."

"Thanks. I know George, but who do I talk to about Monday night?"

"Minnie or Jesus. If you're too tired tonight, here's Minnie's cell number. They'll do everything they can to help."

Isabel paused, then she looked Mike square in the eyes. "I would not have thought you capable of doing what you did with Nick. That was impressive."

Mike laughed. "I didn't know I had it in me, but it felt good. It felt right."

They gathered at the Inn. Pete, the Chief of Police, his wife Janet and their English setter, Cyril. Ray and Cheryl, who owned The Marina and The Escape, and their Portuguese water dog Jock. Clara, from Bloomin' Crazy, her boyfriend Ramon, a saxophonist with a jazz fusion band, and his Bergamasco, Fiamma. Chris and his giant schnauzer, Sis. Annie and her seven cats, Nancy's cat, two neighborhood cats, Simon Finnegan and Oscar McMurphy, and Tillie, the Jack Russell Terrier.

The humans stood in the foyer, looking into the library. Annie said, "We have to stop getting pets."

Janet said, "I think you're right. But if I'm counting correctly, you rescued all of them with the exception of three big dogs and your mother's cat. You're the one that needs to stop."

"They all have homes."

"They do."

"And they're very helpful."

Pete said, "They usually are. Cyril hasn't given me any hints about the arson yet. I might have to solve that one on my own."

Most of the cats had gathered on the cushions underneath the windowsill. They were cat-napping. The dogs were on the other side of the library, probably talking about dog stuff. Tiger Lily was on the windowsill. Annie noticed she looked up intently. She walked behind and looked in the same direction. Apparently she studied the icicles. Nothing else could have caught her attention given the angle of her head.

"They're set. There are water bowls in the kitchen. They all know where to find them."

"Then let's go."

Eight humans left for Sassy P's.

Tiger Lily watched the humans as they walked down the porch steps, took a right and walked the short distance to the winery.

"Do you think we ought to send a spy or two tonight? The air feels like it's popping or something. I bet something's going to happen."

Little Socks yawned. *"What could happen?"*

Sassy Pants said, *"Dose heart peoples, dey say lonely, I say crazy."*

Mr. Bean added, *"And there's that arson, and two or four people that could be doing it."*

"What do they have to do with anything? They're doing stuff out of town, where we never go."

"But we coulds be askted to go an detect."

Little Socks pressed her forehead into the cushions. Then she looked up. *"What are you looking at, anyway?"*

"The icicles. I'm watching them grow."

"Trill!"

Tiger Lily typically couldn't understand Mo, who had not progressed beyond speaking the kitten language he, Kali and Ko used. This time, she understood his intent. She answered. *"Well, I'm not actually watching them grow. I look at them every morning and every evening, and I compare what I see to my memory of them. They're still growing. They get longer, wider and pointier. And none of them have fallen down. I count them, too. Actually, I think we have a couple more."*

"Do you have a favorite?"

"Yes. Here at the corner of the porch, see it? It's the longest and the widest. It has a really sharp point, too. It's almost to the porch rail. It looks like, if you were to pull it down, that it would bring down a whole bunch of ice with it

Kali and Ko said together, *"I see it!" "Yeah! It's a monster!"*

Oscar McMurphy, who lived with her brother across The Avenue at the hardware and computer store, said,

"You get better ones than we do. I think it has something to do with the sun. The sun we get is afternoon sun, and in February, it's pretty puny."

Tiger Lily said, *"Back to the subject, should we send spies out tonight? I think Mommy said they would go to the winery and then to Mo's."*

"Trill!"

Kali and Ko said together, *"That's a good idea, Mo." "Yeah, Mo, go on over and wait for them."*

Sassy Pants said, *"Da winery is my place. Maybe I should goes over."*

"Do you want anyone to go with you?"

"Yeah. Sometimes I forgets someting. It beez easier if someone helps me remember."

"Mr. Bean, can you go with her?"

"Sure. I'll go."

Mo turned to Kali and Ko and trilled softly.

Kali said, *"Mo wants someone to go with him, too. Just in case. Maybe Sis can go with him."*

"We can't get Sis out of here. The only dog that will fit through the cat door is Tillie."

Kali said, *"Well, I can't go. I don't go out after dark."*

"You don't ever go out. Neither does Ko. That's okay. Little Socks, how about you?"

"Why me? Why not Simon Finnegan, or Oscar McMurphy?"

Simon Finnegan said, *"They aren't used to us being in there at night, and we aren't used to being around that many people, unless there are lots of cats."*

Tiger Lily looked at Honey Bear. *"Do you want to…"*

He hissed.

Little Socks said, *"Then you have to go."*

Tiger Lily sighed. She wanted to stay in and nap this evening, but she supposed maybe she should. After all, she considered herself the lead detective.

"Alright. Let's go, Mo. You know if you try to tell me something, I probably won't understand you."

"Trill."

Clara wanted to sit at a cocktail table, giving them a higher perspective as they people-watched. She was an expert. "I want this chair. No, this one. This is the best one."

"They're all the same."

"This is the best one to see who's doing what to whom. Look. I can see everything in here, and all the way into the tasting room."

"We need to get you some cameras."

"Yeah. Why don't you do that?"

Annie sat next to Clara. When Chris and Ramon sat across from them, they both moved their hands and arms. It took a little juggling, but eventually the men were sitting in such a way as to not block their view.

Soon, members from the club began to drift in, mostly in twos. A few singles walked in as well.

Annie said, "It looks like the event tonight was more successful than last night."

"Why do you say that?"

"People are smiling."

At the other end of the table, Janet said, "Chris, Ramon, why don't you move your chairs over here. We might have a real conversation. You know, sports, cars, boats. Clara and Annie are going to drive you crazy with their stuff."

Chris and Ramon looked at one another, stood, and dragged their chairs to the other end of the table. Annie and Clara didn't even notice.

Annie did notice when Sassy Pants and Mr. Bean jumped to the top of the table.

"Kids! What are you doing here?"

She heard, "Meow ick ick meow."

What Sassy Pants really said was, *"We'ze protectin' you, Mommy."*

Mr. Bean said, *"Save me!"*

Clara and Annie stroked the cats and watched and talked. If you can call it talking. It was a combination of pointing, gawking, exclaiming, back-biting and, in minor amounts, positive strokes.

Annie said, "That's Liz. She's staying at the Inn. She's with guy number two tonight."

"Who is he?"

"I don't know his name, but his bank account has to be healthy or she wouldn't be with him. Looks like they're getting along very well."

"He looks like a pumpkin, but happy. It looks like he didn't expect to find anyone so, well, pretty. Who was her guy number one?"

"He's the one that was hitting on Geraldine, too. Oh, look, here she comes."

Geraldine walked into the back room of the winery, scanned the guests, and saw Annie and Clara. She seemed to hesitate, but then she walked toward them.

She raised her nose at the cats on the table. Sassy Pants hissed until Mr. Bean bopped her on the nose.

Geraldine pulled her eyes away from the cats. "Hello girls. Are you all alone tonight, or are those other people at the end of the table with you?"

"We're people-watching, Geraldine. They weren't interested. What brings you out?"

"You know very well what brings me out, Annie. You've seen me go down in flames at least three times in the last three days."

"Really, only two…"

"Oh, don't pander. I suppose I can tell you. Everett may be gone for good this time, and I'm looking for a man that can meet my financial needs. There. I said it. Are you happy now?"

"No, I'm not. Pull up a chair, Geraldine. I need to tell you about him."

"Really? You know something? He's not staying at the Inn…"

"No, but people talk."

Clara stood and dragged a chair to the table. Geraldine sat.

"His name is Dorian, right?"

"Yes."

"I thought you pretty much ended it at lunch today."

"I did. Then I thought better of it. I came to do what I could to make it up to him."

"He's not rich."

"He is."

"He's not. He's on his last dime, and he's looking for someone that can keep him in the manner that he's been accustomed."

Geraldine looked at her. "You don't say."

"I do. Save yourself a little grief. He's not worth it. He thinks Liz has money, and he thinks you do, too."

"And I'm sure you are painfully aware I do not."

"I know nothing about your financial situation, but I do know, if you hook up with him, what money you do have will be gone with the wind."

"Well, I suppose I should thank you."

"You're welcome."

Geraldine leaned in. "Do you, um, know which of these men might be on the wealthy side?"

"Frankly, no. I heard about him, because the women staying with us had a conversation. They were trying to save Liz."

"The leggy blond."

"Yes."

"She's with someone else tonight. I wonder…"

"Geraldine! Stop it! Surely there are other ways of meeting men. If Everett is really gone this time…"

"He is. He actually took half the clothes from his closet this time, and he went to Marsh Haven."

"Not to that apartment that Greg has?"

"It was rented out."

"I'm sorry, Geraldine. Please, don't get yourself into a jam tonight."

"Oh, alright. I suppose I'll go home. I can't get into any trouble there."

As she left, Clara said, "I thought she'd never leave. And what was that thing she had on?"

"What?"

"She had a brooch that didn't match what she was wearing."

"I didn't notice."

Clara stared at Annie. "No wonder."

"No wonder, what?"

"Sometimes I just want to take you to my house and dress you."

Clara looked around the room. Her gaze settled. "Do you know who's at that table?"

Annie looked. "Yes. The woman is Tiffany. She's staying at the Inn. Last night she was the only woman with what looked like an abysmal group of men, with the possible exception of the one that was sitting directly across from her. That's who she's with tonight."

"They look…um…into one another."

"They do, don't they. Something went right tonight. Hey, there's another one of our guests, Elena."

"Where?"

"Table in the front corner, tall, Nordic looking. I think she's Russian. I can't see who she's with. Oh, I can see him now. She's with…oh no!"

"What?"

"I caught some of his conversation last night. He's trying to convince people he's some sort of super spy."

"If you're a spy, you don't go around telling people, do you?"

"No. He's a creep."

"But he's handsome."

"Maybe she's going for something other than, you know, a ring."

"Why pay the money for a lonely hearts club if you aren't going for the ring?"

"Apparently, the group is a disaster. If you ask me, this is probably the last outing."

"What about that couple?"

"Where?"

"Over there, at the front of the room."

Annie said, "Oh, the woman is Charlie. She's the one that is making Travis give her money back."

"What?"

"He wanted to meet her, but instead of calling her for a date, like he could have, he encouraged her to come for the group. And pay for it. And like a fool, he told her."

"Who's she with?"

"I don't know his name. He and another man were mismatched with Elena and Farah last night, two women for whom the word exotic was coined. But he looks perfectly matched to Charlie."

"Who is this guy walking in? Everybody wants to talk to him. Men and women both. It looks like they're thanking him."

"The head of the group, the computer nerd, had a medical emergency. This guy was sitting at the bar at Mo's when it happened, and George convinced him to step in."

"George? Since when is he part of the club?"

"He's not. But the guy, Travis, that was in charge, didn't have any kind of back-up, and George saw something in this guy."

"Must have been the right stuff. Looks like they're happy he's in charge. What's his name?"

"Mike."

"We've seen all we're going to see here. Let's go to Mo's."

Annie turned to say something to Chris, who was deep in conversation with Pete and Ramon. Ray leaned into Janet and Cheryl. They had another conversation going.

Annie got off her chair. "Come on. We'll go in the back way." She looked at Sassy Pants and Mr. Bean. "You two stay with Chris or go home."

The cats looked at one another, jumped down and ran through the winery, apparently headed home.

Annie and Clara went through the door that allowed Mo's Tap and Sassy P's to share a garden area in warmer seasons. Annie, being Annie, had a key.

Clara adjusted her eyes to the dim interior of the bar. "Look. There are two seats right here at the end of the bar. We can see everyone from here."

They grabbed the barstools and jumped up. George gave them a wave to let them know he'd be there and finished an order.

When he arrived, he asked, "Where'd you come from? I didn't see you."

Clara said, "Annie's got a key, man. She can go anywhere."

George laughed. "What do you want?"

Annie said, "Top shelf margarita, rocks."

Clara said, "Same. Anything interesting going on tonight?"

Mo and Tiger Lily materialized on top of the bar. They looked frantic.

George pointed at them. "They came in a little bit ago, but it got so busy, they hightailed it behind the bar. They've been hiding under the well drinks for the last half hour."

"You're safe now, kids. Stick with us. I just sent Sassy Pants and Mr. Bean home."

Mo buried his head in Annie's chest. Tiger Lily leaned into her left arm.

George said, "We have several lonely hearts here tonight. And look, Annie, Geraldine just came in."

Annie and Clara strained their necks until they saw her. With Dorian.

"I told her to steer clear. His silk suit is probably rented. Or stolen."

"He came in with another woman."

"Which one?"

"That tall drink of water sitting at a booth by herself right now, getting angrier by the second."

Annie said, "Her name is Farah. She tried to convince Henrie to…well, I'm not certain what she wanted him to do, but Henrie is happy she now thinks he's gay."

George turned back to her. "She what?"

"Thinks Henrie is gay, because he rebuffed her."

George pointed. "Take a look at her. She is not used to being rebuffed."

Clara said, "Henrie's a hotty, but he's all hands-off."

Without warning, George put his hands on the bar and leapt over, missing everyone in the immediate vicinity and walking quickly to Geraldine and Dorian. He put himself in between the two, facing Geraldine. He said something to her.

Geraldine glared at George, looked past him at Dorian, said something, turned and left.

Clara said, "I wonder what that was all about."

Annie said, "I didn't know George was so agile."

George went behind the bar in a more traditional fashion, walking instead of jumping. He took care of several drinks for his bar customers and servers, eventually coming to the end with two margaritas.

"What happened?"

"She slapped him. I didn't want it to get any more physical."

"What did she say when she left?"

"Something about keeping his lying, cheapskate – and then she named a body part – away from her.

Annie realized she was gripping both Tiger Lily and Mo to her chest. They didn't seem to mind.

Clara pointed. "Do you know those two?"

Annie craned her neck again to see the couple.

"Oh, that's the woman that reminds me of Liz. Tall, leggy and blond. She has a scar that tends to turn men off. But that guy doesn't seem to mind. Wonder what his story is?"

"What are their names?"

"I don't know…"

From behind them came a male voice. "I think you're looking at Tonya and Bob."

Annie and Clara turned to see Mike, the new head heart guy. Annie looked past him to the door. "How'd you get in?"

"George gave me a key so I could go back and forth."

"So what's up with Tonya and Bob?"

Mike looked at Clara, then back at Annie.

Annie said, "She's fine. She's a friend of mine, and she won't tell anyone."

"Well, you know I'm filling in. This is beyond my depth. I'm worried for her. I didn't like what I saw in his profile."

"What did you see?"

"It's what I didn't see. There were a lot of holes. I think he's covering something."

"How do you let her know?"

"I don't have a clue."

Clara said, "Leave it to me." She drained her margarita, said, "Get me another," and started to walk toward the couple.

She turned back. "Silly me. Tell me something, anything about Bob."

"He's from Cleveland. It seems like he's had several jobs. He was a loan officer at a couple of different banks. I can't remember all of it. I read through a lot of profiles today."

"What were the holes?"

"Dates in between jobs, reasons for leaving one job for another. It said he has never married, but he has the look of an experienced philanderer, and those guys are typically married."

Clara left again. It took several seconds to weave through the crowd, but then they heard it. Classic Clara.

"Bob? Bob! It's you! Well, don't you remember me? I'm Clara!"

Annie couldn't hear his response, but his face reflected shock, then confusion.

Clara said, "Surely you remember. You approved a loan for me? When I lived in Cleveland? And then we had such a wonderful week. Until your wife found out. Oh, excuse me. I'm Clara. You aren't married to him, are you?"

The woman, with a shocked expression, shook her head.

Clara scooted her over on the booth bench and sat. "Well, since you aren't married, are you available, Bob? I mean, we had such a good…"

The man, speaking loud enough now that they could hear him, "I'm sorry. I don't remember you. I am on a date with…"

"Being connected to someone never stopped you before. This is my town, Bob. I can show you a really good time."

Annie felt the presence of someone else behind her. It was Ramon. "Oh, Ramon. You're just in time. Clara is throwing a wrench into a lonely heart date."

Ramon stared at Clara. "I thought you were people-watching, not people-playing."

"We're helping Mike. Mike, meet Ramon, Clara's kòkòt."

"Her what?"

"Her kòkòt. Haitian for sweetheart."

"What a great term."

"I thought so, too. Hey, Mike, it's time for you to get in there."

"And do what?"

"Rescue Tonya."

"How?"

"Wade in there and figure it out."

Mike shook his head and waded over. Annie watched as he introduced himself to Clara, then turned to Tonya. They had a conversation. Clara leaned around him and gave a finger wave to Ramon and a thumbs up to Annie.

She slid out of the booth. Tonya followed her, and Mike took his place opposite Bob.

Ramon waited until Clara reached them, leaned in to kiss her on the cheek, and said, "I'm going back there, where it's safe."

Annie watched him as he left. "How'd he get in here?"

She watched as Mo and Tiger Lily jumped to the floor. They followed Ramon to Sassy P's, and, probably, home to safety.

Clara said, "I think Bob may be leaving the program."

Tonya said, "Thank you. Thank you thank you thank you. He thought I had money from the accident! He was so…so…good! I fell for his crap, hook, line and sinker."

"Well sit with us," said Annie. "George, three margaritas!"

As George delivered the drinks, he smiled at Tonya. "Successful escape?"

"Yes. That guy, that Mike, he's really good at this."

Clara grabbed her glass and said, "Me, too!"

"You, too! You were a star!" The three women raised their glasses in a toast.

Annie turned to the front of the bar when she heard a commotion. She couldn't see it at first. Her vision was blocked by George, who, once again, jumped quickly and gracefully over the bar.

Then she saw Dorian and the big, loud, angry guy from the night before. Their fight was physical. Dorian had a cut over his eyelid; blood flowed freely.

George got between the two, facing the big lout. He manhandled him to the door and out. Situation handled, he returned to his post behind the bar in a more traditional fashion.

Annie turned to Clara. "Really. Did you know he was this agile?"

Jim took a deep breath. She was breathtaking. She was perfect in every way. But what was he thinking? He was here to do a job. He couldn't get side-tracked.

If he allowed himself to do it, he could fall in love with this woman. This woman who wanted him only for his money. This woman who would do anything to marry a man to take care of her in style.

He could do that. And maybe he would love her enough to make up for the fact that she wouldn't be able to love him. Maybe.

He would only walk her to her door tonight, for two reasons. One was that, perhaps, she would think kindly of him if he behaved like a gentleman. The other, well, he had another reason, too.

Sassy Pants and Mr. Bean scooted through the cat door, happy to be out of the humid cold and away from the too-many human feet.

By the time they returned, the dogs had moved to the cushions and settled in with the remaining cats.

"Dere was lots of peoples dere, and most of dem was gettin' lovey dovey."

"Yeah. You could really tell its gonna be Valentines Day. Hey, do you think Mo will write another poem for Valentines?"

The year before, Mo had written a siren song. Well, he didn't actually write it, but he composed it in his head. Kali, who promised to recite it word for word as he trilled, actually blushed.

Remembering it, she blushed again. *"Let's talk about something else."*

Ko yawned. *"Let's go to sleep."*

They hadn't slept long before Tiger Lily and Mo ran in.

"Trill!"

"I can interpret that," said Tiger Lily. *"We were lucky to get out with our lives!"*

Mo trilled again. Sassy Pants said, *"He saided George hadded to jump over da bar."*

Tiger Lily added, *"Geraldine slapped the same guy she slapped at the Café. Again."*

"Trill!"

Sassy Pants turned to Mo. *"Which one?"*

"Trill."

"Oh! Mo saided da woman dat wanted to go out wit Henrie is wit dat same man."

Kali and Ko said together, *"That's Farah." "Not Liz?"*

Tiger Lily sighed. *"This is confusing."*

"Trill, trill, trill!"

Sassy Pants again, *"Clara wented over to a boot and maded a scene."*

Tiger Lily took over. *"She saved a woman from making a bad choice. It was kind of fun to watch Clara be Clara."*

They all turned as someone came into the foyer. It was Farah. And that man. Tiger Lily whispered, *"That's Dorian."*

They listened as the two came in.

Farah said, "Let me find my room key. I'll get a cold cloth for your eye." She fumbled in her purse.

Dorian said, "Maybe we can go on up, look for the key there."

"My room's down here. Oh, I've got it." Farah pulled a key out of her purse and they turned toward the back hallway.

The door opened again. A man none of the companions had seen before stepped in. He stopped, looking at Farah. Farah stopped, looking at him.

She said, "Well, this is fun."

"Fun isn't the word I would use." He turned to Dorian. "Who are you?"

"Um…I didn't mean to get into the middle of something. I'll just…." He moved toward the still-open door.

The man didn't budge. "No. Why don't you stick around. It would be worth it to me – if you get my drift – to get some dirt on my wife. You could walk away with a fortune. Cheaper for me than having to pay her the pre-nup."

Dorian stopped in his tracks. "Worth it?" He turned to look at Farah, and looked back at the man. "How much?"

"Couple mil."

"Oh. Well, that…that…" he turned to look at Farah again, who stood, one hand on her hip. If looks could kill, both men would be dead.

"Um, well, here, let me give you my information." He fished a card from his pocket and handed it to the man. The man read the card, put it in a pocket and nodded, moving to make room for him to go.

Dorian left. Farah's expression had not changed. The man approached her, slowly, his facial expression growing more menacing with every step. Suddenly, he stopped.

Without a sound, three large dogs had appeared. They moved slowly, making a semi-circle in front of him, teeth bared, low growls coming from their throats.

He stopped. "Well…it seems you have some…um, protection."

Farah's expression changed to one of rueful satisfaction.

Henrie appeared in the doorway to the dining room. Dressed in snappy tuxedo pajamas and fancy leather slippers, he held a ball bat in one hand and slapped it smartly against the other.

"Welcome to the KaliKo Inn," he said. "How may I help you?"

"Um…just leaving. Farah, we're not finished. I'll get that divorce, and you won't get a penny."

"I think you're forgetting something."

"What's that?"

"In order to break the agreement, I actually have to have slept with someone. I haven't."

"Prove it."

Jock moved to within biting range on the right side.

"You prove that I did."

"I'll see you in court."

Cyril moved to within biting range on the left side.

"It will be a pleasure."

The man was aware the dogs had begun to crowd his space. When he didn't leave, Sis moved to within biting range in front of him. Right in front of him. She was within a second of a very painful location.

"Um, the dogs…"

Henrie said, "Sit."

Three dogs sat, obedient to Henrie's command but with fangs bared. Tillie, who had waited in relative safety in the library, ran out and nipped the man's ankle. He jumped and ran for the door.

Tiger Lily woke with a start. It took her a few seconds to get her bearings. She was still in the library. Pete had been here. He had gone, taking Cyril with him. Jock and Fiamma were still here. Mommy must not be home yet.

What had she heard? She listened carefully but did not hear the sound again.

It's possible, she thought, that she had been dreaming. Mommy dreamed sometimes and woke in the middle of the night, unsure of what had startled her.

That must have been it. She had been dreaming.

13

Henrie put the finishing touches to his winter breakfast bowl. He shredded the butternut squash, added wheat berries that had soaked overnight, dried cranberries, walnuts and honey. With a little water, butter and salt, the mixture went into the oven. It would be finished in plenty of time.

Pete and Cyril walked in through the back door.

"Good morning, Pete. Cyril, come here, I have a treat." Cyril padded over slowly. Some days, he would have come quickly, but he was working this morning He had to show some maturity.

"What brings you out so early? It seems you barely left."

"Oh, business. The station got a call early this morning. We had to go out to the winery again."

"Another untraceable call?"

"Yes." Pete helped himself to a cup of Henrie's perfect coffee.

"From a person that in all likelihood could not see a problem at the winery from the road?"

"Yes, again."

"What was it this time?"

"Have you been out there?"

"Yes, I've driven by on occasion."

"You know how many oversized windows there are?"

"Yes."

"Well, about a third of them are still in one piece."

"No."

"Yes. Someone had to be up close and personal with a sledge hammer or something like that."

"Is the interior damaged?"

"As far as I can tell, only where the glass shattered inside. They'll need to do some cosmetic repair."

"Do they know yet?"

"Not yet. I wanted to let them sleep."

"Did you sleep last night?"

"After taking the report about your – let's call him an intruder – I went home and got into bed. I'll bet I had two hours of sleep. Heck. I can run for a week on two hours."

"I am certain you can. I will call Boone to see if he can be ready to assist with covering the windows."

"Already done. He's getting the material together now. The temperature is already above thirty-two, and rain is headed our way."

"Do you think one of the couples – the one that tried to purchase the winery, or the one that said they would invest – are responsible?"

"My guess is it's the same people."

"How is that possible? This is not a major city. Certainly they would be found out."

"Not necessarily. Let's say the 'real' couple contacted Greg and asked to see the winery. They don't get it, then another couple, let's say brunette instead of blond, or bald instead of bushy, concocted an investment scheme."

"They would scheme to turn over money?"

"They would scheme to get close to the owners, have an excuse to be at the winery while renovations were going on. This didn't start until the work was nearly finished and the building was insured for property damage."

"But you have Greg, Brian and Janet. They have seen these people."

"My guess is that the real people are the ones that Greg met. The fake ones are the investors. My guess is they've used wigs, make-up, theater padding, any number of disguise techniques. There will always be a reason I can't get them together at the same time."

"You are a smarter man than I."

"Not smarter. I've learned to think like a criminal. That smells really good, Henrie."

"Help yourself. There will be leftovers even if you eat. I have cooked for all of our guests. I assume the five women, as is now their pattern, will sleep through breakfast. Annie and Chris, Nancy and Sam, and Brian and Janet will be here shortly, in time for us to go to church."

Pete helped himself to the winter berry bowl, bacon, ham, almond French toast casserole and a large pastry.

"What's this? It looks like a million calories, and I'm going to eat all of it."

Henrie looked. "You have selected the strawberry cream cheese paczki."

"The what?"

"Pete! Do not tell me you have never eaten paczki. This is traditional food."

"Maybe I've just been busy. Did Carlos make this?"

"Yes. Every year, well, this week of every year, he makes them."

"The second week of February? Or is this the third?"

"The week of Fat Tuesday."

"Don't tell me we have Fat Tuesday this week."

"You have been living under a rock. Mo's Tap has been advertising Fat Tuesday specials for a month."

"Well…I learned something today."

Brian and Janet were the first to arrive for breakfast. Pete walked into the dining room and met them. Henrie stayed in the kitchen, but listened to the conversation.

Pete's voice was low, but Henrie knew the content of his conversation. He laid out, slowly and painfully, the extent of the damages, and that, at this time, no evidence pointed to anyone in particular.

Brian's spoke softly, but Henrie could hear what he said. "Well, I suppose we'd better get out there and take a look."

Janet's response was much louder. "No! This can't be happening!" She pushed back from the table and ran from the dining room.

Brian didn't follow. "She needs to get through this. I'll go on out, Chief. I'll leave right away."

After getting his treat from Henrie and listening to Pete talk about his theories, Cyril poked his nose under the detective table. Several cats were there, and they greeted him pleasantly, but he wanted to see Tiger Lily.

He padded into the library. She sat on the windowsill, looking with dismay at something outside.

"What's wrong?"

"My big icicle is gone, and all the ice around it."

"I'll bet most of them will be gone before the day is over. It's warming up now, and it's going to rain almost all day."

"I wanted to watch it fall. It was so big and pretty."

"I'm sorry about that. Do you want to hear about the winery?"

"Yes. Has Pete made progress?"

"Not yet. Someone was out there last night and broke out most of the windows."

From the dining room, they heard Janet wail, "No! This can't be happening!"

She ran out of the dining room and out of the Inn. Tiger Lily watched her progress as she ran through the yard rather than on the sidewalk. Without boots, she ran through snow, now snow and water puddles with a layer of ice on the bottom, to the carriage house. She fell once, picked herself up and ran on.

Then Brian came out of the dining room. He put on his coat and left. They watched him walk to the parking lot in front of the porch and get into his vehicle.

Pete called, "Cyril! Let's go!"

Sis led the way to church. It was now raining in earnest. All of the cats were in the covered wagon, except for Honey Bear. Honey Bear detested the wagon and having to be in such close proximity to all the cats.

Nancy said, "He doesn't go to church at home, so I can't make him go now."

They left without him.

Pastor Teresa's church, Soul's Harbor, ministered to everyone in this tourist community. It was more like a chapel than a church in that regard. Typically, services followed the Christian tradition.

This was the Sunday before the beginning of Lent. Her sermon was based on one of the most recognized passages in the New Testament, John 3:16-17. She always read from the New King James Version.

For God so loved the world that He gave His only begotten Son, that whoever believes in Him should not perish but have everlasting life. For God did not send His Son into the world to condemn the world, but that the world through Him might be saved.

Sermon over, neighborhood cats and dogs sat up from their lounging positions on the floor and in the pews. They loved singing the last hymn with the congregation.

Today, the last hymn was "How Great Thou Art." Annie loved this hymn, and she loved the howls of the dogs on the long, high notes. "Then sings my *hoowwllll!*" always made her smile.

As did "How great Thou *hoowwllll!* How *hoowwllll!* Thou art."

On the way home, Sis splashed through every puddle on the median. She ran ahead and splashed her way back. By the time they pulled even to the Inn, she was soaked.

Chris tried to get her attention. "Sis, come here. I need you to shake it off."

She ran across the street to the Inn, then back, hitting the water gathering at the edges of both sides of the road.

Chris stood, shaking his head. "You are so wet. You're going to soak Henrie's furniture."

In answer, Sis ran back across to the Inn, then started a trip around the house. She stopped at the edge of the steps and nosed her way into the bushes.

Then she jumped, ran in three tight circles, sat down and howled.

Annie asked, "What? Is she still singing that hymn?"

"No, I don't think so," said Chris. He walked past the steps and into the bushes. He looked down, then backed away, taking Sis by the collar as he did.

"We need to call Pete."

Annie, from the top of the steps, looked down and over.

There was a body of a man, lying on the frozen ground and surrounded by the morning rain.

14

Pete sent Marco to investigate the murder. Henrie had knocked on each guest door and informed them of the need to stay in their rooms and to speak to no one until a police officer came for them.

Now, Annie, the cats and Sis were alone in the library. Chris was in the dining room; Henrie was in the kitchen; Nancy and Sam were in their suite in the carriage house. Brian was still at the winery, but Janet was in the room.

Annie sat on a sofa, surrounded by her cats and Sis, drinking a cup of Henrie's cinnamon and vanilla tea. She was numb. Once again, the Inn was caught up in a murder. She had lost track of the crimes that had been committed in and around the Inn, and by or against a guest.

Sis was on the sofa with her, huddled onto her lap. She was an awfully big dog to be on her lap, but Annie knew she was not fully recovered from the shock of her own beginning in Chelsea.

She wished she could understand what the cats and Sis said to one another. All she knew for certain was that finally, Sis had stopped shaking. She was awake, but breathing easily.

Little Socks, stretched out on top of Sis, said, *"That's good. Go to sleep now. Really, it's not always this exciting. You just came at a bad time, and we had a little set-back today. You'll be fine."*

Marco came into the library. "Okay for me to sit?"

"Sure, Marco. How can I help?"

Marco handed Annie his cell phone. He had snapped a photo of the dead man. "Do you recognize him?"

"Oh! That's Dorian. He's one of the lonely hearts guys."

"What do you know about him?"

"Well, what I know is hearsay. You'll have to follow up with others. I heard he used to be rich, now he isn't. The first night they were all in town…that was Thursday…I saw him at the winery with Liz, one of our guests."

Marco took notes as she talked. She went on. "Jet told me he'd hit on several women until Liz came in, then Liz kind of took over. From talking to her, I picked up that she had a list of rich guys and started at the top."

"The top?"

"This is purely guessing. I think she listed them by portfolio amount first, looks second."

"Okay. Gives me an avenue to question. You saw the two of them together?"

"I did. They had a glass of wine, maybe two, then they left together. I'm not sure where they went, but a half hour, forty-five minutes later, he came back. Without her. That's when he connected with Geraldine."

Annie looked up at Marco. "You remember that scene at the Café on Saturday? That was him."

Marco nodded, but said nothing.

Annie thought about it. "Then the next time I saw him was Friday around noon at the Café. He met Geraldine, and was seen by several Hearts On Fire people. That afternoon, our guests talked about it, said he was doing something 'outside the box.' Dating outside the box. Apparently that's frowned upon."

"By whom?"

"It's one of the rules, or guidelines, or something, from the club. Anyway, that afternoon is when I heard that he was rich, now he's not."

Annie neglected to say that Liz had become angry. If she were called upon to be specific, she would. She continued. "On Friday night, there was a scene at Bon Vivant. Dorian was seated at a table with Liz and two others. But he had invited Geraldine to come. She did, but she's not a member of the club. She was kicked out."

Marco looked up from his notes. "Geraldine was kicked out of your restaurant?"

"Not by me. By the guy in charge. Travis."

Marco nodded and continued taking notes.

"And then Liz stopped talking to him. She almost turned completely in her chair to have her back to him and she talked to the other guy all evening. At least when I saw them."

"Is that all you remember about Friday?"

"Yes. If I remember something else, I'll give you a call. Let's see. On Saturday, you saw what I saw at lunch, and that night when I saw him, he was at Mo's Tap. It was after their dinner-dance thing. He was with Farah, another one of our guests, and Geraldine came in. I hate to say, but there was another scene with her. George had to intervene."

"What did George do?"

"He had to get in between them, and he told Geraldine to go."

"So whatever happened, she instigated it?"

"I hate to say, Marco. That would be my best guess, but really, you need to talk to George. And after that, a big guy, a lout, one of the lonely hearts guys, came in and punched him. George had to kick him out, too."

"George was busy."

"He was. Very. Hmmmm….. And then, when I looked around again, I didn't see him or Farah. I don't know if they left together or separately, but maybe George saw them. They ended up here together."

"How do you know that?"

"There was an incident, Henrie called Pete, but you may not have had a chance to catch up. Farah is married. Her husband showed up here. Henrie didn't see him, but as Pete took statements, it came out that Dorian was here when the husband showed up."

"Why was Pete called?"

"Henrie and the dogs had to force the husband out."

"Henrie? And the dogs?"

"Yes. Henrie with his ever-present ball bat, and, um, Sis, here, Cyril and Jock. And Tillie, I think, nipped at his heels."

Marco closed his eyes and shook his head. He took a deep breath and said, "Can you remember anything else?"

"No, not really."

"Okay. It looks like I need to talk to all of your female guests – well, I'll talk to everyone, to make a timeline – but to focus on this Dorian character, I need to talk to the lonely hearts guests, Henrie, George, Jet, Geraldine, this Travis guy…"

"He's in the hospital."

"Excuse me?"

"Travis became ill during the day on Saturday. You'll need to talk to him, but a guy named Mike took over on Saturday."

"Okay. Travis, Mike…who else should I talk to from Bon Vivant?"

"Isabel. She worked with Travis Friday night and with Mike Saturday. And you should probably talk to Candice, who would have been on the bar floor, and maybe Jesus and Minnie."

Annie and Marco had been through a period of time in which they were – to put it mildly – not getting along well. They had put this behind them, and now, for the most part, Marco kept an open mind as Annie was concerned. Sometimes, Marco reverted to type. Like now.

"You just seem to always be in the middle of it, don't you."

Annie didn't answer.

Marco handed her a notebook. "Write it down. Everything you remember, days, times, places, and people that may have witnessed what you saw or heard."

He left, and as Annie made her statement, she hated to add the name of her mother, who had heard the story of the fake millionaire. Then she added Clara, who was people-watching the night before.

When she heard Pete come in, she breathed a sigh of relief.

Pete sat in the dining room with Chris. "You're isolated?"

"Yep. I probably have the least knowledge of anyone. I saw the photo. He's a lonely hearts guy."

"Not a guest?"

"Not a guest."

"Connected to a guest?"

"I think, connected to two."

"Oh, boy. Well, I have an appointment in Marsh Haven. You guys will be sitting alone until tomorrow afternoon unless I get some help in here."

Pete called the state police. "Do I have any juice with you guys? I have a couple of investigations. One is a murder that is mushrooming. I need people who can interview...um...maybe up to twenty people. Right away."

"You've got juice. I'll send three."

"Thanks." Pete gave them the address.

Pete found Marco and asked him to bring Henrie to the library. There, with Annie, they discussed logistics.

"We need to do these interviews quickly, while memories are fresh, and we don't have enough space at the department. Why don't we figure out a way to interview everyone here?"

Annie said, "We don't have enough space to keep everyone separated."

Marco offered, "We could bring everyone in here, and post an officer to make sure they don't talk to one another."

"Good idea. At least three state officers will be here to help interview, and our own officers can pick people up and bring them in. Do you have places for them to conduct the interviews?"

Everyone looked at Henrie. "If you would leave the dining room and kitchen free, I could begin to serve coffee and canapes. That leaves the all-season porch and the landing on the second floor. I will add a privacy screen."

Annie added, "As long as there will be an officer at all times, both my kitchen and dining room can be used."

Pete nodded. "Henrie, please gather your guests, including everyone from the carriage house. Marco, do you know how to find everyone else?"

"I do. I'll get on it."

George and Candice walked down the sidewalk toward the Inn. They turned when Felicity called, "You guys get called in, too?"

They continued to walk, but backwards and slowly, while Felicity and Trudie caught up. Candice said, "Yes. We're on the list. But we're not supposed to talk about it."

"Right," said Trudie. "Oops, watch out!"

George, walking backwards, almost ran over Isabel. "You too?"

"Yes. I was right in the middle of it Friday and Saturday nights. And in the afternoons. Oops. Can't talk about it."

Jesus and Minnie joined them on the sidewalk and motioned for Jet, who was walking across The Avenue, to join them.

George looked at Jet. "You, too?"

"Yep. We all served nearly everyone at one time or another, but..." everyone said together, "can't talk about it!"

As they reached the Inn, they heard a voice behind them. Turning as one, they saw Clara, trotting across The Avenue to catch up to them. "I'm here! Too bad I can't talk about it!"

In Marsh Haven, Pete and Cyril got out of the car. Pete looked at the house. He had driven through the neighborhood to get a feel for it. Somehow, the neighborhood didn't appear to be the kind that would lend itself to people with money to invest. He reminded himself to keep an open mind.

"Ready, Cyril?"

Cyril's tongue rolled out of his mouth.

"Let's go."

He knocked on the door. It was answered by a roundish woman with puffy cheeks and brown curly hair that surrounded her face. She opened the door wide to reveal a man that looked surprisingly like her. Except that his curly hair was gray.

Pete and Cyril walked in. The two looked at Cyril but said nothing. Apparently they had heard of Cyril.

"Thank you for seeing me. Right now, I'm casting as wide a net as possible, just to get a feel for the situation."

"Sure, sure," said Dan. "Have a seat. We made coffee."

"Thank you. Cyril, stay."

Dan and Jenny led the way to a dining table. The room was shabbier than their clothing would suggest, but homey.

"Now, explain to me your connection with the Thomases."

"Well," said Jenny, "we were driving around the country. It was so pretty. The hills, the vineyards…"

Dan added, "And they had done wonders with the building. Before, it was rundown. It looks great now, and the terrace and deck have doubled the size."

Pete let them run on, taking mental note of chinks in their armor. One thing he noted was a southern accent. He hadn't heard it on the telephone.

Jenny was talking again. "So, one day we saw them, and we stopped and talked. We told them we had a secret desire to own a winery, but we didn't think we could handle the work."

Dan added, "So, we drove by every weekend. Every now and then we'd see them, and eventually, Brian asked if we wanted to invest."

Jenny said, "And of course, we said yes. We set up a meeting…"

Dan said, "It went well. He told us how they were doing, about the vineyards, about the renovations."

"And we were waiting to hear back from him."

Pete asked, "That's how you left it? He was to reach out to you?"

They looked at one another and nodded their heads.

Pete asked, "And he would get back to you because…"

"He hadn't named a figure. We thought he was, you know, thinking about it."

"And then you heard about the fire."

"Yes. We saw it on the news."

"Which news station?"

"The one with the roving reporter."

"WQVX."

"Yes."

"On their morning show."

"Yes. We watch news at breakfast, then get on with our day."

"Is there anything you can tell me?"

"What could we tell you?"

"For example, did you see anyone else when you drove by, or did you ever hear anyone say anything about the winery?"

They looked at one another and shook their heads.

"Okay. Thank you for your time. I'll leave my card. If you think of anything, please give me a call."

Back in the car, Pete looked at Cyril. "I think they did it. How about you?"

Cyril's tongue rolled out of his mouth and he smiled.

When Pete got back to the office, he called the Marsh Haven police department. He asked them to do a check on the address of the house and email the results.

Liz and Farah passed one another in the hallway. After an awkward pause, Liz asked, "Want to get a cup of coffee?"

Farah nodded, and they went down the stairs to the Keurig corner. Coffee in hand, they walked back up to the second floor landing and settled into comfortable chairs.

Liz said, "So, your date ended badly last night."

"It did."

Silence.

Farah finally said, "In a million years, would you have guessed…"

"No! Who do you think did it?"

"I told the police about my husband, that he offered Dorian two million to testify against me."

"Two million?"

"That would have been a lot cheaper for him than paying out my pre-nuptial agreement. But Dorian would have had to lie. I didn't sleep with him."

"He would probably say you had intent."

"I could pass a polygraph saying I'd offered to take him to my room to get a cold cloth for his eye."

"Have to say, I would have loved seeing Nick deck him."

"It was rich. Of course, I knew Dorian was scamming everyone. He didn't know I knew, but…actually, it was kind of fun. I wasn't trying to make a good impression. I was just being me, you know?"

"That's so refreshing. I won't get to be 'me' again until I get a ring."

"Are you sure that's the life you want?"

"I'm taking pointers from you. I'll have a great pre-nup."

"The key is to have a good attorney. Start there. Do you think Jim would do that? Are you going to try to go the distance with him?"

"I might. I think he genuinely likes me. That's a good start."

While waiting to hear from Marsh Haven, Pete logged onto the internet and looked up Hearts On Fire.

He stared at the page and Dorian's picture. In the lower left corner, he was the Monthly Flame. The upper right corner had the picture of a woman.

He looked through the menu and found a page for the Valentine's Day Mixer. He found the schedule, name of venues, schedules, dates and times, and a listing of local hotels, motels and B&Bs.

Pete thought, if I were a conspiracy theorist, my list of suspects would have quintupled. If I could figure out who might have been looking for him.

An email arrived. The home he had visited was owned by Dave and Jessica Emerson – the wrong couple – and was rented to someone else. One more nail in the coffin.

15

Tiger Lily sat with the other cats in the windowsill of the third floor apartment. They were without extra cats and dogs, police officers, Mommy's staff, crying guests, and dramatic townspeople. Thank goodness!

All afternoon, they had to stay underneath the detective table. It was crowded, because the neighborhood companions had to come over. There was such excitement! But with Oscar McMurphy, Simon Finnegan, Tillie and Honey Bear…well…it was cozy with seven cats. It was tight and stuffy with ten cats and a terrier.

Now that they had space, she decided it was time to detect. *"Did we learn anything?"*

Honey Bear actually had something important to say. If he wasn't so officious when speaking, it would almost be pleasant to include him in their detecting.

"I heard Marco and Pete talking. First of all, the body was kind of stuck to the ice, so it had been there for several hours. And this may be important. They can't tell what the murder weapon was."

"Did they say anything about it? Anything at all?"

"He was stabbed with something, right in the heart. He bled a lot. He was probably dragged into the bushes, but any evidence of dragging was washed away."

"Darn it. But it was a knife of some kind?"

"If it was a knife, it was a strange one. More like a tool, but it didn't really have a shape they could determine."

Little Socks said, *"No shape? How could it have no shape?"*

Honey Bear sighed. *"How should I know? I'm only reporting what I heard."*

Tiger Lily asked, *"Did you hear anything else?"*

"Yes. There was a heart pin in his hand."

"One of the women's pins? The black heart with flames?"

Honey Bear thought about it. *"Well, now it makes sense."*

"What?"

"There must be women's pins and men's pins."

"The women wear a black heart with flames; the men wear a plain red heart."

"That was the other thing, then. There was a black heart in his hand, but no stick pin on his shirt. There was a hole where it should have been."

The cats looked around at one another. Eventually, their gazes settled on Little Socks.

"What?"

Kali and Ko said together, *"You can burgle the rooms."* *"You can look for a man's pin."*

Sassy Pants added, *"You can looks and seze if one of dose womens losted a pin."*

All of the cats turned to look at Sassy Pants. Tiger Lily, gently, said, *"You can't look for something that isn't there."*

"But, okay, you can tell Pete, and he can makes all da womens show him dere pins."

"Now that's a good idea!"

The cats turned to the important business of cleaning themselves. Except for Tiger Lily. She gazed down at the roof covering the front porch. A few icicles clung to the edge. The ones that did were the bigger ones. Hers should have still been there. It was the biggest.

What was the thing in the back of her mind? Something…she missed something…what was it?

She wanted to pace, but she couldn't. There were too many cats on the windowsill. She jumped to the table and paced from one end to the other. Back and forth.

She heard Mommy come in. Grandmommy was with her. Grandmommy was saying, "It's such a nightmare!"

That was it! Her dream! What was it, again? She heard something. A raised voice. No, two raised voices, A crack, then a loud crackle and something that sounded like glass breaking, then a scream. Then she woke up and heard nothing.

"I know what the murder weapon was!"

16

Annie and Henrie were in the kitchen. They were alone.

The cats were upstairs. Nancy and Sam were doing something with someone. Chris and Sis went home.

If they were alone on a Sunday night, they indulged in a guilty pleasure. Breakfast.

Tonight, they had eggnog French toast with cranberry-apple compote, a bowl of fresh melon and strawberries, and sparkling wine.

While Henrie finished preparations, Annie ran through more terms. She did it out loud tonight, since Henrie knew what she was doing.

"Hot Stuff, Hottie, Hot Lips. No. Too hot."

"Good Lookin', Gorgeous. No. He is those things, but no."

"Stud, Stud Muffin, Studly. No. Sounds like he's a carpenter."

"Sexy Thing. Gross."

"Prince Charming. Romeo. No. Too Disney."

"Dreamboat. Doll Face. No, no, no, no, no."

Henrie waded in. "I have the perfect solution."

"You do? What?"

"Chris."

"Yes. A term of endearment for Chris."

"My point, exactly. Call him Chris."

"Oh, Henrie. Let's talk about something else. Like the murder. What did you learn?"

"You heard they cannot identify a murder weapon?"

"Yes. And the body was frozen to the ground, so it was there for a while."

"You heard the stick pin is missing and a brooch was in his hand?"

"Yes. Have you heard about suspects?"

"Marco was on the telephone to Henrie stating his preference for Geraldine."

"No!"

"Yes. She was angry with him, and she has no alibi for last night."

"Everett left her. If she was home alone, she wouldn't have an alibi."

"That is another nail in her coffin."

"I have no idea why that upsets me so."

Minnie served crab cakes with remoulade and dirty rice. Jesus poured sangria. Nancy and Sam sat with a notepad and pens.

Sam said, "Are you sure you want to do this?"

Jesus answered. "Yes. We are very happy here, but having a piece of a vineyard and winery, that's something, too. And it would be a secret. We would make the same arrangement with Chateau Simon that we do with every other regional winery. No special favors."

"You understand you would have no influence on their decisions. Silent partner means the silent part first."

Minnie said, "Jesus grew up in a vineyard. He really doesn't want to be a decision-maker in that life."

Nancy leaned forward. "What do you think about a fine dining restaurant on the weekends?"

"It's a great idea, but I'm not sure Chelsea could afford two. During the busy season, yes, but…"

"But if something were to change, you might think it was a good idea?"

"Is something…"

"No! It was just a thought. It sounds like you're ready to go. When will you talk to them?"

"Do you have a suggestion?"

"The sooner the better. Those poor young folks are getting awfully discouraged."

"Does Pete have a suspect for the trouble out there?"

Sam said, "I think he knows who it is, but he doesn't know how to catch them."

"Them?"

Nancy said, "It may be a couple."

Sam added, "It sounds to me like it's someone that wants to force them to sell, and drive the price down in the process."

Minnie and Jesus looked at one another. Jesus said, "Think we can take a trip out there tomorrow evening?"

"We'll be too busy tomorrow evening, but maybe mid-afternoon?"

"I'll ask Jet to cover for us."

"How are we going to keep this a secret?"

Nancy said, "We won't tell a soul. Not even our daughter."

Tiger Lily and Little Socks huddled. *"Do you think you can do it tonight?"*

"I'll wait until they leave tomorrow. They usually go somewhere for lunch."

"Good idea. I'll go to work early. I hope Pete and Cyril will be there for breakfast. Cyril can help me tell Pete about the icicle."

"You can't spell it?"

"Are you kidding me? I don't have a clue how to begin."

17

"Henrie, did you see Tiger Lily this morning?"

"She had bacon and ran out the front door."

"Hmm. I wonder what she thinks she's doing."

"We had a murder. She is detecting. Waffle?"

"No, thanks, Henrie. It smells wonderful. Gingerbread?"

"Yes, with whipped cream and, or, molasses."

"I hope Felicity has something similar. Like Tiger Lily, I think I need to get to the Café. Will you be getting more paczki today, or should I stop on the way home?"

"Carlos is setting a box aside for me to pick up this afternoon. It will be our Fat Tuesday breakfast."

Annie glanced at the television. It was on, the sound muted. The day's weather was displayed. "It's going to be warmer, Henrie, but it drops to single digits tonight."

"The ground is still frozen. The water has nowhere to go. A sheet of ice will cover everything tomorrow morning."

"I hope Mom plans to stay in. Hey, Skype meeting around ten."

"I will see you then."

Annie lifted the cloth of the detective table. "Come on, kids. Let's go."

Obediently, five cats walked out. Annie lifted the cloth again and leaned over. Little Socks rolled over and went back to sleep.

"Are you coming, Little Socks?"

Little Socks stretched, licked her right paw, and went back to sleep.

"Okay. I'll tell Diana."

Annie walked up The Avenue, dropping cats off as she went. She stopped at the yoga studio to tell Diana the little girl stayed at home.

At the Café, Tiger Lily wasn't at her post. Annie walked behind the hostess stand, and there she was. Cyril munched on a treat – probably from Trudie – and Tiger Lily meowed and purred into his ear.

Annie stopped at the coffee bar. "I need sustenance. I didn't take time for coffee at home."

"Here. Have a cup of Rose."

"Thanks. The cardamom will wake me up. Anything going on this morning?"

"Look out there. I think we have about thirty flaming hearts…"

"Hearts On Fire…"

"Yes, them."

Annie turned to look. Most of them had turned and were looking at her. Over her shoulder, Annie asked, "Why are they looking over here?"

"They all seem to know he died at your Inn."

"But I didn't kill him."

"The jury's out on that. There have been a fair number of people talking about your, um, history."

Annie turned fully. "And what history is that?"

"You know. Murder. Mayhem. All that."

Annie's eyes rolled up and back. Dear heavens. She was channeling her mother. She then stood tall, squared her shoulders, and walked through the dining room, smiling and saying hello on her way. She stopped when she reached Pete. He sat with Greg.

"Am I interrupting?"

"Yes, but please, sit. I was just making arrangements with Greg to give me a hand."

"With those horrible winery folks?"

"Yes. Them."

Greg said, "I get to look through the window."

"The two-way? That's so fun!"

"You get to do it a lot. This will be a first for me."

"Be brave. You can see them, but they can't see you. When are you going?"

Pete said, "They called this morning. They'll be here in about a half hour. I'm just coordinating timing."

Annie looked Pete square in the eye. "Pete, I have it on good authority..."

"Henrie?"

"Sure. Anyway, is Geraldine at the top of your list?"

"She's up there."

"Why?"

"She was angry with him. And there's something about a pin that she shouldn't have had but maybe she did and now she doesn't."

"That's nothing!"

"Annie. I told you more than I should have."

"She didn't do it! She couldn't!"

"You're protecting the woman that you had to take to court?"

"Well…that was something else. Just think about it. If she did it, there would be stiletto tracks in the mud…"

"Maybe there were."

"No, there weren't. I live there, remember? And she has a strong personality, but she isn't a strong woman. She couldn't drag him behind those bushes."

"Maybe she had help."

"Who?"

"I don't know. Maybe Everett."

"Everett left her. He lives in Marsh Haven now."

"Well…."

"What?"

"He came back to town."

"For what?"

"He decided to use Valentine's Day to make up with her."

"But on Saturday, she said…"

"She didn't know. He got in late, so he got a hotel room."

"Maybe Everett did it."

"Annie, stop being a detective. Leave that to your cats."

Greg laughed out loud. Annie realized she had forgotten he was there. He wheezed out, "Yeah. Detective cats. That's a good one, Pete."

From across the room, Tiger Lily hissed. She was too far away for them to hear.

Tiger Lily was happy she had gotten to work early. Cyril was already there. He had a loopy smile. *"They did it. I know it, and Pete knows it. And he thinks the people we're meeting this morning are them, too."*

"What people? What did they do?"

"He thinks the people we met yesterday will be the people we meet today, and they don't think we know they're the same."

"I'm not following you."

"Oh. Mr. Bean must not have followed the conversation."

"This was the conversation from yesterday? Start at the beginning. But before you leave, I have something important."

"Okay. I'll keep it simple. Your guests…"

"The lonely lovers?"

"No, the winery people."

"Brian and Janet."

"Them. They bought a winery that, let's keep it simple, couple number one, wanted to buy. Greg showed it to them, they couldn't afford it, and eventually, Greg sold it your guests."

"I'm with you so far."

"Okay. Then after your guests started the renovations of the main building, couple number two started driving around, pretending they were just wandering, and they introduced themselves."

"Why?"

"They were pretending they wanted to invest."

"Oh! Those people. And they started the fire? And broke the windows?"

"Yes. Then they met us in someone else's house pretending it was where they lived, but they don't, and now…"

"Stop! You're losing me again."

"Oh. Sorry. They told Pete where to meet them, and pretended it was their house. Pete asked the Marsh Haven police about it. We were meeting couple number two, remember? The house is owned by couple number one, but it was rented to someone else."

"Oh, I see." She didn't. But she didn't want to let Cyril know she was lost. She was supposed to be a great detective. She decided to pay better attention.

Cyril continued. "And we think they were wearing wigs and maybe had something stuffed in their clothes and in their mouths, to make them look heavier."

"It would make them look lumpier."

"Exactly. Anyway, couple number one called early this morning and made an appointment. They're coming here, and Greg is going to look at them, to make sure they're who he remembers."

"And then what?"

"First, I'll smell them to make sure they're the same people. Then, we need to figure out how to get someone to make a mistake."

"How?"

"We have to do it legally. I was thinking maybe you could help."

"How?"

"*I don't know.*"

Tiger Lily thought about it. She thought she had kept up. "*Maybe you could get me in front of couple number two, and maybe I can get tangled up in a wig or something.*"

Cyril looked at her with interest. "*You're really good at this. We just have to figure out how to do that. So what do you have for me?*"

"*I know what the murder weapon was.*"

"*You do? What was it?*"

"*A big icicle.*"

"*An icicle?*"

"*There was a big one on the corner of the porch, and I didn't know it at the time, but I heard it come down. And I heard voices.*"

"*How didn't you know it at the time?*"

"*I was asleep. I thought I was having a dream.*"

"*So how was that the murder weapon?*"

"*It had a sharp end. Someone strong could have shoved it through his chest. And then it melted.*"

"*That makes sense. It's an odd shape, and it just turned to water.*"

"*In the rain.*"

"*Wow.*"

"*How do we tell Pete?*"

"*I don't know. I'll think about it. What about those voices? Did you recognize them?*"

"*No. Maybe I'll hear something that will strike a memory.*"

"*Keep an ear out.*"

Marco settled Greg into Pete's office. "I'll knock when it's time for you to come out. If it's them, just nod. If not, shake your head. Either way, come back here and write out your statement."

"This is so exiting!"

Marco chuckled, left the office and closed the door. He nodded at Pete, and the outer door opened, right on time.

Pete welcomed Dave and Jessica Emerson. She was shapely with a blond bob. He was trim with hair shaved close to his head. They were about the same height as the other couple.

Pete led them past Cyril on the way to the interview room. Cyril sneezed to cover his sniffing. When they were safely in the room, Marco opened the door to Pete's office and escorted Greg to the two-way mirror. Greg looked, nodded his head, and went back to the office.

Marco touched Cyril's head softly as he walked by. He didn't need to watch the interview. Pete had that. Marco sat at the reception desk and went through his murder notes.

He looked at cards with information on each suspect – Marco was quick to remind himself there could be more – in no particular order.

The first one was Farah. She knew that Dorian was considering taking money from her husband to testify against her. Was she strong enough to stab someone in the heart and drag him into the bushes? What kind of murder weapon would she use?

The next was Farah's husband. He had been interviewed via Skype with his attorney present. They had gotten very few answers from him. Perhaps Dorian told him he wouldn't do it. Perhaps he wanted more money. Perhaps he wanted money up front. He couldn't be sure, but the man looked strong enough to drag a big man several feet.

Geraldine was still Marco's favorite, but she would have had to have help dragging him. It's possible she and Everett hooked up to do it, but what would Everett get out of helping her?

If Geraldine and Everett still thought he was rich, they had nothing to gain with him dead. If they learned he was not, which, according to Annie, Geraldine had, it could have been out of anger.

Geraldine could not control her temper. Neither could Everett. It was possible Everett saw the two of them together. It was possible they planned it together in a fit of rage. Well, you don't plan things in a rage.

The other lady lonely heart, Liz. According to her, she was embarrassed that she had been taken in by his line. She may have had motive, but again, was she strong enough?

Someone who was strong enough was Nick, the big guy who gave him the black eye. According to witnesses, he was angry that Dorian had hooked up with three attractive and apparently wealthy women, and he had hooked up with zero.

Did the coordinator have a reason? No. The original coordinator, Travis, was in the hospital. Mike, the new guy, was too new and too green.

Annie? Nah….

Chris? Not a chance.

Henrie? His weapon of choice was a ball bat. It was hard to stab someone with a ball bat. And Henrie was, well, Henrie. He would not have left the man to be found in front of the Inn.

What they really needed was that warrant to get a look at the computer files. As if that would tell them anything.

18

Annie set up her laptop in the back dining room. Felicity and Trudie brought refreshments. Annie loved her life.

Tiger Lily jumped to the top of the table, inserting herself in front of the monitor.

Soon, people up and down the street appeared. Diana at the yoga studio, Little Socks sitting on the keyboard. Diana's screen shimmered in protest.

George, Georgia and Candice at a table. Mo lounged in front of the computer, like Egyptian royalty.

Carlos and Isabel were at a table with both Mr. Bean and Tillie. They tried to stay away from the computer. No, that was a lie. Isabel held Tillie back, and Carlos held Mr. Bean.

Minnie and Jesus sat placidly behind Sassy Pants, who sat on the keyboard and pawed at the monitor. She touched the faces of everyone, apparently trying to get a response.

Henrie and Hilly were in the kitchen. Kali and Ko were behind them, visible in the monitor from the kitchen table.

Everyone was present.

After working through the week's scheduling issues, Annie made a note. "Ask accountant about overtime for the year. Have we used up budget? It's only February."

Tiger Lily rolled over. What a boring meeting. So much happening around town, and they were talking about schedules.

Annie finally gave a deep sigh. "I have something serious to discuss. It affects almost everyone here. Well, actually, probably everyone."

She looked into the monitor. "What do you think about Bon Vivant? Has it run its course?"

She was met with silence. Complete silence. Then Carlos spoke up. "I think it's been a great money maker. It's something the community wanted, even though they didn't know it until we opened. It has gotten all of us additional business. But…it has also been a strain. I'm glad Cookie decided to cut down on options. That was helpful."

George was not noted for sugar-coating. "This week's been hard. And there have been a few other times that it's been hard. I'd like to say keep it open and hire staff just for the weekend. But how can you keep a fine dining place open with only part-time staff?"

Georgia added, "It's great. I've learned a lot and I've pulled a lot of overtime. Good news for me, it's more money. Bad news for me, I have a child."

Felicity chimed in. "I agree. This week was a challenge. We stretched everyone to the limit. We're all beat. And we've eaten up a lot of overtime."

George got a wicked grin. "We'd have less overtime if you stayed in town this week."

Candice dug an elbow into his ribs. Felicity blushed. Annie looked at Henrie but saw no visible response.

Slowly, Jesus said, "I think Chelsea likes the idea of fine dining. If we close, it's possible someone else will pick up the slack."

Henrie said, "The unfortunate circumstance of losing Cookie has presented an opportunity. A decision can be made either way. If I could offer one observation, it is true this weekend has created an unusual strain. There are times during the tourist season that strain has been apparent as well. Should the decision be to remain open, perhaps staffing changes could be considered."

Annie said, "To date, it's been profitable. That's not a reason to keep something open. Show of hands, who would prefer that it close?"

Slowly, every hand went up. Even Sassy Pants voted that preference, although it could be argued she was only mimicking what she saw online.

Annie noticed that Jesus and Minnie only raised their hands after looking at one another for a long moment. And after Sassy Pants weighed in.

Annie was acting as hostess when Geraldine and Everett came in. As she led them to their table, she made a rash decision. She sat with them.

"I beg your pardon," said Everett.

Geraldine said, "Stuff it, Everett. What's up, Annie?"

"Are you aware that you're a suspect?"

"They haven't said so in that many words, but they came on strong during questioning."

"Who questioned you?"

"Some state police officer. I don't remember his name."

Tiger Lily, shocked that Annie had sat down, jumped from the hostess stand and walked over. Nonchalantly, she wandered among the feet underneath the table, keeping an open ear.

Annie asked, "Did you…well…incriminate yourself in any way?"

"No!"

"Were you completely honest?"

"Of course I was."

"I only ask because I know you haven't always been. You know. Honest. When the police have questioned you."

"Oh, for heaven's sakes. I've always been honest. Sometimes I've been misunderstood."

Everett said, "This is none of your business…"

"I know it's none of my business, but I hate to see them make a mistake. These flaming hearts" – Annie was saying it now, too – "are going to leave town and you'll still be here. If they don't solve it before Wednesday, you'll be the only one easy to get to."

"What do you suggest?"

"Can you remember anything? Anything that might point a finger toward someone else?"

"I honestly cannot."

Annie slapped the table softly, but hard enough that Geraldine jumped. "Why did you go to Mo's? I thought you were going home."

"I was on my way home. I was going to my car, and I saw him from the window. I was so angry. I wanted to tell him what a skunk he had been."

"You shouldn't have done that. That's the last thing a lot of people remember."

"I heard someone else took a punch at him after that."

"Yes, but that was man on man. It's wrong, but people don't think as badly about that as they do if a woman is involved. And George had to separate you."

"That was unfortunate."

"And where did you get that pin?"

"What pin?"

"You're doing it again. You just can't help yourself. That pin! The one you had on at the winery. The cloisonné brooch."

"Oh. That. It must have fallen off someone. I saw it on the sidewalk outside the winery. I picked it up, and, well, I didn't know if you had to be a member to get in, so I put it on."

"Everyone knows you're not a member, Geraldine. Everyone has seen you, all week, and, well, people talk. So, really? Just, really?"

"Stop it. You know why I was there. I told you. I wanted to make it up to him. I'm sorry, Everett, but you were gone."

"Yes, I was gone. We've gone through these episodes before. Sometimes you, sometimes me. No need to apologize. I've heard it all anyway."

Annie looked at him in surprise. Everett cleared it up by saying, "I've been interviewed twice. I'm probably a suspect, too."

Geraldine said, "You're the reason I don't have an alibi."

"It was late. I didn't want to wake you. And, frankly, that's why I don't have one either."

Annie looked back at Geraldine. "What did you do with the pin?"

Geraldine sighed. "As I left the winery, I took it off and threw it into one of those flower pots on the sidewalk."

"Did you go look for it?"

"The police did. I was certain they would find it, but no. They looked at all of them, not just the one I pointed to."

"Then someone must have picked it up. Think, Geraldine. Was anyone around when you threw it?"

"The sidewalk was almost as busy as the winery and Mo's that night. Lots of people were around."

"Was anyone watching you?"

"Not that I recall."

"What do you recall? About the pin, I mean."

"I walked outside, stopped, undid the pin, tossed it in the pot in front of the bakery, looked up and saw Dorian through the window at Mo's. So I went in."

"No. That's not right."

"What?"

"It's not right." Annie closed her eyes. She paced her words to match the steps she imagined Geraldine had taken. "You left Clara and me. We were at the far end of the back room. You walked all the way through that room, then the tasting room. You opened the door and went out. You stopped, took off the pin. You started walking again, tossed the pin, looked up, maybe took a few seconds to think, and then you went into Mo's."

"Yes. That's what I said."

Annie opened her eyes. "Not possible. Clara and I looked at and talked about at least two couples...three? Yes, three. And then we talked about the new coordinator. You know Clara. She doesn't talk; she chatters. Then we decided to go to Mo's. I tried to get Chris's attention, gave up, and we left. We were there before you were. You did something or talked to someone in between. Think!"

"Stop badgering me!"

"Geraldine, listen to me. If you can't figure out who might have taken that pin, you could be charged with the murder. Think!"

Geraldine sat back, a mixture of anger and confusion on her face. "Why would you do this?"

Everett added, "Yes. Why are you bothering her at all?"

"That's not what I mean, Everett. Annie, why are you trying to help?"

"Lord knows. Anyway, think about it. When you figure it out, call Pete. Maybe he can help."

Annie rose, weathered the slings and arrows of the lonely hearts club members who somehow thought she was involved in the murder, and seated four impatient people. Honestly. They'd probably only waited for a couple of minutes. Three or four at the most.

Peggy gathered the others together and suggested a visit to Gema's Creations, then lunch.

Farah said, "I went in there Saturday. She has beautiful things. I had hoped to get a bauble from Dorian, but...guess that won't happen. I'm not above buying something for myself."

As they walked to Mo's, Elena said, "I'm surprised you're still here. Aren't you worried about your husband?"

"Not really. He made his point. Today, he's huddling with his attorneys, and I've already made a call to mine. If he tries to divorce me, he'll have to pay."

"Can he keep you from traveling in the future?"

"No, not really. Part of the contract was an annual stipend that I can spend as I wish. Frankly, I have him by the yo-yos."

Liz said, "Good for you. I want something like that."

At Gema's counter, they took turns taking Gema's attention while they talked about their Sunday evening.

Liz said, "Jim and I were going to spend the day together, but we ended up going to a town down the coast for dinner and drinks."

"He has a car here?"

"We used Uber."

"What's he like?"

"He's really very sweet. It's too bad he's not good looking, but his bank account is healthy. I may have to shave some of my scruples."

"Where does he live?"

"Milwaukee. Not the best, but not impossible."

"Milwaukee has lakefront, it's close to Chicago, and it has a great zoo."

"Well, I guess there's that."

"What business is he in?"

"He wouldn't say."

"What?"

"He wouldn't say. I asked, and his answer was something like 'pretty little women shouldn't trouble their heads.'"

"And you're okay with that?"

"If part of being a pretty little woman is getting set up, yeah. I'm okay with that."

Peggy asked, "How about you, Tiffany?"

She smiled. "I think this time, I might have found someone."

"Brent? What did you do last night?"

"He rented a car. He was disappointed we couldn't have the entire day. He planned a trip up the coast, looking at lighthouses. Instead, we found a nice restaurant about a half hour up, in Marsh Haven."

"What's he like?"

"Well, he just got a new job, and he's making more money than he knows what to do with."

"You could help him with that."

"No, not really. He said he wants to buy a house. A small house, but big enough for a couple of kids, with a big yard. And he wants to invest about two thirds of his pay every year."

"And you like that? That he would save his money? Not spend it?"

"Yeah. But what I like most about him is that he didn't mention the difference in our races. Not once."

Tiffany turned to Peggy. "How did it go with Paul?"

"Surprisingly well. I had paid no attention to him, but Mike, the new guy, got us talking. Frankly, this was going to be my last time out, and I didn't think anything would gel."

"Are you going out with him tonight?"

"Yes. I have to say, I was convinced this group outing would end like all the others, but…maybe…just maybe…. You know, he said the sweetest thing."

"What's that?"

"He said he only wanted someone to love, and that maybe I was the one."

The women were silent for a while. Then Tiffany asked, "Elena, how your date go with Fritz the super spy?"

"He was surprisingly attentive. Really. Surprisingly."

Peggy wanted details. "Tell us everything."

She did.

Before they left, Peggy surprised everyone. She put one thousand dollars on the counter and purchased a sapphire and diamond necklace and earring set in white gold.

While she completed the purchase, she sent a silent thank you to Fritz for the money. She wouldn't spend all of it. She would make her mortgage payment as soon as she got home.

And the electric. Yes. She would pay that. Most of it.

Her credit cards would have to wait.

In the back of her mind, a thread of worry started. What about Elena was so important that he would pay for the information?

19

The cats rushed home in the early afternoon. The rain had turned to sleet, and it was beginning to leave an icy residue on the sidewalk. The temperature seemed to plummet, but it could have been the wind off the lake.

At home, they found Kali, Ko and Little Socks on the windowsill in the library. They jumped up.

Tiger Lily asked, *"Were you able to get into their rooms?"*

"All of them. I found great stuff."

"Good. Let me tell you all about Cyril first, then you can tell us everything."

Tiger Lily filled them in on the conversation with Cyril, about the two couples that might only be one couple, and that she might be called upon to help unmask them. *"And if I'm not available, one of you will have to do it."*

They nodded in solemn agreement. Then she told them that Cyril would try to help them with the icicle problem.

"Here's some news. Mommy is trying to help Geraldine."

"What?" "Why?" "Trill!"

"She thinks Geraldine is innocent, and she wants to help her."

"Maybe dat place down below frozed over."

"Maybe. What did you all think about Bon Vivant?"

"Ize sorry it closes. Whats Mommy and Chris do on weekends now?"

Kali and Ko said, at the same time, *"What they used to do." "Eat somewhere else."*

Little Socks said, *"Maybe Mommy will cook."*

"Trill!!!!!!"

Mr. Bean said, *"Even I know what that meant. If Mommy tries to cook, let's go across The Avenue and eat with Simon Finnegan and Oscar McMurphy."*

Everyone agreed. Tiger Lily turned to Little Socks.

"So...what did you find?"

"I went to the back room first. That's Farah's room. I found lots of stuff, but I don't know that any of it makes her guilty of anything. She has a gun and lots of money."

Tiger Lily said, *"That's all for protection from that husband. But so far, nothing to incriminate her."*

Little Socks turned to Kali and Ko. *"Who's in the room that faces The Avenue?"*

Ko said, *"That's Liz."*

"That makes sense. She has lots of make-up and fancy clothes. It looks like she's spent a lot of time on the balcony."

"It's too cold for that."

"I know, but maybe she's watching for people. She has all kinds of papers on the dressers. You know those big cross things that people put on things, when they're done with them?"

"Xes?" asked Tiger Lily.

"Yeah. She put big Xes on several of them."

"I'll bet the papers are the file things they talked about, and the ones with Xes are the ones that don't have enough money."

"Or aren't handsome enough."

"Yeah."

"So then I went into the room that faces the winery."

Kali said, *"That's Elena's room."*

"Okay. She had a gun and lots of money, too. Here's the important thing. Do you remember the first clue I ever found? The first time I burgled a room?"

"Trill!"

Kali and Ko said together, *"A passport!" "A passport!"*

"Yes. She had three of them."

"I tot peoples only hadded one at a time."

Tiger Lily said, *"That's the way it's supposed to be. Did you find anything else?"*

"No. That's enough to keep an eye on her. The next room was the one facing the state park."

Ko said, *"Peggy."*

"She had a computer, and a drawer that had lots of money thrown in, loose, like she'd picked up stray bills on the street and didn't put them in neat stacks."

"Everbody knows you gots to puts bills in stacks. Dat's da way you do it."

"Right. But it's like she got it all of a sudden, and she just wanted it out of sight."

Tiger Lily mused, *"I wonder if she needed it out of sight in case a police officer came in after the murder?"*

Kali and Ko said together, *"She had time to put it away." "Those policemen didn't come for quite a while."*

"So, nothing of interest."

"Apparently not. The last room was the one facing the lake, so that has to be Tiffany. There wasn't a single thing in her room that was interesting."

"So you went through all their rooms, and there wasn't a stick pin anywhere."

"Nowhere."

"But if one of them did do it, they could have gotten rid of the pin."

"Or they could have it in a purse, or a pocket."

Disappointed, they cleaned themselves and curled into the cushions for a nap.

Mem looked up. A young man – one of the lonely hearts – entered CyberHealth, a computer in his hands.

"Can I help you?"

"Are you Mem?"

"Yes."

"George told me you could help."

"I'd be happy to."

"Did you hear that Travis, the, um, coordinator of the club, got sick?"

"I did. You're Mike, the one that took over."

"Yes, ma'am, I am. I have his computer, and, well, I thought it was just slow, but now, I wonder if there's some kind of virus?"

"Let me take a look."

"I guess, well, George told me I should tell you that the police say they'll have a subpoena this afternoon for the computer."

"Oh. My. Is there some reason you don't want to give it to them?"

"Oh, no, ma'am. I think they need it to help solve their case, but I don't know all the legalities, you know. This is filled with all kinds of private information. You know, of people who aren't involved in this at all."

"I see. Well, I suppose the best thing to do is to call the Chief, let him know what I'm about to do, and then I'll take a look."

Minnie and Jesus got out of the car. They stood and looked at the nearly-finished building, almost finished but for the large deck, and scarred with broken windows.

She said, "Let's go in."

As they walked toward the lower level entry, it opened and Brian stepped out. "Good afternoon. Is this the first time you've seen it?"

"First time since the former owners were in charge. You've done a lot of work. We're very sorry for all of your troubles."

Brian escorted them in. "The adjuster seemed to think there would be no problem. I just need to send him the police reports."

Brian walked them upstairs to the tasting room. Minnie took a deep breath. "The view is outstanding."

Janet stood from behind the bar. Once again, she was painting. "It is. And next year, there will be more grapes out there. That always makes a good view even better."

Brian led them to a table by the windows and they sat. They had gotten to know one another over the last few months and had a comfortable, friendly relationship. All, however, were nervous as teenagers on a first date.

Jesus led with, "I assume you know why we're here."

Brian answered. "I hope we know why you're here."

"We'd like to invest fifty thousand. We understand the terms you're offering, and we agree. On a couple of conditions."

Brian looked at Janet, then said, "We're listening."

"The 'silent' in silent partner goes two ways. We put the money in a bank upstate, with no connections to Chelsea. The deposit will be made in the name of Great Lakes Wine. If people ask who your backer is, that's the name you give. We don't tell you how to conduct business, and you tell no one we're backing you."

"Done."

"We'll make arrangements to sell your wine with the same deal we give every other regional winery, if you'll sell to us."

"We will," said Janet.

Jesus and Minnie looked at one another, smiled, took deep breaths, and began to breathe normally. Minnie wondered how she had been able to transact business without having done that in the first place.

With renewed warmth, she turned to Janet. "We have it on good authority that the Bon Vivant Grille will close at the end of the month."

Janet had warmed as well. "This calls for champagne. We've had a bottle on ice for just this occasion."

Peggy left the group of women and walked up and down The Avenue, looking first into one shop, then the next. She was window-shopping with a purpose.

At CyberHealth, she saw Mike hand the woman a computer. This had to be the shop's owner. That had to be Travis's computer.

She kept going until she reached the church, Soul's Harbor. She went in to browse the charity gift shop. Two people were there: the volunteer behind the desk and one customer.

"Hey, Fritz. Shopping or just looking?"

"Just looking around. I kind of like some of this local art."

"Oh. Wow. This is nice. Who's the artist?"

"All I can see is a 'C' in the right-hand corner."

Peggy looked around. The volunteer concentrated on something in her hand. Her phone, probably. Fritz put his back to the volunteer, reached into his pocket and pulled out an envelope. He turned and handed it to Peggy, using their bodies to hide the transaction.

Peggy whispered, "We have to talk. Trouble."

Out loud, Fritz said, "Why don't you join me for tea? I hear there's a nice tea shop here."

"No, not there. Let's go somewhere else." She widened her eyes to let him know not to argue. At least, not in front of the volunteer.

Pete returned Mem's call. "I can't spare anyone now, Mem. I'm going to have to trust you to do what you need to do and document everything."

"Okay, Pete."

She turned to Mike. "Let's go."

Mem turned on the computer, entered the password, and got to work. Within minutes, she said, "You have a Trojan."

"What's that?"

"Someone's been messing with you, reading everything. It doesn't look like anything's been changed, but, for example, whoever's on the other end can see every file. And they can monitor your clicks. They can see how many times you visit any one file."

"What would that tell them?"

"Right now, I'm not sure. I don't want to give them any food for thought right now. Let me see what I can do to get rid of it before they realize what I'm doing. Otherwise, you could have even more problems."

At Mr. Bean's Confectionary, Fritz ordered two plain coffees and one rose hip paczki. "We can share, right?"

"Right. I don't even need half the calories."

At the furthest table, Peggy leaned in and told Fritz what she had seen through the window at CyberHealth.

"I think he found the Trojan. Or at least he realized something was wrong, and he took it to an expert."

"I thought you said he was too stupid."

"Travis was. That Trojan had been there for almost two years. This guy, Mike, must be smarter."

"So they'll be able to figure out, what, exactly?"

"Well, they'll trace the Trojan to me, probably, and then, I don't know, they might figure out what I've done with it. If they interview me, I don't know how I can keep quiet about you."

"That's not good."

"Well, if you were planning on following her home, you know, stalking her or anything, you might want to rethink your plan."

Fritz smiled. "That won't be a problem. Plenty of fish in the sea."

When Peggy left, Fritz sent a text to the same untraceable number. "Must be tonight."

20

Annie waited for Chris in the kitchen. When he and Sis entered through the foyer, she was surprised to hear the cats – it sounded like all of them – say hello.

Chris came to the kitchen, Little Socks hunched on top of his shoulder, snuggled into his face. "I love the way she comes to me now. I'm not sure how or why it happened, but…she loves me."

"So do I."

"But you don't climb to my shoulder. She loves me more."

Little Socks purred. Another milestone.

Chris looked at Henrie. "How about you, Henrie? Do you love me? What to climb on my shoulder?"

Henrie looked at Chris, turned, and poured a cup of coffee. He added a touch of Kaluah.

"Okay. This is good." He took a sip. "How is everything since, well, you know. Yesterday."

Annie said, "Pete thinks Geraldine did it."

"You're kidding."

"Nope. I tried to talk to her today, to get her to think about that night. Somehow she got hold of a pin, a pin – maybe or maybe not hers – ended up in the dead guy's hand, and she can't find the one she had."

"Bummer. Sorry. I can't muster any feelings about it, one way or the other. I don't want her to be charged with murder, but she's put you through an awful lot in the last couple of years."

"How are your guests?"

Henrie said, "It is surprising how well this oddly-matched group of women get along. They spent most of the day together."

Annie added, "I saw them on The Avenue. It looked like they had come from Gema's. I saw a couple of pretty bags."

"They bought jewelry themselves? Didn't wait for men to do it?"

"Some of them have decided to do things their own way. Let's just hope Hearts On Fire dies a much-needed death this week."

"Is tonight's gathering a Hearts-Only thing?"

"No, not really. They will eat and drink for free, but they have to wear their pins. Chris, let's go. I want to be there in case anyone comes in without one."

Chris looked at Henrie and shook his head. "She's getting to be as bad as the cats."

Little Socks purred again.

Chris put the girl on the floor and she ran to the foyer to coordinate the evening.

Sis listened as the cats made their plans.

Tiger Lily said, *"Little Socks, keep your eyes open for the pins. Figure out who doesn't have one, and watch who talks to who."*

"I know what to do. Sis will have to help."

"But I don't know who anyone is," said Sis.

"If you hear or see something suspicious, point them out to me. If they're important, I'll know who they are, or I'll know how to figure it out."

"Okay. Do I stay with Chris, or wander around the room?"

"We might have to wander. Can you do that?"

"I'll try. I'm still nervous around strangers."

"You'll get used to it. This is a tourist town. There will always be strangers."

Annie and Chris were out of the house before men arrived to pick up their dates. The women had gathered in the foyer, anxious.

Henrie walked among them as they sat, handing out coffee, tea and water.

Jim was the first to knock on the door. Henrie, like an overprotective father, answered it.

Henrie stood aside while Jim entered. He didn't say a word. He walked to Liz, pulled a box out of his pocket and opened it. The box contained a ring. Henrie knew his jewelry. He saw a two-carat heirloom ruby with two one-carat diamonds, one on either side, set in white gold.

Liz raised a hand to her mouth, then she looked at Jim. He stood in front of her, solemn, short, round and frumpy. She reached for the ring and put it on her right hand. It fit perfectly. She smiled, stood to her full height, looked down into his eyes and said, "It's beautiful. Thank you."

Jim nodded to Henrie and spirited Liz out the door. In one short minute, he had made a huge impression on every woman there while looking like a pumpkin and uttering not a single word.

Henrie held the door as they left, and left it open as two men entered. They nodded at Henrie and walked in.

At the same time, Peggy said, "Hi, Paul," and Tiffany said, "Hello, Brent. I'm ready."

As they left, Henrie nodded and closed the door.

He refreshed coffee cups while they waited for the last man. Fritz the super spy. He didn't knock on the door. He walked in, dressed to kill. He swept the room with his eyes and held out his hand for Elena. She rose and walked to him, took his hand, and walked out with him.

Farah stood. "Well, Henrie, I'm on my way. My date tonight is named Tonya. We're going to show the rest of them how to have a good time. Want to join us?"

Henrie smiled and opened the door.

Tiger Lily sighed with relief. They were all gone. Finally! Unfortunately, she had not heard a single voice that sounded like those in her dream.

A sign at the door to the back dining room said "Hearts On Fire Members Only."

Annie and Chris sat at the tasting bar. Little Socks sat in front of Chris, and Sis sat on the floor, beside Annie. She had a clear view of people coming in. Jet was behind the bar.

"Where are Minnie and Jesus?"

"Minnie's in the kitchen, Jesus is at the back bar."

"Busy night tonight."

"'Tis."

Mike came in, looking a little jumpy.

Annie said, "Hello, Mike. You're still nervous?"

"It's not that. I wanted to wait out here for a couple of folks. Mind if I sit?"

"Please. This is my...friend...Chris. Do you mind if I gossip?"

"No. Please do. It might help me."

Chris said, "Jet, get this man a glass on me."

As the Inn's guests arrived, one by one, Annie pointed them out to Chris again, with names and the names of their male friends, and what she could remember about them.

She was surprised to see Farah and Tonya together. Mike stood and motioned them over.

"Farah, I'm really sorry to hear how your evening ended Saturday."

"Thanks, Mike. I'm getting over it."

"That's good to hear. Tonya, I, um, I have someone in mind for you to meet. When he comes in, will it be alright if I bring him over?"

"Sure. I'm open for anything."

"Great. See you in there."

Mike turned to Annie. "She lied, you know. She said she wasn't married. I'm going to have to kick her out of the group, but after the week is over. She's had a shock."

"It's good to hear you'll continue as the coordinator after Wednesday."

"Oh. It did sound like that, didn't it. Huh. Guess I didn't mean to...excuse me."

Charlie and Thad arrived. Mike motioned them over as well. "Charlie, where's your pin?"

"I can't find it."

Annie and Chris looked at one another. Little Socks and Sis looked at one another as well.

"Well, okay. I know you're a member, but, gosh, please look for it again."

A man came in, and Mike jumped up. "Tom, it's so good to see you. Come with me. I have someone I want you to meet."

As Mike disappeared into the room, Annie looked up to see two men enter. "Uh, oh."

"What?"

"Remember Nick, the loudmouth from the restaurant?"

"Yep. And there he is."

"He was kicked out of the group last night."

"Certainly, Mike will take care of it. Who's the other guy?"

"Bob. He's the one that lied to Tonya. I think he got kicked out, too."

Raised voices came from the back room. Jet excused himself and headed in that direction. Chris followed. Sis started to get up, but Annie touched her head. "Stay here, girl."

Voices grew louder, a few chairs hit the floor, and soon, Chris and Jet came from the room, hands gripped around the arms of Nick. They were followed by Mike and Jesus, escorting Bob in a similar manner.

Before they left the room, Annie heard Mike say, "This was your last chance. I'm calling the police now, and I'll file a protection order tomorrow morning."

Little Socks trotted down the bar until she was directly above Sis. *"We can't hear anything from here. Now that the excitement's over, do you want to go inside?"*

"Sure," said Sis. *"I'm getting used to this."*

Later that night, Tiger Lily asked Little Socks how the evening went. *"We didn't learn anything, but I had some crab-stuffed mushroom, an oyster, Mommy said it was a Rockefeller, and a piece of filet mignon. Sis had what Chris called beef burgundy. I'm going to sleep now."*

Annie went downstairs Tuesday morning to the smell of – something – what was it?

Henrie was in the dining room, setting out a plate of paczki. That wasn't what she smelled, but it looked great, nonetheless.

Annie walked to the buffet and, with great difficulty, contained her drool. Some were glazed. Some were covered in granulated or powdered sugar. She saw traditional plum and wild rose hip, Bavarian cream, custard, strawberry, blueberry, raspberry, and apple. Some of the fruit ones had cream cheese; some didn't.

"I can't choose just one, so I guess I'll have to have whatever I smell in the kitchen."

"Good choice."

Annie turned to go into the kitchen. "It's freezing out there, Henric. I went out to the balcony this morning, and there is a sheet of ice everywhere."

"And there will be no sun. None. If any of our guests suffer from SAD, they will have a rough time today."

"Sad?"

"You are not aware of seasonal affective disorder?"

"Oh yeah. That. What did you make?"

"Winter brussels sprouts."

"What?"

"I appear to be on a walnut and cranberry journey this week. This dish has grilled brussels sprouts, bacon, shallots, cranberries and walnuts. It also has bourbon, maple syrup and balsamic vinegar."

"It sounds wonderful. It appears you have cooked for all of our guests. Do you expect any to appear?"

"If the week holds true, we will see your parents and the Thomases."

"Strange women. They pay for breakfast, but so far, they have eaten nothing."

They turned when they heard a frantic scream from outside. Running to the front door, Annie held Henrie back before they both ran onto the ice.

Nancy was on the ground, on her knees. She was screaming, "Help! Help me!"

Beside her, Sam was flat on his back, screaming in agony.

Pete had far too much on his plate today. And now he had to deal with Mike – again – about a protection order. Mike turned over all of the particulars about the men and noted that, according to the hotel in which they registered, both had checked out that morning.

"We will register the complaint, but since they have left town – supposedly – let's not go to the trouble of getting that order."

"Are you sure?"

"No, but…let's talk about that other thing."

"The computer?"

"Yes. I'll give it to a forensic technician. Maybe he or she will be able to tell who was doing what."

"Mem didn't do that?"

"No, but Mem protected the computer from further intrusion. Let me ask, in the short time you had it, did you see anything that would give you ideas about these crimes?"

"All of them?"

"Well, the murder, number one, and then this Trojan."

"They weren't the same thing?"

"I don't think so. I have a list of suspects for the murder longer than your right arm, but none of them look good for the Trojan."

"I don't think I can tell you anything. Have you tried to talk to Travis?"

"He's in critical care."

"What?"

"I didn't want to put a damper on your party, so I didn't say anything."

"What was it?"

"Jennifer said it was series of TIAs, you know, the precursors of a stroke. And he had a big one at the hospital. Suffice it to say that had George not caught it, he'd be somewhere else."

"Oh my, oh my, oh my."

Pete's phone rang. "Chief."

"Chief, I'm Detective Joe Miller with the Omaha Police Department."

"Nebraska?"

"Yes."

Pete opened a file and looked at his murder notes. "What can I do for you, Detective?"

"I have information that an Elena Long may be in your town. Some kind of lonely hearts club. Do you have any way of knowing where those activities are being held?"

"As a matter of fact, yes. Do you need to contact her?"

"We do. We've tried to reach her by cell, but her provider must not work very well in your area. Think you can help?"

"I can. Do you want me to have her call you, or do you want me to relay a message?"

"I'd prefer if you'd relay a message. It's not pretty. Her parents were killed last night. There was an explosion in their house. It's being investigated as murder."

"Any suspects?"

"Not a one."

Pete took Detective Miller's contact information and rose. "Come on, Mike. We have a notification to make."

They walked toward the Inn, passing the Café. Cyril jumped to the window, padding it for Tiger Lily. Seeing him, she jumped down and ran out the cat door.

"You have to come to the police station at one o'clock."

"I can't tell time."

"I'll figure out a way to come get you."

"Okay."

Annie waited in the hospital with Nancy. Sam was in surgery. He would probably have a new hip before he came out.

"Mom, please. Stop pacing. You'll need a new hip yourself."

"I told him we should wait before leaving the suite, but no, he just had to see Henrie and get paczki."

"That's not a bad excuse to leave the house..."

"He's not a spring chicken."

"Neither are you. Frankly, you're the one I was worried about."

"I may seem like a nitwit, but Sam is the one that needs help on occasion."

"Really? What do you mean?"

"Oh, he has spells, sometimes, when he loses his balance. I didn't want to say anything, because he doesn't want anyone to worry."

"Mom. I'm not 'anyone.' I'm your daughter."

"I know. And, well, we've been talking, Sam and I, about making a change."

"What kind of change?"

"We saw a little house, in the neighborhood where Martha lives, and we were thinking of downsizing. Buying that and moving here."

"Really? What's the house like?"

"It's small. Big enough for Sam, me and Honey Bear. One bedroom, a den, an eat-in kitchen and a living room. Oh, a laundry room. There's a full bath off the bedroom and a half bath off the kitchen. Everything is on one level; there's an attached garage. The yard is very small. Cute, but very small. Very little maintenance."

"How long have you been thinking about this?"

"Oh, just a little while. Remember the other morning, when Sam went to Marsh Haven for Gema?"

"Yes."

"Greg was free, and he decided to go with him. They started talking, and Greg said he had the perfect little house in mind. And he did. It was."

"I've wondered why I've seen so little of you in the last few days."

"Well, you've had your hands full with all kinds of exciting things. Murder, vandalism."

"I think I know the house you're talking about. It is cute. Are you sure you want one that small?"

"That's where you come in, dear. Whenever we have family visiting, we'll rent rooms from you."

"Family is always welcome, Mom, but what happens if they're coming and all the rooms are booked?"

"We'll cross that bridge when we come to it."

"I'm happy for you. And you know we'll help in whatever way we can."

"I'll be happy to downsize. I'm already thinking about things I don't need to bring with me."

"What about your friends?"

"Oh, so many of them have moved to their winter homes, and so many others are so…small-minded."

"You haven't said anything about it before."

"Well, it's been slow to make itself known. We go home and tell everyone about our friends and our life here, and then, sometimes, noses go up, or invitations stop coming. You know how it can be in a small town."

"I suppose so. I'm sorry to hear that. Really sorry. But I would love to have you here. And so will Chelsea."

The doctor came out, and the conversation ended.

Pete and Mike entered the foyer. Henrie heard them and met them before they reached the dining room door.

"Pete, Mike, how can I help you?"

"We have to see Elena. Is she in?"

"I believe so. Allow me to check. Would you care for coffee? A fresh pot is brewing in the kitchen."

"Thanks."

Henrie returned from the second floor with Elena. Pete motioned to a chair and a cup of coffee. Elena sat. Henrie left.

The conversation did not go well. Pete expected shock, pain, denial, anger – any number of traditional responses to news of this sort.

Instead, Elena jumped from her chair and ran to her room, without asking for details. Henrie materialized from the kitchen, as only Henrie could do.

Pete, facing the way Elena had run, spoke to both Henrie and Mike. "Let's give her a little time to process this. I don't mind waiting for a while for her to calm down. Then I can help her get home."

Pete checked his watch. He thought about twenty minutes had passed when she ran down the stairs, out the door, and into an Uber that had just pulled up.

"Huh," said Pete.

"Ditto," said Henrie.

Mike asked, "Is this how it was supposed to go?"

As they left, Pete asked Mike, "Is she on television or something?"

"Not that I'm aware."

"Huh. She sure looks familiar."

22

Annie got to the Café when lunch rush was on the downswing for locals and the upswing for lonely hearts. She gave Tiger Lily a hug and whispered, "Grandpoppy is fine."

She noticed Cyril behind the hostess stand and turned to look. She saw Pete and Ray at a table in the middle of the room.

She accepted a cup of coffee from Trudie and told her how Sam and her mother were doing.

Trudie said, "I'll send a text blast to let everyone know. What should I say about visiting?"

"Tell them not now. Thanks."

Annie went to Pete's table and asked to join them.

"Sit. I only have a minute, though. I have an interview in ten minutes. An important one. And a few after that."

"Murder, property damage or something to do with lonely hearts?"

"Property damage, then murder. It will probably have something to do with lonely hearts. How's Sam?"

"New hip. Some embarrassment. He'll be fine, thanks."

"Did you hear about Elena?"

"Henrie sent a text. I understand she left town already."

"She did. I can't shake the feeling that this had something to do with this club."

"When Henrie sent the text and told me about the explosion, I couldn't help but think about the translation of her name."

"What?"

"Elena said that in her parent's home country, Elena means 'torch'.'"

"What home country are you talking about?"

"I'm guessing Russia."

"Her last name isn't Russian."

"Long is probably an Americanization of their original name. And another thing, she had just hooked up with a guy. That's so sad. It was going to be a Hearts On Fire success."

"Who is the guy she hooked up with?"

"Fritz, the super spy."

"Super spy?"

"Don't ask."

"Now I remember where I saw her. Her picture was on the website as the monthly something."

"Monthly Flame."

"Yeah. Dorian's picture was there, too. Could be, if anyone was looking for either of them, or searching the web for keywords…"

"Pete! You're a conspiracy theorist, pure and simple."

"I just have a mind for details, and I have to go."

Pete left, taking Cyril with him. And Tiger Lily?

Annie ran to the door. "Tiger Lily, where are you going?"

They were nearly at the door to the police department. Tiger Lily stopped, turned, waved her tail at Annie, and followed Cyril into the building.

Pete registered the presence of Tiger Lily but didn't have time to deal with it. The people scheduled for an interview waited in the lobby.

"Mr. and Mrs. Evans. Thank you for coming. Give me just a minute, and I'll…"

Tiger Lily had jumped to the reception desk, to the bookshelf, then down to the head of Mrs. Evans. She held the wig with all four paws, claws digging in. Mrs. Evans held on to the wig with both hands, but Tiger Lily wiggled just enough to make it fall backwards and off her head. By the time Pete got to the screaming woman, he was looking at someone whose short, blond hair was held in place by a net.

"Pleased to see you again, Mrs. Emerson."

Mem waited on the freckled redhead. "Can I get something for you? Perhaps tea?"

"Sure."

"What kind do you want?"

"Um, I don't know."

"I'll make something for the season."

Mem brewed a Ceylon black tea flavored with chocolate and strawberries. When she served it, the woman said, "Do you have a minute to talk?"

"Certainly." Mem got another cup, sat down and poured. "Can I help you with something?"

"I hope so. Maybe. I feel so…well…did you hear that one of our Hearts On Fire members had a tragedy in the family?"

"No, I didn't."

"Elena – she was staying where I am, at the Inn down the street – her parents were killed last night."

"How awful. What happened?"

"I heard it was an explosion, and it's being investigated as murder."

"How dreadful for her."

"I'm wondering if I did anything to, um, cause it."

"What?"

"I saw Mike in here with his computer. I figure maybe he was smarter than Travis. I figure he found the Trojan."

Mem said nothing.

"My name's Peggy, by the way. I put the Trojan there. I did it to mess with Travis, but…well…."

"Do you think we should continue this with the police?"

"I think that wouldn't be a bad idea."

Mem pulled her cell phone out of her pocket. She dialed the number of the police department and got Marco.

"Marco, I'm in need of an officer at CyberHealth."

"We're pretty busy here, Mem."

"You'll want to make time for this."

"Mem, really…"

"You. Will. Want. To. Make. Time."

"Okay. I'll leave Pete to his interviews and be right over."

Pete nodded to Marco. He had read the note, pressed against the door's window. "Mem has emergency."

For the first time, Pete wondered if the moon was full. No, that was a couple of weeks ago. There's a new moon now. Why are all the crazies out?

He turned back to Charlie. "Tell me again, everything you remember about losing your pin."

"Well, I had it on when I got to the buffet and dance, because Mike, the new guy, was checking everyone. I had it on before I left, because I went to the restroom and saw it in the mirror. After that, I don't remember."

"Where did you go after that?"

"To the winery. Mike introduced Thad and I, and we went together."

"When did you realize it was missing?"

"When I dressed for the Monday evening event. I looked all over for it, and couldn't find it."

"What about Thad? Did you ask him if he saw it at any point of the evening?"

"I didn't think to do that."

"Do you have a number for him?"

"Yes."

"Could you ask him to meet you over here? Please don't tell him what it's about."

"What if he asks?"

"Tell him your purse was stolen."

"Why?"

"Sometimes, when people are asked a question and don't have time to think about it, the truth pops right into their heads. If he has time to think about it, he'll imagine seeing it, and he could be wrong."

"Okay."

She sent a text and received a response right away. "He'll be here in ten minutes."

"Great. Wait right here. I've got to do a couple of things."

Pete went to the front room and looked down The Avenue. Marco was coming from Mem's shop. He escorted a redhead, one of the lonely hearts, probably. What was up, now?

He looked down at Cyril, who looked back.

"You did a very good thing today, Cyril. Thank you for bringing the head detective to the interview."

Cyril opened his mouth, and his tongue came out.

Marco reached the door. Pete stood aside while they entered. "This is Peggy. She has a story to tell us about Trojans and Russians."

Pete smiled and nodded his head. "Get the statement started, and as soon as I finish with this, I'll be in. Well, as soon as I finish with a couple of things."

A Marsh Haven deputy was at the door. "You got a transport?"

"We do. The couple in holding is charged with arson and felony mischief."

"From those winery incidents?"

"Yep. Do you need our help? We've got interviews piling up."

"You need more officers."

"Tell that to the Town Council."

"I might do that."

Pete gave him the keys to holding and held the door open for another man. "Are you Thad?"

"I am. Is Charlie okay?"

"She is. I need you to come with me, please."

Pete led the way to the interview room and opened the door. He gestured that Thad should sit beside Charlie.

"Your purse was stolen?"

"No…"

"Let me do this, Charlie."

"Okay."

Pete turned to Thad. "Neither you nor Charlie are being accused of doing anything, but it's very important that you listen to my questions and answer them as honestly as you can. Do you understand?"

Thad nodded his head. A sweat broke out on his forehead.

"Saturday night, you met Charlie at the buffet/dance. Do you remember seeing the heart pin on her?"

"Yes."

"What was she wearing?"

"Um…" Thad looked up and to the left. "She had on black slacks and a silk blouse, red, with big white flowers."

"And where was the pin on her blouse?"

Up and to the left again. "On her right shoulder, on top of one of the flowers, like it was the center of the flower."

"Good. Do you remember going to the winery?"

"Yes."

"You're sitting at the table, drinking a glass of wine. Look at her now. Is the pin on her blouse?"

Thad looked up and to the left. He raised his arm as if picking up a glass of wine and closed his eyes, relaxing into the memory. "No. It's not there."

"Can you pull up a memory of the last time you saw it?"

Thad closed his eyes, looked around in his memory again, and said, "I remember seeing it when you came back from the restroom, then right after that, we put on our coats. We walked to the winery, we took off our coats, and it wasn't there." He opened his eyes again.

Pete asked, "What kind of a coat do you wear, Charlie?"

"It's right here. It's a cape."

"So it's possible, if it came loose, it could have fallen to the ground?"

Both Charlie and Thad nodded.

"Good. This has been very helpful. Thad, I have to ask, why is your memory so good?"

"I'm an accountant. We have to remember things. Like today, we remember things we don't even remember."

Pete pulled Marco out of the interview room. As Marco brought him up-to-date with the story, Pete made notes. He pulled a sheet of paper out of his notebook and handed it to Marco on his way into the room.

"Warrant, rooms, Elena, Dorian, Travis, guy named Fritz."

Marco nodded and left.

23

Brian entered the foyer. He had a cat carrier in one hand. He put Simon on the floor and walked to the dining room, expecting to see Henrie in the kitchen.

Instead, Henrie called from the second floor. "Good afternoon, Brian. Can I be of assistance?"

"Oh, hello, Henrie. I just came to tell you when we plan to move out."

Henrie was at the bottom of the steps. He noticed Kali and Ko approach the cat carrier. "Did the sale of the house go through?"

"It did. Everything's looking up. Pete made an arrest, we have investors, and the house will be in our possession by the first of March."

"Wonderful. We can keep the room available to you for as long as you need."

"The first of March is fine. Most of our things have been in storage. We have certainly appreciated the room and everything about it, particularly the lowered rate."

"It is always worth it when good people move to town. Even better when a business opens. Our miniscule investment will reap benefits in months to come."

Brian turned to look at the cat carrier. A large, orange, long-haired cat sat quietly on top. Simon hissed and growled.

"I thought Simon would get along with your cats. I'm disappointed he doesn't. I hoped they would visit the winery."

Henrie said, "This is not one of ours. Trust me. When they visit, everything will be fine."

Kali and Ko approached Simon carefully. They stopped a respectful few inches away and stretched, forelegs toward the case, back legs away, and tails straight out behind them.

Whiskers twitching, they sniffed.

Simon leaned forward in the case. He was not afraid, merely curious. Like his hostesses.

He knew something about Kali and Ko. He smelled them in the room. And other cats. He had been wanting to meet them, but his humans had not thought it important.

There was one cat he did not want to meet, and the scent of that cat was in this room. He hissed.

Kali and Ko jumped back, turned and almost ran into Honey Bear. They hissed, too, then ran to the library.

Honey Bear walked to the carrier, pawed at the door, hopped to the top and lay down. His fluffy tail hung down in front of the case, blocking Simon's view and imbuing the case with his scent.

Simon continued to hiss, adding some growls to the mix.

Suddenly, the tail was gone. Simon was stunned to silence. As Brian picked up his case and turned to go, Simon saw the tall man holding the orange cat. His opinion of the tall man rose.

Tiger Lily gathered the cats and led them home. She wanted to tell them of her great success with Pete's arrest.

They arrived to find Kali and Ko having a bitter argument with Honey Bear. The argument was filled with words the girls had been taught better than to use.

Tiger Lily and Mo waded in. Tiger Lily pushed Kali to the ground and Mo pushed Ko. Mr. Bean and Sassy Pants tried to take Honey Bear to the ground, but didn't succeed until Little Socks jumped into the mix, knocking all three of them over.

By the time Henrie got to the library, things were relatively quiet. Tiger Lily and Mo sat tall on two dilute calico rumps. Honey Bear was buried.

Henrie sighed. He knew what had happened. To be honest, he didn't know about the language Kali and Ko had used, but he knew the sentiment.

He looked at Honey Bear, whose eyes glared through layers of fur. "This is what comes of your high bearing, Honey Bear. I suggest you take your afternoon snack upstairs in the apartment. I will take it up myself."

The cats didn't get off him until they saw Henrie go toward the stairway with a small dish in his hand. Reluctantly, they rose, and Honey Bear stood. He shook his hair out and walked, regally, to the steps, up, and out of sight.

Tiger Lily sighed. *"When will he be out of our hair?"*

Kali said, *"We were meeting Simon, and he ruined it."*

Ko added, *"He was going to be our friend. I bet he won't speak to us after this."*

"Maybe weze be able to fixted it. We coulds go up dere, to his room, and talks to him tru da door."

"He's not there now," said Kali. *"He left with Brian."*

Ko said, *"They're moving. They bought a house."*

"Trill!"

Kali interpreted, *"Now we'll never get to meet him."*

Tiger Lily said, *"I'll bet Mommy takes us to his winery sometime."*

"All of us?"

"Maybe one or two at a time. We'll all meet him. Sometime."

Kali spat, *"That dratted Uncle Honey Bear."*

Tiger Lily said, *"At least you cleaned up your language."*

Little Socks asked, *"Did I see you coming back from the police department? Without an escort?"*

"Cyril watched for traffic while I crossed. He would have jumped out to save me."

"You have to be careful crossing that street. It's good on The Avenue. Everyone watches out for us."

"What you duz over dere?"

"This is really great news! You know the people that were doing bad things to the winery?"

"The two couples that were really one?"

"Them! They came in disguise today, and Cyril took me over. I knew they wore wigs. I jumped on the woman's wig, held on for dear life, and I was able to wiggle it off."

"And that helped Pete?"

"Yes. He could prove they were the same couple. Cyril said short of them admitting it, something outlandish like that had to happen."

Kali and Ko said together, *"I wish I'd seen it!" "We should have been there!"*

Mr. Bean said, *"I could have done it, too."*

Tiger Lily looked at the strong little boy. *"You could have. And you could have done it more quickly."*

Kali and Ko said together, *"Did you hear about Elena?" "Elena's parents were killed!"*

Unfortunately, none of the cats had much information. Kali and Ko heard about an explosion and murder, but then, Elena was gone. They heard nothing else.

Little Socks asked, *"Did Mommy say how Grandpoppy is?"*

Tiger Lily nodded. *"She said he's okay, but that's all I know. I think he's still in the hospital."*

"Where's Grandmommy?"

"She's staying with him. She'll be back tonight."

They napped for a while, until Mr. Bean woke and said, *"It's Fat Tuesday. Do you think Mommy will let us go to Mo's?"*

24

Annie brought Nancy into the kitchen. Henrie had supper on the table. For two.

Nancy said, "Oh, don't bother setting a place for me, I'll make something…"

"Mom, this is for you and Henrie. Remember, I'm going to Mo's tonight for Fat Tuesday. Henrie wanted to do this."

Chris and Sis got to Mo's early, to get a table. He was able to get the large setting with comfortable chairs and coffee tables. It would also afford Annie a view of the entire bar, if she sat with her back to the wall.

Chris ordered two pitchers of aperitifs. One was French Monaco, pomegranate lemonade with an artisan beer. The other was Soul Train, tequila and cardamom with lime and grapefruit juice. Both were specially made for Fat Tuesday.

Pete and Janet appeared with Cyril, followed shortly by Ray, Cheryl and Jock. Clara arrived alone. Ramon was back on the road, playing in Chicago for Valentine's week. Laila, Annie's best friend and owner of the grocery store across the street, arrived next.

"Annie just got home with Nancy. She should be here any minute."

Chris said, "I expect her to bring the cats."

"All of them?"

"Probably not Kali and Ko. They don't like to leave."

Laila said, "Chris, you are becoming more and more like Annie every day. You're assigning thoughts to the cats."

"Not just thoughts. They have feelings, too."

Clara said, "I need a cat. Maybe if I had a cat, I wouldn't get so lonely for Ramon."

"A cat that gets along with big, matty-haired dogs," said Ray.

Cyril and Jock drooled. Sis said, *"Gracious. Fiamma isn't even here, and you guys go loopy."*

Jock said, *"She's beautiful."* Cyril added, *"And flirty."*

Annie walked in, pulling a wagon behind her. When she got to the table, the cats pushed their way out, opening the wagon's lid from inside.

Five had come. Chris was right. Kali and Ko preferred to stay home. And thankfully, Honey Bear wasn't interested.

Henrie opened lids on the fragrant dishes he prepared for Fat Tuesday. He toned down the spice for Nancy. She loved spice, but Henrie thought she should take it easy for the time being.

It was still fragrant. He served shrimp and grits, shrimp and sausage gumbo, hush puppies, and bananas foster for dessert.

"This is wonderful, Henrie. Did Annie tell you our surprise?"

"No. We have had no time to talk. What is it?"

"Sam and I are going to downsize. We're going to sell our house and buy a little one here in town. Greg found a darling home in Martha's neighborhood."

Henrie put down his fork. "That is wonderful. You will come for breakfast often, I hope."

"Well, not every day, but I hope we can. Often."

"Will your plans be on hold while Sam heals?"

"No, I don't think so. Greg made arrangements with a realtor to sell our house, and I've talked to Patti. She'll take a week off and pack for me. She'll know what to keep and what to sell or give away. She'll Skype me with any questions."

"Are you certain you want to do this without saying good-bye?"

"Certainly. I can let go."

"What about Sam?"

"He said it would be alright."

"It will not. Do not argue with me. I will hire a vehicle large enough to hold some of your things and comfortable enough for Sam to ride, when the doctor says he may travel. We will take at least a week."

"Henrie…"

"Do not argue. We will work it out. Your house will not sell overnight, and that will give Patti additional time to do what she must."

Nancy put her head in her hands and began to cry. Henrie let it go for a moment, then said, "You are home, Nancy. This, Chelsea, is your home."

Mike sat at the end of the bar closest to the door. He was visibly nervous.

George gave him a beer and asked, "Need help, Mike? Anything I can do?"

"Um, no…I'm kind of watching for two guys. Three."

"Which ones?"

"Nick, the big guy, the one that hit Dorian. Bob, the guy that lied to Tonya. I kicked both of them out of the club. They checked out of their hotels, but they still might show up and make trouble."

"Who is the third?"

"Did you ever see the guy that tells everyone he's a spy?"

"Yeah. Fred…no, Fritz."

"Him. If you see him, don't say anything, but call the Police."

"I'll let Pete know. He's in the back room."

Mike turned to look. "Oh, yeah. That's good. Okay, well, that's settled. I'll mingle."

Laila watched Annie's cats and the dogs mingle with the Fat Tuesday guests. Sis was getting the hang of it. She was learning who welcomed the approach of dogs and who didn't. Who was sloppy with their food and who wasn't. How to stay out of the way of servers as they made rounds with trays.

She, Clara and Annie sat where they could see everyone. And gossip. Clara asked, "Who are we watching for tonight?"

"I'd like to see if Fritz comes. He was seeing Elena. She's the one that had to leave town."

"I heard. Her parents blew up."

"Their house."

"You know what I mean. Oh, look. There's the woman I saved."

"Tonya. She's seeing Tom now. She met him yesterday at Sassy P's."

"He's not anything like Bob."

"No. Bob was on a mission to get money. This guy is looking for a commitment."

"Maybe better for Tonya."

"Maybe. Oh, look. There's one of my guests, Peggy. She's still with – what's his name?"

"Paul. She doesn't look too happy."

"No. She doesn't. She keeps looking over here."

"Did you wave?"

"She's looking in this direction, but not at me. She knows me. I can't stare. Who is she looking at?"

"Wait for it."

Annie took a drink and a picked up a baby crab cake.

Laila said, "Oh. She's looking at Pete."

"Is he looking back?"

"He is. It's not a friendly look."

"Unfriendly?"

"No, more businesslike."

"Huh."

Clara said, "Another one of your guests is here, the tall, pretty one."

"There's more than one tall, pretty one. The blond?"

"Yeah. And she's still with the pumpkin."

"Henrie told me that pumpkin gave her a wowzer ruby ring."

"Henrie said 'wowzer'?"

"More like 'very expensive and tastefully created.'"

"That sounds like Henrie."

Annie stood quickly and walked behind Pete. She pointed and he looked up. Laila looked to see who had been pointed out.

"Who are they?"

Clara told her, "The big guy, his name is Nick. He hit Dorian, you know, the guy that died, and the other one, he's the one I outed as a lying liar. I saved a woman that night."

Pete walked to the men as Clara continued her explanation. Annie sat down again. They watched as Pete showed them his badge.

"What's he doing?"

"This is a public place. It's not private to the club, just free to club members. He's telling them he's going to keep an eye out, and if they interfere with club members, he'll ask them to leave."

"It looks like Bob is leaving."

"But not Nick. He doesn't look happy."

"What's he doing? Where's he going?"

Nick made a beeline to a table in the middle of the room. It was set with appetizers on one end, sides and entrees on another. A large, colorful king cake was in the middle.

Nick moved like a bulldozer straight to the king cake. What happened next could possibly have been avoided if Pete had arrested the man right away. Or if Chris and Ray had made it to the table in time. Or if George had gotten over the bar just two seconds sooner.

But none of those things happened.

Tiger Lily cornered Cyril before he left. Pete was taking two men to jail. Pete needed Cyril's help, but she had to tell him. *"I heard the voice!"*

"What? Say it quick. I have to go."

"I heard the voice of the person that got the icicle!"

"Great! We'll talk tomorrow!"

Jock was leaving with Ray and Cheryl. Ray limped, favoring his right leg. He should have stayed out of the way of that foot. Jennifer was arguing that he should see a doctor, but Jock finally growled that she should just mind her own business. Jennifer didn't understand what he said, but she got the point.

Sis was beside Chris on the floor. At least he was finally sitting up. Marie had a cold pack to his eye, and Sis howled her disapproval. Mommy was there, too.

People were leaving the Tap. Tiger Lily couldn't see the person whose voice she had heard.

She called Little Socks and Mr. Bean over. *"Tell the others. We need to look for a short guy who's almost as round as he is tall."*

Before going to bed, Henrie sent a final text message. "Tomorrow cannot arrive soon enough." He watched it go and deleted it from his history.

Brian and Janet relaxed at Sassy P's. They had not had a night out for weeks, and tonight was special. They sat at the far end of the back dining room, so as to minimize contact with Jesus or Minnie.

They shared small plates of Fat Tuesday food: dirty rice, crab cakes, shrimp and grits, and colored pancakes topped with icing and sprinkles.

Janet said, "We should go to the hospital to visit Sam."

"Do you think he wants visitors?"

"We can check with Nancy first. It's kind of sad."

"What?"

"We're moving to town, and we've been so busy, the people we've connected with the easiest will be leaving soon."

Brian looked at Janet. "No they won't."

"What?"

"I saw Greg today. Nancy and Sam bought a house in town. They're moving, too."

"How nice! It will be like having parents nearby."

"Really nice, since ours have been gone for a while. I miss having that mature perspective."

Janet laughed. "We have a mature perspective."

"You know what I mean."

They ate a little, drank a little, and looked around the room. Janet said, "It's awfully busy in here. I expected everyone to be at Mo's for Fat Tuesday."

"It's good to know there's enough to go around. Do you think fine dining on Friday and Saturday will be enough?"

"I'm wondering about opening only one night a week. Maybe Friday."

Brian said, "Saturday is date night."

"Friday's the end of the week, the beginning of the weekend."

"We have plenty of time to decide."

Janet said, "We do. What about a name?"

"A name?"

"For the restaurant."

"I kind of like Chateau Simon."

"That's the name of the winery."

"We need to keep it simple. Easier to brand, keep marketing to a minimum."

"You're right. Oh look. There's Greg. Let's invite him over."

Greg was in the company of three other men. They sat at a table, but Greg approached the couple. He and his friends had been laughing from the moment they entered the winery.

"What's so funny?" asked Brian.

"Oh, you guys are gonna love this town. Next door, they're having a fight with king cake."

"Part of the entertainment?"

"Yes, but it wasn't planned. You picked the right place to come tonight. Is this a celebration?"

Janet said, "It is. Criminals captured – thank you for the help – investors secured, and new home purchased. We're good."

"Who are the investors?"

"A corporation, Great Lakes Wine."

"Great! How'd you get together?"

Brian looked at Janet. They hadn't decided on a cover story. He pushed ahead. "They said there was chatter on the winery circuit. They drove out and liked what they saw."

"Are you comfortable with them?"

"Yes." Brian thought quickly. He couldn't say very much, or the secret would be out. "They gave us the money."

Janet quickly added, "And they want to be silent partners. Even better."

"The best. Well, let me know if you need anything. Don't forget our closing appointment."

"We won't."

When Greg left, they breathed a sigh of relief. "We need a story."

Janet said, "We need names and faces."

"Maybe a Facebook page."

"Can we do that?"

"I think so."

Minnie came to the table to pick up drinks and take another order. She whispered, "Greg is telling his friends you have investors."

"Yeah. We blew him some smoke, but we need a story. We're going to make a fake Facebook page."

"Don't worry. I did that this morning. I got busy and was going to tell you tomorrow, but…go out and look for it and 'like' our page. I made it private, so nothing shows up. When we get some 'friends' and can make it look better, we'll do that."

"Okay. Let's talk later. Maybe you can come out…"

"No. Some morning, tomorrow or the next day, come around the back way and up to our apartment."

"Tomorrow."

"Good. Is ten okay?"

They nodded and sighed. Brian said, "Don't worry about that drink order. We're headed out."

As soon as the fight started, Jim stood, put cash on the table and escorted Liz out of Mo's Tap. His thought was, "I can't afford to be questioned as a witness." What he said was, "We don't need this. Come. I'll escort you home."

He knew he was taking a chance. It was not typical for him to stay in town once a job had been done. Then again, nothing was typical about this job.

First, the opportunity to finish the job presented itself early in the week. He saw the man, the perfect weapon was at hand, and some local gave him a way to throw investigators off the track.

Second, he found himself falling in love. Or something. Probably the or something. A beautiful woman needed his money as much as he needed something pleasant on his arm.

Third, if he left before the week was over, suspicion would fall on him. He did not think he could erase all evidence of his presence if the police started to take a look at him.

The best he could do at this point was avoid the possibility that he would be asked questions about an incident he had only observed.

Tomorrow, he would give Liz the necklace and earrings he had already purchased. They were waiting at the jewelry store, safely marked "sold." He had spent almost as much in gifts for her as he made this week.

Tomorrow night, he would ask her to marry him. Was it too soon?

No. Everything was going right for him. He was on a roll.

Felicity reached for her phone. She saw the text message, smiled, and deleted it from her history.

Liz got to her room, opened a bottle of wine, and sat in the overstuffed chair. She took a deep breath.

This man was different than any she had dated before. He had given her an expensive ring. He talked to her about the future. He had demanded nothing of her in return.

At least, not yet.

Friday, Saturday, Sunday, Monday, now tonight. He had walked her to her door, given her a sweet kiss on a cheek – although tonight it had been placed gently on her lips – and he left.

Tomorrow had to be the night. He would commit to something. He would ask to see her again, at her home, or at his, or somewhere else, or not.

They planned to spend the day together, at least from mid-morning to mid-afternoon. He promised something special.

It could be more jewelry. It could be – dare she think it – something as large as a car or SUV. Certainly not. But the ring on her hand could have paid for a small vehicle, certainly.

But tomorrow night, something would happen. Or not. Now, all she had to do was to decide – if a question was asked – what her answer would be.

25

The cats gathered underneath the detective table on Wednesday morning. The day, a day made for lovers everywhere, was dismal: very little sun and a combination of snow, sleet and rain.

The cats were beginning to show signs of SAD. For more reasons than just the weather.

Tiger Lily said, *"So, just to recap our glorious evening, most of the food on the floor was king cake and we don't like that; we didn't learn anything from any of the conversations; and we lost the guy whose voice I heard. Does that sum up our experience?"*

"You'ze forgettin' 'bout Chris. He gots a black eye."

"Trill...trill."

Kali translated. *"He said George got a busted lip, and Candice has to buy a new shirt."*

Mr. Bean added, *"And Ray hurt his foot. Or his ankle. Or his leg. Something."*

"That was pretty bad."

Ko asked, *"How many people did Pete take to that holding place?"*

"The big guy, Nick, and his friend, Bob."

"Yeah. I was surprised to see him come back in. They were pretty stupid."

"Yep." "They were." "Trill."

Mr. Bean said, *"It was a bad night, but we've done some good work this week. We took out the winery criminals."*

"Yeah, and we're pretty sure none of the people at the Inn murdered the guy. That's progress."

"We don't know how to find the guy that did."

"And we don't know how to tell Pete about the icicle."

Kali and Ko said together, *"Elena was our guest, too."*
"What about Elena?"

Tiger Lily asked, *"What about Elena?"*

"Can't we help find out who blew up her house?"

Little Socks pushed her forehead into the floor and said in a strangled voice, *"The last time I checked, we don't live anywhere near Omaha, wherever that is, and we don't have friends there."*

"Dat's too bad."

"Trill."

Tiger Lily said, *"Let's not forget that Henrie is leaving today, and he's probably going somewhere with Felicity."*

The cats grew silent.

Henrie poured coffee when Brian and Janet arrived for breakfast. "Good morning. Did you sleep well?"

"Yes," answered Janet.

Henrie was too polite to accuse her of lying.

Brian said, "It's nippy out there today. What do you have for a cold winter morning?"

"I made chai spiced winter porridge today, to go with eggs and bacon and gingerbread French toast."

"It smells good. What's in it?"

"Oats, spices to mimic chai tea, maple syrup, spiced pecans, and pomegranate seeds. I added chopped firm, ripe bananas and chia seeds."

"The worst thing about moving into our own home will be missing breakfast at the KaliKo Inn."

"You are always welcome to visit."

"We'll bring a bottle of wine each time."

"Thank you. I will look forward to it."

"How's Sam today?"

"He is anxious to leave the hospital. Nancy left a while ago to spend the day."

"I hear they're moving to town."

"One can scarcely keep a secret in Chelsea for long."

Pete was on the phone with Detective Miller. "I think we have some information for you. Are you in front of a computer?"

"I am. What do you want to show me?"

Henrie gave him the web address of Hearts On Fire. When the detective found the site, Pete said, "See that picture? That's her. Did she ever show up?"

"She did not. This is the same photo we have of her, so I know we're looking at the right person."

"I got a warrant and searched her room. She left most of her luggage when she left town. She also left her credit cards and cell phone. We checked with Uber, and they say they dropped her at the regional airport in Marsh Haven. We've checked all the airlines. No one by that name purchased a ticket, and no one recognized her photograph. This is a small airport."

"So, what are you saying?"

"I have more. One of the Hearts On Fire members put a Trojan on the organizer's computer, and she received money from a Fritz Falcone for any information she could get on Elena. She gave him the last name, the town, and a guess on the ethnic background. We're pretty sure he passed that information on to someone who followed through."

"You're kind of out there in left field, Pete. What pushes you there?"

"Her nickname, Torch. A simple word search on Google would pick that up. The fact that this Fritz fellow is gone. He left town without checking out of his hotel, and he left his cellphone as well. And my sixth sense. You need to check into your dead family's Russian connections."

"You know, I talked to the state police about you. They said you were whacko."

"They said that about me?"

"Well, I think, to be honest, they said you always had theories out in left field, and that you solved more cases than anyone else they knew."

"So your interpretation of me is 'whacko.'"

"Yep. I'll run your theory up the flagpole and see what we can find out."

"Send me the paperwork, and I'll pass on everything we have on Elena and Fritz, including what we got from the rooms."

Brian and Janet put their cards on the table. Brian said, "We want to honor your wish to stay silent, but in the short time we've been here, we've learned there is no way a secret can be contained in this town."

Janet added, "That's both a positive and a negative. We're looking forward to being a part of this community, but...I don't see how we can keep your names a secret."

Brian took over. "We can make this fake page, and put fake pictures on, and we can add things every now and then to make it look good, but...it's going to fall apart. And then all of us will have lost the trust of the community."

Jesus and Minnie sat back and looked at one another. Jesus took a deep breath and said, "You're right. There's one way we can save this. We can tell a little lie. The story could be...." He looked up and to the right, thinking.

Minnie picked it up. "I know. We sent a front person, so you didn't know it was us. After the deal was finalized, we introduced ourselves to you."

Janet said, "I like it. But what about selling our things at Sassy P's? What will the other wineries think?"

Jesus said, "We formed the corporation to make the investment. We'll make that known to everyone, and we'll be upfront about the silent partnership, that we have no decision-making power."

"And that we have the same deal with you as with everyone," added Minnie.

Jesus said, "And we'll put all of that on our new Facebook page."

Annie hung around the Inn later than usual. She sent the cats to work, but found several excuses to be in the library, in the kitchen, on the all-season porch, back in the library….

Henrie used the back kitchen door when he put luggage into the Inn's car. Annie knew this because she was spying.

Henrie finally said, "Annie, do you want to ask a question?"

"No, Henrie. No. I just hope you have a wonderful date, um, night, um, I want you to have a wonderful time. Can I do anything for you? To help JoJo, maybe?"

"I believe she is ready for anything. She will arrive mid-afternoon to prepare and set out afternoon canapes. She plans to sleep in the basement suite, and the breakfast menu is set."

"Okay, then, I guess I'll go. Have a good time."

Henrie didn't like to keep secrets from Annie, but he needed to know where he stood with this woman before talking to her. He did not want another disaster like his last romance.

As he pulled onto The Avenue, he saw Brian and Janet coming down the back steps from the apartment above Sassy P's.

He had been correct. Minnie and Jesus were the silent partners. Henrie hoped fervently they found a way to let the secret out.

He turned right onto Main Street and right again into the alley behind Annie's businesses. He executed a perfect three-point turn and stopped, facing Main Street again. Before he came to a stop, Felicity was at the door, luggage in hand. She opened the back door, put it in, jumped into the passenger seat and turned to him.

With a brilliant smile, she said, "Let love begin!"

Annie got to the Café to find everyone in the weeds. Already. Tiger Lily sat on the hostess stand, stiff, unmoving. Seeing Annie, she erupted into meows and yowls.

Trudie said, "Annie, I know you don't go to the kitchen, but please, go to the kitchen! They need someone to tell them what to do!"

Annie went to the kitchen and found pandemonium. And trash. She said, "I'm taking the trash out, then we're going to take a deep breath and start over!"

She pushed open the back doors, two heavy bags in her hands, and lugged them to the bin. She pushed up the lid, threw in one bag, then the other. The bin sheltered her from view. She was sure Henrie didn't see her. Nor did Felicity.

She had been right.

She didn't know whether to rejoice in their happiness or worry for them and for her own businesses.

Henrie and Felicity were off to enjoy Valentine's Day together. And she couldn't tell anyone.

Pete decided to look at one last thing before going to the Café for lunch. Once again, he pulled out Travis's computer, the one found at the Ace Hotel.

He found Fritz Falcone's file and looked through the information.

He lived in Buffalo, New York. He listed the Rand Corporation as his employer. That was probably a fabrication.

On a whim, he looked up the Rand Corporation. They did not have a facility in Buffalo, but a company called Rand Capital Corporation did.

Pete looked at other items: marriages and divorces (none listed); children (none listed); home (stated a home was owned on Boston Avenue).

Pete sighed. There was no need to waste time on this. It would go to Omaha. This was their case, not his.

As Pete closed the computer, his eye was drawn to a date on the top right hand corner. Date of Membership. According to the file, Fritz didn't join until mid-January.

Pete smiled to himself. Fritz, or someone for whom Fritz worked, spent time every now and then searching keywords, looking for people. And they found Elena.

Maybe he would pass that insight on to Omaha. They might not catch it.

Then Pete had another thought.

26

Gema had thought twice – no, three times – about getting extra help for Wednesday, but she was glad she had done it.

Ben, dressed in his finest millennial duds, light blue denims, a bold horizontal striped t-shirt and red sports coat, helped two couples try on rings. She worked with three other couples. She sold a ruby necklace and earring set, an emerald tennis bracelet and a diamond brooch with earrings. And that was just during this hour.

So far, no one had special-ordered anything. Her investment in stock had paid off.

On occasion, she heard Frank's cash register ring up a sale, but she didn't have time to look.

No one left for lunch. Frank called Mr. Bean's, and Isabel dropped by with soup and sandwiches for everyone. She said, "Everybody's strapped today. We were all busy for breakfast, now lunch. And Felicity is gone."

Gema laughed. "This would be a day for Henrie to step into the Café to cook."

From the far corner of the jewelry counter, Ben said, "He can't. He's gone, too."

Gema and Isabel stared at him. Gema finally said, "Where is he?"

"Don't know. I only know that JoJo is taking care of things at the Inn this afternoon and tomorrow morning."

The women looked at one another.

Isabel said, "You don't suppose…"

"No…couldn't be…"

"But it's so unusual…"

"Is it possible?"

Gema remembered the floating diamond solitaire pendant in platinum. The one Henrie special ordered. The one he picked up last week.

Pete and Cyril stopped at the Café to pick up a to-go order. Cyril waited while Tiger Lily jumped down.

"I heard the voice. I don't know his name, but he's almost as round as he is tall."

"Could it be a guy named Jim?"

"I don't know. Who's Jim?"

"Pete can't find out. He pulled Mike in this morning and showed him the picture."

"If he doesn't know anything about him, why does he think he's the one?"

"He checked the dates that people joined the club, and this guy joined in January. Like he joined just to find someone."

"Does Pete know anything about him?"

"He's seeing some woman from the Inn, Liz."

"That's right! I saw him there, too!"

"But you didn't hear his voice?"

Tiger Lily thought about it. Slowly, she said, *"He came in and looked at her, then pulled something out of his pocket – it got all the women excited – and then he held out his arm and they left. He didn't say anything."*

"It sounds like Pete is on the right track, then. But we still have to tell him about the icicle. If he can't find a murder weapon, he won't be able to make an arrest."

Annie had not expected to see Geraldine in town until the Hearts On Fire group left. Geraldine surprised her.

"Hi, Geraldine. Table for one, or are you meeting someone?"

"I'm meeting Greg."

"He's here. He's in the back room."

"I'll find him; thanks."

Annie wondered...but she got busy again.

She seated locals. She seated flaming hearts. She couldn't stop saying or thinking "flaming hearts," after correcting almost everyone else.

She delivered drinks, bussed tables, carried orders from the kitchen to the dining room. She greeted friends; she seated some of her guests from the Inn.

She had to hold onto her jaw when she seated Liz and her frumpy pumpkin, Jim. First, she saw the ring Henrie had told her about. Then she saw the necklace and earrings. Henrie had described the ruby as heirloom. The ruby in the necklace looked the same as the ring. According to Henrie, it was very expensive.

Geraldine was leaving as she seated Liz and Jim. Annie noticed Geraldine staring as well. She must have liked the look of the jewelry.

The lunch rush didn't end until mid-afternoon. When it did, finally, Annie sat, rubbing her calves with her feet. She gratefully accepted a cup of Rose coffee. Trudie sat with her, putting her feet up. Tiger Lily joined them, flopping on the table like a dead fish.

Georgia came in, saw them and sat. "Sorry I'm late."

Annie asked, "Are you late?"

"I am. I wanted to be here by one to get dinner ready. Does anyone have a reservation count?"

Trudie said, "Given the rocky start, I was surprised that we have twelve couples."

"Twenty-four people. Great. I can do that in my sleep. Almost."

"Plus Chris and me. Do you have all the people you need?"

"I do. And Isabel is running the dining room. Our servers are going to be dead tired when they finally get home tonight."

"They are. Speaking of that, I'll send them home to get some rest. I'll finish up the dining room."

Annie had just wiped down the last table as Isabel came in to set the room for Bon Vivant. Essentially, that meant putting bright linen cloths and napkins on the tables. She would set the lighting on low, and tonight, she would turn the sound system on to contemporary lovers' music. Whatever that meant. Annie didn't ask.

She looked at Tiger Lily. She slept on top of the hostess stand, either too tired or too lazy to walk around and "help."

Isabel said, "It's lover's night tonight, Annie. Are you going to have any energy?"

"I'm the last person to worry about Valentine's Day, Isabel. It's my least favorite holiday."

"Why is that?"

"The hype, the build-up, the false expectations of a perfect love. So many people have the idea that their Valentine's Day should be as perfect as what they see on television."

"Well, you're right about that."

Annie picked up a red linen cloth and fluffed it over a table. Isabel said, "You've done enough. Go home."

"Alright. You twisted my arm."

Annie grabbed her coat and stopped at the hostess stand. "Ready to go, darlin'?"

Tiger Lily yawned, stretched, sat up and cleaned her right paw. And then, Geraldine walked in.

"I know you're closed, well, you're getting ready for tonight, but can we talk?"

Annie sat at a table, cup of coffee in front of her. She had moved from Rose to Chocolate Cherry. At this point, she dreamed that a shot of one hundred proof cherry cordial had been added.

No such luck.

Pete was at a back table with Geraldine. Four of her cats, wondering why she was late in going home, had arrived and they sat, with Tiger Lily and Cyril, under and on top of the table.

Oh, how she wished her cats could talk to her. Tell her how this conversation was going.

It appeared another guest was embroiled in a crime, if only peripherally.

Geraldine had not been looking at the ruby jewelry worn by Liz. She had been looking at the washed-out pumpkin of a man that had given her the gift. Jim.

Annie played the conversation in her mind again. Geraldine said, "They followed me out of the winery. I turned around to look at them just as I took off the pin. This man, he had the eyes of a snake, saw me look. He stared at me, and my blood ran cold. I don't know why I didn't remember it. Anyway, he was still looking at me when I turned and tossed the pin into the flowerpot. I was so shaken, I stood there for several seconds, not focusing on anything, and then I saw Dorian through the window. Well, you know the rest."

Annie stopped her. She put Geraldine at a table and called Pete.

Tiger Lily sat close to Geraldine on top of the table, listening carefully to everything she said. At one point, she gazed down at Cyril.

"Pete's getting good. He already knew who did it, without our help. And now he's building a case."

"He still needs to know what the murder weapon was."

Tiger Lily looked outside. The day had produced a new crop of icicles. She looked back at Cyril.

"If you can get Pete to the Inn, and get him to the porch, maybe I can figure out a way to show him the icicle. Maybe he'll understand."

While Annie sat at the table, her cell phone rang. It was JoJo. Before she could answer, she saw a frantic woman run from the alley behind her building toward the police department.

"Pete," she said, "You've got another problem. I think…"

A gunshot rang out, and the woman went down.

27

A car raced up the street, around the police department and out of town while Pete ran outside. Marco came from inside the department, and the sound of the ambulance starting up at the end of the street added to the cacophony.

Annie missed JoJo's call, so she called her back from the safety of the Café.

"What happened? Farah was shot!"

"This man came, he demanded…well, she heard him, and she came out of her room, and he…he chased her back and…and…she must have run out that back door."

Annie remembered Farah was in the downstairs guest room, the one that had an exit to the beach and the back garden.

"Calm down, JoJo. Take a deep breath. That's right. Now another. Keep breathing. I can't leave here now, until Pete says I can go. I saw it happen. I'll get someone there to stay with you."

Annie tried to think. Too much was happening. She couldn't remember who was where, and she didn't want anyone to have to walk near the police department.

She practiced what she preached and took two deep breaths. She could think again!

She called Minnie, who answered on the first ring. With no greeting, Minnie said, "What happened?"

"There's trouble at the Inn. The man that fired the shot is gone. JoJo is there alone, she's scared, I can't leave…"

"I'm on my way."

Annie knew her first responsibility had to be to her guests at the Inn, especially since Henrie was gone. Darn him! Why did he have to fall in love, or whatever it was he had done!

She fidgeted and fretted until Marco came in and asked what she had seen. She told him, with as much detail as possible, then ran to the Inn, five cats in hot pursuit.

Farah heard her husband in the foyer. He was browbeating that young woman, the one that was filling in for Henrie. Apparently Henrie had a love life, after all. This young thing didn't deserve what her husband was dishing out.

She opened her door and strode down the hall. When she got to the foyer, she stopped. Something was wrong. She called him by name, and he turned. His eyes. Something was wrong with his eyes.

And then he pulled a gun.

Farah turned and ran back to her room, not thinking. She got there and locked the door behind her, took a frantic look and noticed the back door. She had opened it once, when she arrived, and she knew it went to the beach.

Hesitating only as long as he got to the door and started pounding, she ran to it, out, and veered left around the back of the building. She ran past the back of the carriage house, and then up the alley behind the long building. She remembered the police department was just past this building.

If she could just get there….

Pete opened the interview files from Dorian's murder. Several pages in, he found what he needed. Contact information for Farah's husband, a description, and a screenshot from the Skype interview.

He called an all-points bulletin to the state police, giving them what he had, checked with Jennifer and Marie before they drove away in the ambulance, and drove his car to the Inn. He needed to stay nimble today. No walking down the street this time.

He and Cyril entered to find several people in the foyer.

Nancy was back from the hospital. He hoped she had been in the carriage house when this took place.

Brian and Janet were there, consoling her.

Annie sat in a deep sofa in the foyer, next to Minnie and JoJo. JoJo was curled into Minnie's lap. She was still sniffling, but it appeared as if she had calmed.

The rest of Annie's guests stood in a huddle near the stairway. He recognized Liz, and of course he knew Peggy. He didn't remember the name of the third one. He had seen her around town and had seen her picture attached to her computer file. Tabitha, maybe. No, Tiffany.

Annie asked, "How is she?"

"Hit in the shoulder from the back. She lost a lot of blood, but the sisters say she'll be okay. Who can tell me what happened?"

"You need to start with JoJo, if she's able."

JoJo nodded, sat up and followed Pete to the dining room. She turned at the doorway and looked at Annie, her eyes still red with tears.

Sniffling, she said, "You might want to give the guests something. I made two kinds of rumaki for the first time ever. They're in the kitchen. Henrie thought they would be good for this afternoon."

She sniffed again, rubbed away a tear, and turned back to the dining room.

Nancy didn't look well. She was worried about Sam, probably not sleeping well, and making plans to move from a house she'd lived in for over forty years. She was moving away from the town of her birth. The town in which she had lived all her life.

Many years ago, before Annie was born, her father had asked that she leave and move to Chelsea with him. She didn't then. Eventually, the marriage disintegrated and they divorced. And now, she was leaving home for Chelsea.

It was too much for Annie to consider now. She moved to her mother to give her a hug.

Nancy said, "Don't worry about me, dear. Take care of your guests."

"You're one of my guests, Mom. Let me take care of you."

"Tell you what. Why don't you let this nice young couple take care of me, if they're willing, and you do what you need to do."

Janet sealed it by putting her arm around Nancy's shoulders. "Come on. We'll go to the carriage house, and Brian will get us something for supper."

Annie turned to her guests. She took a deep breath and asked, "Is everyone okay?"

They stared at her, then turned, one by one, and went to their rooms.

She sank back into the sofa beside Minnie. "What else can go wrong?"

"Well," said Minnie, "you might start hearing a rumor about Jesus and me, so I may as well go ahead and tell you now."

Tiger Lily heard Marco coming up the porch steps. She ran to the porch and jumped as high as she could, landing on his chest.

Reflexively, Marco held her, and from his grip, she climbed to his shoulder. He was in the perfect position, if only she could get him to turn around.

She reached as high as she could over his head, and he turned, to see what had her attention.

She shifted just enough, so that she could continue to reach for the large icicle that formed in the same corner as before.

He moved closer, so she could touch it, and she did. She touched it several times, looking at Marco as if to say, "Let's play!"

Marco reached out to touch it. It was strong, firm.

He grabbed it and pulled. Ice that had gathered at the base of the icicle shattered to the ground.

Tiger Lily recognized the sound. If only Marco was smart enough….

It took him several seconds, but then he said, "That's it!"

He put Tiger Lily on the floor of the porch and ran into the Inn, icicle in hand. "Pete! Pete! I know what killed him!"

Tiger Lily huffed in pleasure. Marco would never know that she had provided him with a sixth sense about the weapon.

28

Chris arrived to take Annie to dinner. She asked if they could go to church first.

"On Wednesday night?"

"It's Ash Wednesday. You don't mind being seen with me if I have a smudge, do you?"

Chris held her coat. Annie had dressed up. She wore the purple dress she had purchased for the grand opening of Bon Vivant. It was a strapless, shimmery, low cut, tight-fitting dress in tones of rose and lilac. And even in the sleet, she wore strappy, glitzy purple sandals with a two inch heel.

"If you had told me, I would have worn my tux. I still have the tie and cummerbund to match this dress."

"I didn't realize I was going to wear it. I just thought, well, after this week, I wanted to look and feel special."

"You always look special."

"Stop it."

They walked up The Avenue toward Soul's Harbor, leaving Sis with the cats.

Annie knelt in front of Pastor Teresa, received the ashes, and walked with him to the restaurant.

Chris whispered, "No one is as fancy as you tonight. Strapless dress and a smudge of ash on your forehead. You are my dream come true."

"I'm glad, because someday I'll be dust. Will you still care?"

"I will. Until dust do we part."

Chris noticed that Isabel had everything under control tonight. She and Mike greeted couples as they entered the Café, all dressed to the nines.

He counted twelve tables. "Who's here?" he asked Annie.

"You don't remember anyone?"

"Too many people. I'm leaving that up to you."

"Well, there are Liz and Jim. See those rubies?"

"Pretty. Do you want some?"

"No. No. No."

"Okay. Who else?"

"I haven't gotten the names of everyone, but I know a few. Let's see…Over there is Peggy, and her beau is Paul. Would you like to be called my beau?"

"What?"

"Never mind. Anyway, things seem a little tense over there. This may be the end of the line for them."

"Why would you say that?"

"Look at his face. He's trying to be polite, but his jaw is so tight he might need a dentist."

"You're right. Is she the one that stirs the pot all the time?"

"Yeah."

"Maybe she stirred it a time too many."

After a brief silence, Annie said, "There's Tiffany, with the man of her dreams, Brent. How about man of my dreams? Do you want to be called that?"

"Are you sure that was ash she put on your forehead?"

"Oh, there. The couple that just walked in. That's Charlie. She got off to a rocky start, but she's finishing strong. I think his name is Thad, and look at the diamond on her left hand."

Servers delivered aperitifs to those who had ordered. Chris gave the Charleston Fizz – grapefruit and elderflower liqueur with tarragon – to Annie, and he had a Negroni.

"Oh. There. In the corner. Tonya and Tom. She has a new tennis bracelet. I think it's got emeralds and diamonds."

"Are you sure you don't want me to get you jewelry like that?"

"Really, I don't need it. I love what I have."

Chris sighed. "What are you going to do with your time when Bon Vivant closes?"

"I think I need a vacation."

"Really? I know this campground…"

"Camping? I don't think so. Did you order wine?"

"I did. It will be here with the shrimp cocktail."

"Good. I'll bring you up to date. Are we deep enough in a corner that no one can hear us?"

"As long as we keep our voices down, yes."

"Geraldine recognized Jim, the round guy with Liz, as someone who may have taken the pin. You know, the heart pin that was in the dead guy's hand."

"Does that mean that he…"

"Don't know. Pete's not saying. Did you hear about the shooting today?"

"I did. I figured you'd tell me about it when you were ready."

"That was Farah, the woman that the dead guy was out with before he became dead."

"She shot someone?"

"No. Her husband shot her."

"I haven't kept up at all."

"You've been too interested in talking to your friends all week while I've done the hard, nasty work of spying on all of these flaming hearts."

"Hearts On Fire."

"Yeah, them."

"So, apologies to Farah, to whom I have been egregiously negligent, how is she?"

"Stable. Bullet wound in the back, through the shoulder."

"Where's the husband?"

"Long gone, I hope. I don't think he had any other business in town, especially since he knows her date is dead."

"How would he know that?"

"Pete had to interview him as a suspect. Or Marco. Someone interviewed him."

The shrimp was gone, replaced by cold cherry-raspberry soup and white chocolate raspberry scones.

Annie thought some more, then said, "And Peggy? The sweet-looking freckled redhead?"

"Yes…what about her?"

"She put a Trojan in the lonely hearts database. She did it to mess with Travis…"

"Who?"

"Travis. Remember? The computer guy who was the coordinator…"

"Oh, yeah, and George called an ambulance…"

"I think he was finally moved out of critical care…"

"Just to focus the conversation…the redhead put a Trojan in the computer to do what with Travis?"

"Mess with him."

"And did she?"

"She did, but worse than that, she got money from – do you remember the super spy guy?"

"Nope. She got money from him, though?"

"Yes. For information on that other guest of mine whose parents blew up."

"You mean their house blew up."

"Yes. Torched. Like her nickname. And now she's gone with the wind, and so is the super spy."

"Together?"

"Probably not."

The soup and bread plates were removed to be replaced with winter root vegetable pancakes and crab risotto.

Annie asked, "Did I tell you the murder weapon was probably an icicle?"

Chris took a deep breath. He looked up to the ceiling, decided nothing up there would be any more understandable, and asked, "Anything else happening?"

"Oh, nothing much. Jesus and Minnie are the new investors of the Chateau Simon Winery."

"No!"

"Yes. They thought they could keep a secret, and they formed a corporation called Great Lakes Wine."

"They…"

"Go out and 'like' them on Facebook. They're silent partners, but they had to go public before it blew up in their faces."

"Silent as in…"

"They don't say anything about how it's being run."

"That sounds like fun."

By now, Chris had filet mignon with garlic shrimp cream sauce and Annie dug into crab-stuffed lobster tail.

Chris said, "I'm going to miss this restaurant."

"Me, too. Oh, Mom and Sam bought a house."

"What?"

"They'll stay at the carriage house until their furniture gets here. They're downsizing, so they won't bring everything, but I think they're going to buy one or two antique pieces from Frank."

"Where's the house?"

"It's that cute little one across the street from Martha."

"Nice. How's Sam, by the way?"

"Cantankerous. He wants out."

They ate in silence for a while, until the cheesecake-stuffed strawberries arrived with snifters of brandy.

"What would you think if I called you my treasure, or the man of my dreams?"

"What is this about, Annie?"

"Everyone has a name for the person they introduce, like partner, fiancé, friend, kòkòt…"

"What?"

"Kòkòt. It's Haitian for sweetheart."

"Why don't you just call me Chris?"

"That's what Henrie said. Oh, that's probably the last thing."

"Do I want to know?"

"I don't know. I think Henrie and Felicity are dating."

Chris put his snifter on the table and stared at Annie, who was staring out the window into the darkness.

She finally said, "It's a secret. Don't tell anyone."

29

Annie rose early on Thursday to help JoJo with breakfast. JoJo was ready.

"Henrie said you were absolutely not to help, but if you would like, you can take things from the kitchen to the dining room."

Annie stared at her.

JoJo stared back.

"He insisted."

Annie shook her head and took breakfast meats to the dining room. The warmer was ready for them. All she had to do was put the dish inside. Useless. She was just plain useless.

JoJo came out with breads in one hand and something that smelled heavenly in the other.

"Henrie also told me to tell you that you are not useless. Not at all. You just can't cook. You can do lots of other things that none of the rest of us can do."

"Name one thing."

JoJo turned to look at her. "Well, you can…you can…. I know there are things you can do that we can't."

"Right. What did you make?

"Avocado toast."

"What's in it?"

"Avocado, bacon, brussels sprouts, goat cheese, parmesan cheese, some chopped orange, pomegranate seeds."

"And toast."

"Yes. And toast."

"Did you bring this recipe with you?"

"No. Henrie looked it up, and I thought it would be easy enough."

"I can't even make pizza."

"I was here that day. You can make great pizza. You just have to remember to take it out of the oven. I was kind of out of it yesterday. What was Marco going on about, something about an icicle?"

"They think Dorian, the guy that was killed, was done in by an icicle."

"How'd they come up with that?"

"Remember, the wound had an odd shape, and they couldn't figure out what it was. Then Marco was on the porch and saw an icicle. He just had a brainstorm and figured it out."

"Marco?"

"Yep."

"Not Pete?"

"Odd, isn't it?"

"Maybe he's developing that sixth sense that Pete has."

Annie wondered about that and looked down. Tiger Lily had just sat down on her foot.

Liz put her luggage into the elevator and pushed "down." She could have gone downstairs to get the cart, or asked that someone bring it up, but she was too excited.

He had popped the question the night before. He had actually asked her to marry him! And now, he would drive her home, where she could pack what she wanted to keep –

basically her clothes and jewels – and then she would live the life she deserved to live! The life she was born to live!

Annie must have heard the elevator, because there she was.

"Oh, Liz, let me get the cart."

"I don't need it. I'm down now."

"But you still have to get out to a car. Did you call a taxi? The airport shuttle?"

"Jim is coming. I'm getting married!"

"Congratulations."

Liz thought her wish was a bit strained, but maybe it was her. Maybe she was too excited and needed to be toned down.

Annie was already coming with the cart, and that young woman, Joe, or something. They were putting luggage onto the cart, and then the door opened. She turned, expectant.

Her smile went away. It was that Chief of Police. She couldn't get out of this town quick enough. It seemed there was murder and mayhem everywhere she turned, and the Chief was always here. It all centered on this Inn!

He was pleasant enough, but…oh, well. She was leaving. He was saying something. To her!

"Excuse me?"

"Are you expecting Jim to pick you up?"

"I am. He should be here any minute."

"I am here to extend his regrets."

"Excuse me?"

"His regrets. It seems he's quite taken with you, and he regrets not being able to leave with you today."

"Do I need to wait for him? Can he leave tomorrow? Why did he send you?"

"I'm sorry to have to tell you this, but I've arrested him for murder."

"What?!"

"Murder. He had a contract to kill Dorian. And he did."

"Dorian? A contract?"

"He's a killer, Liz. This wasn't his first, and unless we can keep him behind bars, it won't be his last."

"But…"

"I'm sorry. If you'd like to talk to him, he'll be in the holding cell for another hour or so, then he'll be transported to the county jail."

Liz found the back of a chair and walked around it so she could sit down. "I could kill him. I could just kill him."

"I reckon so," said Pete.

Liz barely registered the warmth of Peggy and Tiffany on either side of her. Mo jumped into her lap, offering his special kind of solace. She hugged him to her breast and sobbed.

Annie walked to the carriage house. She knocked on the door of the honeymoon suite and waited until Nancy came to the door. She looked better this morning.

"Did you sleep, Mom?"

"I did. Janet gave me something, and I slept like a baby."

"Hungry?"

"Yes! Breakfast at the Inn?"

"I think we need to leave the women alone today. They've had a hard week, and Liz is having a terrible morning."

"Don't tell me about it today. Let's only talk about happy things. Come on. Are we going to Mr. Bean's or Tiger Lily's?"

"You choose."

"I haven't been to Mr. Bean's for breakfast for a long time. Let's go there."

Mr. Bean had gone on to work and greeted his Grandmommy as only he could. He waited until she chose a seat, and jumped into a chair beside her. Annie picked a cranberry-cherry scone and a cinnamon roll to share and sat next to Nancy.

Nancy reached across the table and took Annie's hand. "I understand you know who the investors are."

"You knew?"

"Yes. Sam and I played matchmaker with them. Just like that flaming heart fellow."

"Hearts On Fire."

"Yes. Him. The one that does a good job. Or so I understand."

"He did do a good job. Unfortunately, I don't think he got paid for it, and now it's over. He seemed to really like it."

"He must have some other job."

"I'm sure he does. He'll probably just go home and pick up his life where he left off. Have you heard from Patti?"

"Yes. She'll be at the house in a couple of weeks. Did Henrie tell you he plans to take us?"

"Yes. He can have the week and more. JoJo said she'd be happy to fill in, and she's done well, considering."

"She handled herself well, that's for sure. I don't know that I could have stayed for the police interview, much less stay the night and push on with breakfast."

"She did more than that. Henrie gave her specific instructions on what I could and couldn't do and how to handle me."

Nancy laughed. Finally, Annie laughed about it, too.

"You need a vacation, dear."

"I do. Chris wants to take me camping."

"You should go."

"Not on your life."

Isabel came to the table. "Annie, do you have a minute for me?"

"Sure. What's up?"

"Well, since Bon Vivant will be closing, I wondered if George could use another cook. Someone to help Georgia. I assume Georgia will be promoted to Cookie's role."

"I think so, yes. He was waiting to get through the week. Have you talked to George?"

"I haven't. I wanted to make sure it was okay with you first."

"One thing you'll have to learn around here, Isabel. I'm the last person to know, the last person to ask, and the last one to make a decision. Everyone else takes care of it."

Isabel laughed. "You only think that's the case. Thanks, Annie. I'll talk to him."

George wondered what he was going to do about replacing Cookie. Promoting Georgia was a no-brainer, but he didn't have a strong second that he trusted.

Take this morning as an example. Here he was, taking out last night's trash. He had been surprised that no one he considered capable had answered the ad, or come in to ask about the position.

Several had come in. Several that would make good, competent cooks. But none to equal Cookie or Georgia. Maybe he would have to lower his standards. Or not. He would give it a couple more days. He could limp through the weekend. He could probably make it to the end of the month before pulling his hair out.

He threw the last bag into the garbage bin, reached back to close the lid, and heard a car.

He peered around the corner. No one should be back here on a Thursday.

Well. What was this? Felicity getting out of Henrie's car? Leaning through and giving him a kiss on the cheek?

George was stunned. This wasn't gossip material. This wasn't teasing material. This was flat-out, unforeseen, potentially calamitous material.

30

Annie left her mother and went to the Café. She had been there just a short while when she turned to a commotion at the door.

Juanita, a reporter for the local paper, and Dan Tapper, a despicable on-site reporter for the regional television station, WQVX, argued at the door for first dibs on Annie.

As the door opened, Annie heard Juanita say, "You don't have exclusive rights to anything!"

"I do. I'm always first on the scene!"

Annie sighed and tried to get to the kitchen before they saw her. She didn't make it.

Mike sat at the bar with a sigh. George put a beer and a menu in front of him. "Long week?"

"Sure was. I just worked through a vacation for which I paid dearly."

"I wondered about that. Any chance you can get a refund? And payment?"

"Maybe. Maybe even better. We'll see."

"What could be better?"

"Travis is out of critical care. Marco had to interview him about that Trojan, so he took me with him to the hospital. Travis is going to hang it up, so…I figure…what do I have to lose?"

"What are you talking about?"

"Travis said he can't afford to give me a refund or pay me, but he's going to give me his two computers and his files. I'm going to take over."

"Really? You're really going to be the new Flaming Heart?"

"Head Heart On Fire."

"Oh yeah. Right. Congratulations. Would you do me a huge favor?"

"Sure, anything, George. You've been my best friend here."

"I'm glad you feel that way. What I want you to do is to never, ever, ever, in a million years have an event like this in Chelsea. Never. Ever."

Annie finally escaped the Café. She and Tiger Lily went through the back door and came in through the kitchen at Mo's. She noticed one of the part-time cooks at the grill. Oh, right. Georgia was at the Café.

Weren't Henrie and Felicity due back soon?

George was surprised to see her come out the kitchen door. She scooted Tiger Lily out from behind the bar and sat on one of George's resting stools. He rarely got to use one, but they were always there.

George said, "Hey."

"Hey."

"What ya doin'?"

"Escaping Dan Tapper and his mad cameraman. If they come in here, I'll go to the kitchen."

"Noon news?"

"It's too late for that. I'd check the evening edition."

"Can I get you anything?"

"No...."

Silence.

George finally asked, "Is Henrie back yet?"

"I don't know. He should be back, or back soon."

Neither George nor Annie looked at one another's faces.

Finally, George said, "You know, it's hard to keep a secret in this town."

"You heard about Jesus and Minnie?"

George looked up. "What? What about them?"

Annie looked up. "You weren't…oh, I'm sorry. You haven't heard. They've invested in the new winery, Chateau Simon."

"Great. Was that a secret?"

"They were trying to keep it that way."

"They should know better."

"Yeah. So, what secret were you talking about?"

George took a deep breath. "I saw them come back to town." His eyes kept contact with Annie's.

She finally said, "I saw them leave."

"How long have they been dating?"

"Who knows? They were both out late one night last week. Valentine's Day had been planned for a while."

"Did they think we wouldn't find out?"

"Maybe. Maybe they'll tell us now."

"Maybe."

"Or not." Annie was silent for a moment, then asked, "Did Isabel talk to you?"

"She did. We'll work out a schedule after Bon Vivant closes."

"Is this a good thing?"

George showed some of his typical animation. "Oh, yeah. Imagine what she'll bring. Authentic Mexican cuisine, her baking skills – she learned from Daniela just like Carlos did – and she has a real style. She'll class up the joint."

"Will she and Georgia work well together?"

"Sure. Georgia is over the moon about it."

"By the way, did the social media stuff get out about Bon Vivant?"

"Yes. All channels. We're closed this weekend, and we will have one last weekend celebration and close for good."

The ambulance pulled up at the carriage house. Jennifer got out and removed a wheelchair from the back. She and Marie helped Sam out and settled him in the chair.

Nancy and Annie stood by, watching. Annie, trying to keep it light, said, "I expect Sam to work for his room and board until you leave. He has to go through every inch of the Inn and tell me if it's ADA compliant."

"He'll be happy to, dear. Say, did you take time to get your guests off this morning?"

"JoJo stayed to take care of that. The airport taxi was supposed to arrive around ten. I hope Liz hadn't cancelled her ticket."

Annie followed her mother into the honeymoon suite, watching as the sisters made sure Sam knew how to transfer from his chair to another and back, and from his chair to the bed and back.

"Mom, if he has difficulty, do not attempt to help him. Call me, or Henrie, or Hilly, or…"

"I know, I know. Anyone on The Avenue. Oh, I knew I was going to forget something."

She went to a catalog on the coffee table and flipped to a dog-eared page. "Here, dear. Show these to Henrie."

The page had photographs of cast brass signage for doors. They looked vintage, circa eighteen hundreds, the era the house was built. They were elegant. They were casual. They were perfect.

"Thanks, Mom. Speaking of Henrie, I need to see if he's back."

The cats gathered on the windowsill in the library to watch icicles grow.

Mo said, *"Trill,"*

"I agrees," said Sassy.

Little Socks asked, *"What did he say?"*

Kali and Ko said together, *"This is boring." "We could die of boredom."*

Tiger Lily said, *"You don't understand the concept. What you do is look at them in the morning, measure them, count them, you know, and then look at them in the afternoon. That's how you watch. You can't sit here and see them grow."*

Mr. Bean said, *"Why didn't you explain it to us?"*

"I did. A few days ago."

"I didn't remember."

Honey Bear said, *"I didn't listen."*

Little Socks asked, *"When are you moving back to the carriage house?"*

"When that horrible cat, Simon, leaves."

Tiger Lily sighed. *"That's almost two weeks."*

"I'm sure you will miss me. I would, if I were you."

Tiger Lily said, *"You aren't so bad. Just look. You're sitting here with us now, and actually talking to us."*

Honey Bear seemed to realize the truth of the statement. He jumped down and made his royal walk to the stairway. *"I prefer the windows upstairs."*

Sassy Pants watched him go. *"He'ze a royal pain in da butt."*

Tiger Lily sighed. *"Did we help Pete enough this week?"*

Little Socks said, *"He's getting pretty smart. He won't need us after a while."*

"It was great what you duz wit Marco. Marco duzn't knows it was you, but he gotted it right."

Kali and Ko asked, together, *"What's up with Mommy and Henrie?"* *"Are Mommy and Henrie mad at each other?"*

"What?"

Kali said, *"They're in the kitchen now, but they aren't talking to each other. Just sitting there, mostly."*

"Maybe Mommy's mad about Felicity."

"Why would Mommy be mad...?"

"Quiet!" said Tiger Lily. *"Wait here. I'll check it out."*

Henrie poured coffee and sat with Annie. They said little. The television was on. The early evening news would start soon, and neither wanted to miss it.

Tiger Lily padded in, jumped to the table and lay between them, slapping her tail every now and then.

Henrie rose and went to the refrigerator. He plated two kinds of rumaki and put them in the convection oven.

"She must have made twice as many as she needed."

"She didn't need any. I don't think they were touched."

"Why not?"

"Oh. Henrie, I'm sorry. I'm in my own little bubble. You've been gone, and you don't know what happened."

"Tell me."

"Poor JoJo. She had such a time of it, and she did it so well. I had Clara send her flowers with a personal note this afternoon."

"Do not leave me in suspense."

"Okay. Well, first, that husband of Farah's came back. He demanded to see Farah, but JoJo wouldn't tell him which room she was in. Farah came out, and that's when he pulled a gun…"

"A gun!"

"Yes. And she ran back to her room, locked the door, went out the back way and was almost to the police department when he shot her. He must have figured out she wasn't in there, and he ran out the front way. He must be a good shot…"

"How is she?"

"She's in the hospital. I sent flowers, by the way. She was shot in the back, through the shoulder. She asked that we pack her things. JoJo did that last night and sent them to her."

"Was he arrested?"

"He got away. Pete put out an all-points. While this was happening at the Inn, Geraldine was telling Pete that she recognized Jim. You know, Liz's friend?"

"The short, round man."

"Yes, him."

"The one with excellent taste in jewelry."

"Yep. By the way, he got a necklace and earrings to match that ring. At least Liz got them before he was arrested."

"What?"

"Pete arrested him late last night for the murder of Dorian."

"Liz's second date, Jim, murdered her first date, Dorian, so he could have Liz to himself?"

"No, Jim murdered Dorian because he's a hired killer. There was a contract on Dorian. He owed the wrong people a lot of money, and Jim was sent here to do the job."

"Chelsea hosted a contract killer?"

"Yep. He signed up with the club just to do it."

"Thank goodness it was not Geraldine. The town would have been miserable. They love to hate her, but this would have been too much."

"It's a funny town that way. Oh, speaking of the town, you know how secrets have a way of coming out?"

Henrie said nothing.

"Minnie and Jesus fessed up to being the investors in Chateau Simon, so that's all out in the open."

"Thank goodness. I did not want to have to keep that secret."

"You, too? Mom and Sam did the matchmaking and hadn't said a word."

"I did not know for certain. I merely pieced bits of information together."

"I've done that on occasion. For several things."

"I am sure you have. What else happened?"

"Well, Pete told Liz about the arrest as she waited for Jim to pick her up this morning. Turns out, Jim had asked her to marry him. Again, JoJo stepped up."

"Backing up to the murder, did Pete discover the weapon?"

"Marco did. I think Tiger Lily helped him, but he doesn't realize it."

Tiger Lily thumped her tail twice and purred.

"What was it?"

"An icicle."

"An icicle. I have no words." Pete paused. "I can say that quite a lot happened in my absence."

"Yep. Oh, Isabel is going to work for George after Bon Vivant closes, and that young guy, Mike, who took over the flaming hearts…"

"Hearts On Fire."

"Yes, them, he's going to take it over for good."

"Excellent. There is hope for lonely hearts everywhere with him in charge. I trust he will never hold an event in Chelsea again."

"George took care of that."

Henrie picked up the television remote. "The news is on."

The opening segment came with soaring music and photographs of on-air personalities flipping in and dropping out, or arcing in and dropping out, or fading in and dropping out. It always gave Annie a bit of a headache.

Anchor Charles Veritone filled the screen. "Good evening! Welcome to the Lake Region's good news station! We begin our good news with ace onsite reporter Dan Tapper. Dan was in Chelsea today. Dan, what good news do you have for us this evening?"

The screen changed to show Dan with the KaliKo Inn in the background. He wore his "I'm a bona fide reporter" face. "Hello, Charles. This is a taped-live segment. We caught up with Chelsea's news grabber, Annie Mack, at her restaurant..." Dan looked at his notes, "the Tiger Lily Diner."

Annie groaned.

"What you see behind me is the ka-LEE-ko Inn, a local bed and breakfast, also owned by Annie Mack. The Inn was the site of a gruesome murder last weekend, and details are finally coming to light. You may recall this Inn has been the scene of dozens of murders, rapes and kidnappings in the past."

Annie pushed her cup toward Henrie, who poured more coffee and a stiff shot of Kahlua.

Dan paused, looked away from the camera, and came back with his "this is impossible to believe" face. "The local police department is withholding information regarding this murder. They would have us believe they are confirming the murder weapon, but truth be told, this department has always been tight-lipped when Ms. Mack is involved."

Dan turned to be shown by another camera. This placed an up-the-street view of The Avenue behind him and gave him time to reconstruct his face. Now, he wore his "this is serious business, folks" face.

"And this wasn't the only crime. In a period of less than a week, in addition to the murder and in circumstances involving businesses owned by Annie Mack, there were several assaults, a possible poisoning, the shooting of a woman, and a connection between the ka-LEE-ko Inn and a house explosion in Nebraska."

Dan looked at his feet and shook his head, then looked into the camera again. He had used the moment to construct his "are we kidding ourselves" face. "When will this town come to its senses and rid itself of this queen of crimes?"

The screen dissolved to an incredulous Charles Veritone looking at a smug Dan Tapper. Behind them was the horrid photo of Annie from a previous run-in. Her face, which was in actuality moving to a cry of anguish, appeared to be that of a movie star monster. Her hair was straggly, sweat streamed from every pore, and cat hairs were stuck to her chin and chest.

Charles said, "Did I hear you correctly, Dan?"

Dan nodded earnestly. "Yes, Charles, it appears..."

"Did you just call for the assassination of a Chelsea citizen?"

Dan stopped nodding. "Uh, no, Charles. I merely suggested Chelsea should consider asking her to move..."

"That's not what it appeared you said, Dan."

"Certainly, that's what I said." Dan faced forward and said to someone, "Roll that part of the tape again..."

"I think we've seen enough. Let me ask you a few questions, Dan. You say the KaliKo Inn..." he pronounced it correctly, "is connected to an explosion in Nebraska?"

"That is my speculation, yes."

"Funny. I didn't hear that word, speculation. And then, you say the police department shields Ms. Mack from the crimes of, did you say 'dozens of rapes, murders and kidnappings'?"

Dan cleared his throat. "Well, again, Charles, the real numbers are speculation, because she is shielded..."

"Yes. Shielded by a police department led by a man with incredible arrest leading to conviction statistics."

"Again, Charles, this is speculation. This is an op-ed piece, which can lead to..."

"You are the roving news reporter. News, Dan."

"I'll give you some news, Charles. In some respects, the town has come to its senses. The crimes have forced the closure of the Bone-VIE-vent Grille. That's news."

Charles Veritone faced the camera. "To Ms. Mack and the people of Chelsea, including their fine police department, let me say that I had no control over the showing of that video. The control lies with Mr. Tapper's father-in-law, the owner of this station. I hope you will accept my personal apology for the heinous lies that were told here tonight. It is possible this will be my final broadcast. But for now, Felix, what's happening with the weather?"

Tiger Lily herded the cats upstairs. *"Mommy's in the news again with that bad man. We have to take care of her."*

"Did Henrie say anything about Felicity?"

"Shush."

Annie had already turned off her telephone. She had no plans to touch a computer tonight. Before Henrie got the Inn's landline turned off, one call came through. It was Jenny, her attorney.

"I'm going to file an injunction tomorrow. Please don't stop me. I'm going to file, then I'm going to sue the whiskers off them."

A beaten Annie almost whispered, "What good will it do?"

"I can make them stop maligning you, the Inn and any of your businesses. Most important, I can make them stop using that photo."

Henrie put a hand on her shoulder, then turned her in for a hug.

Darn him. She wanted to be so angry with him, but there he was, being her rock once again.

Annie dabbed at her eyes and pushed herself upright. There would be hundreds of calls, texts and messages with which to deal in the morning.

Annie lay in bed in the dark, surrounded by her cats. Even Honey Bear lay on the far corner of the bed. She didn't think she would ever sleep.

She heard the door open and soft steps come toward the bedroom. She didn't move. She continued to stare at the ceiling.

Soon, the bed rolled a bit under the weight of a giant schnauzer. Sis pushed a few cats out of the way to lay firmly against her side. Chris joined them, on the other side of Sis.

"I figure a dog is better comfort to you now than I can ever be," he said. "So I brought her over."

"Thanks."

They didn't say another word, and sometime after the moon was on the other side of the house, she fell asleep.

31

Chris and Sis were gone when Annie woke. She arrived downstairs in time to see eight cats finish little dishes of crumbled bacon.

Henrie was home, but he was not in the kitchen.

He came in through the foyer just as she walked out to look for him.

"Henrie, did you sleep well?"

"I did. I woke up quite refreshed. I just delivered breakfast to Nancy and Sam."

"It smells wonderful, as usual. What is it?"

"Croissant French toast with sautéed bourbon pears."

"Yum. Have you eaten?"

"I have not. Brian and Janet ate early and are gone. Will you join me in the kitchen?"

"I will."

Henrie said nothing as he served. They shared space in companionable silence.

Finally, Henrie asked, "Have you turned your phone on?"

"No."

"Computer?"

"No. Is the telephone on?"

"The message utility will answer calls today."

"Do you think I should check texts?"

"You will be surprised to see the percentage of people in your corner."

Annie changed the subject. "I asked Mom to have Sam test all the rooms – guest and common – with his wheelchair, while he is legitimately in it, so he can tell us if we're compliant."

"She said as much. We will tour the rooms today. She wants to see her quilts in the newly-painted rooms."

"Hilly cleaned them all yesterday. Since we have no guests, she probably won't be here today."

"We do not have guests coming until next week. We have a long weekend ahead of us."

"Great. Please don't make breakfast tomorrow or Sunday. Please really take it off. We can give Brian and Janet free meals at the Café tomorrow, and give them a coupon for somewhere else on Sunday."

"That is a pleasant thought. Perhaps I will, um, go somewhere for a couple of days. But only if you will be alright by yourself."

"I'll be fine. Go."

"By the way, here is the morning paper. You are page one. Again."

Annie looked at the headline and read the story. As always, Juanita got it right.

"Contract Killer Comes To Chelsea." The photograph on the front page was the Hearts On Fire website. Juanita focused on the murder. She noted the body was found in front of the KaliKo Inn, but clarified that neither the victim nor suspect were registered as guests. The Inn appeared to be a location of convenience.

High praise was given to the Chief of Police and his department for the arrest of a killer during a crime-filled week.

A smaller article announced the arrest of a couple from Marsh Haven for the arson and felony mischief of Chateau Simon. She noted the winery would be open for business in the spring.

An even smaller article noted the shooting of a tourist, in town for a convention, by her husband.

Nothing was said about an explosion in Nebraska.

Three column inches were given to a newsworthy announcement. "Due to staffing changes, the Bon Vivant Grille will host one more weekend and will then close. Plan to dine on haute cuisine on Friday or Saturday evening, February 23 or 24. Make your reservations as soon as possible."

Annie said, "I like her. I really like her."

Henrie said, "As do I. Tell me, what are your plans for the day?"

"The committee has a planning meeting for the block party. We'll meet at Mem's after morning rush. After that, I don't know. Chris and I will take a drive down the coast this evening. Tonight is Chinese New Year, and he made reservations at a great oriental restaurant."

"The weather will be perfect. We will warm to nearly forty degrees today, and the sky will be clear. You will see the stars."

"We will. I need a starry night."

"You need a vacation."

"I'm working on it Chris has proposed something that doesn't sound very vacationy to me."

"You only live once. Or so I have been told."

Pete and Marco went over their reports from the week of lonely hearts. "This has been quite a week," said Marco. "I don't think we've ever been so pressed."

"We have to ask the town council for more officers."

"How will you justify it?"

"Think of all the tax revenue they have from the hotels, restaurants, B&Bs. I think they're holding out on us. I'm going to take Joan to lunch one day next week and talk about it."

"Joan, the council president?"

"Yeah. If you can't start at the top, don't start at all."

"Say, Pete," started Marco, "I've been thinking about telling you something."

"What's that?"

"You remember I had the idea about the icicle…"

"Yeah, and the coroner agreed. It was a good call."

"That day, well, Annie's cat jumped up, you know, jumped high, so I caught her at my chest?"

Pete nodded.

"And then, she just kept wanting to play with the icicle. She kept reaching for it, so I took her closer, and all of a sudden, it came to me."

Pete smiled to himself. He hoped it didn't show.

"I know you and Cyril have a way of communicating. Do you think that cat put that idea in my head?"

Pete started to answer, and Marco cut in. "Oh, forget it. It was a stupid thought. Okay, what's next?"

Gema ran to Mem's. She thought she was late for the meeting, but it turned out she was not the last to arrive. She gave Annie a hug.

Annie said, "Thanks. Let's not discuss it."

Mem said, "Trudie and Felicity will be here in a bit. The lunch rush went long, because you're in the news again. It's Gossip City over there. Gema, help yourself to tea. We're celebrating The Year of the Dog."

"What kind of tea, Mem?"

"Roasted oolong, and I have walnut cake, too. Tiger Lily and Little Socks approved."

Indeed, Tiger Lily and Little Socks, sunning themselves on the windowsill, were still cleaning their faces. Cake crumbs were in evidence.

Gema looked around. Mem and Annie, Isabel, Candice, and Minnie. They were missing only Trudie and Felicity. She decided to jump right in.

"You know, for all of the issues the lonely hearts brought to town, I made out like a bandit."

"I saw some of that jewelry."

"It was beautiful."

Gema said, "I sold one of the prettiest pieces the week before."

Annie turned to look at her. "To whom?"

"To Henrie."

Everyone stopped what they were doing, which was eating and drinking. They looked at Gema.

She looked around the room. "It was a diamond solitaire necklace. In platinum."

"Whoa." "You're kidding." "Henrie?"

Gema looked at Annie. "Is he dating Felicity?"

Annie looked at her tea, desperately hoping a leaf or two would tell her something. Nothing spoke to her.

Candice said, "George saw them together."

Annie said nothing.

Gema said, "Well, it isn't our business anyway. But I guess we'll know if we see that necklace...."

Trudie and Felicity ran through the door. Trudie said, "Sorry we're late!"

Felicity looked around. "Only women? How did we end up with only women on the committee?"

"Just lucky," said Minnie. "Hey, did you hear about Geraldine?"

"What?"

"She put her house up for sale. It's mortgaged to the hilt, but it's one of the historic homes in the neighborhood. Greg thinks he can make a profit for her."

"What will she do then?"

"She's going to buy a small house, one of those in the neighborhood where Nancy and Sam are going to live."

"No!" said Annie. "She'll be Mom's neighbor?"

"Yes. And she has a job."

"Doing what?"

"She's a buyer for a major department store – I don't remember which one – that's beefing up its online presence. They're going to pay her to go everywhere! New York, Paris, San Francisco, Los Angeles, Rome. She'll go everywhere that fashion is hot, bring back the ideas, and they're going to make affordable knock-offs."

"So she travels, takes photos, maybe, and…what?"

"She sends the photos to them with ideas about material, colors, changes in design, accessories, and her impressions about audiences that will go for it."

"That's a perfect job for her. It's not nine to five, she gets to live her dream. And wear her wardrobe."

"She'll probably get deals on what they sell, too."

"Just what she needs. More clothes."

"Think she can keep her claws in?"

"I hope so. Long enough to keep her job, at least."

Felicity toyed with her earrings. Gema saw them. "Wow."

Felicity looked up. "What?"

"I know my jewelry. That's a pair of sapphire and pavé diamond halo stud earrings, in eighteen karat white gold, if I'm not mistaken. I never am, by the way."

Felicity smiled. "My new guy gave these to me."

"Your new guy?"

"Yeah. Thanks, again, Annie, for giving me the time off. I really, really had a good time."

"Are you going to say who?"

"No! For now, he's my secret, but you can admire the earrings all you want."

32

The February block party was on a Wednesday, the last day of the month. The temperature had gotten to forty degrees during the day, but by the time of the party, it was below freezing. A fine drizzle permeated the air.

On the second floor of the Café, Chris tied a colorful scarf around Sis. It was the scarf Annie had given her the day she was rescued. Fiamma wore a similar scarf. Tillie ripped hers off, over and over, until Isabel gave up. Cyril and Jock wore purple bow ties around their necks.

They walked through the crowd, accepting well wishes from all who attended. This was the Year of the Dog, after all. In Chelsea, they knew how to celebrate the important things of life.

The room was filled with animals. Tiger Lily and her siblings hosted all of their friends. Simon Finnegan and Oscar McMurphy had come with their humans, Holly and Jolly. Speckles and Daryll came with Martha, Georgia and Little Fred. Frank brought his haughty white cat, Claire, who canoodled all night with Honey Bear. Mo sulked.

Around the room were signs of good fortune regarding dogs. Tiger Lily read most of them to her friends. The ones she could understand. If she didn't understand it, she made something up.

They stopped in front of one. Tiger Lily read, *"If a dog comes to a house, it means good luck."*

Sis said, *"They don't have to write that down. Everyone knows it's true."*

Tiger Lily read another one. *"A dog's lucky colors are red, green and purple."*

Cyril said, *"That's why we have purple ties."*

Tillie said, *"That scarf had all the colors. I was luckier."*

"You took it off."

"I don't need to wear it to be lucky. Anyway, it was dragging the ground. I kept tripping over it. That's not lucky."

Tiger Lily saw another sign. *"This one says, 'dogs are loyal and kind.' I guess you are."*

Fiamma threw her hair in that fetching way she had and said, *"Always."*

Sassy Pants asked, *"What do dat one say?"*

Tiger Lily looked. *"Dogs are always ready to help others."*

Jock said, *"That's true."*

Little Socks pointed to another one. The words in that one were long and complicated. Tiger Lily said, *"The best friends for dogs are cats."*

Cyril looked at her. *"You made that up."*

"Did not."

"Did so."

"Did not."

"Read it again."

"Cats are the best friends for dogs."

"That's not what you said the first time."

"Is so."

Cyril huffed. *"I guess it's true. You're a pretty good friend."*

Mr. Bean said, *"It might have said something bad, and she was just making it better."*

"Maybe. Oh, well. Let's see if we can get treats."

Annie took a deep breath. The smell of oriental cooking – one of her favorite cuisines – permeated the room. She helped herself to noodles, the sign said they signified happiness and longevity; dumplings, signifying wealth – she took another, just in case – sweet rice balls, for family togetherness; tangerine and orange sections, representing wealth, again; and finally fish, representing prosperity. The fish was sea bass, steamed and served with scallions, ginger, and seafood soy sauce.

She asked Chris, "With so much of this food signifying family, wealth and prosperity, do you think I'm going to find a long-lost family member who'll give me millions?"

"That's probably exactly what it means."

"Thanks. I needed to hear something positive."

"Thinking of positive things, tell me again about this lovely outfit."

"I told you."

"I don't believe you. Or maybe I misheard you. Please, tell me again."

Annie wore a stunning red silk dress with a design of white snowflakes, ivory flowers, gold stars and black tree branches. It was fitted, but not tight.

"This was a gift from Geraldine."

"I still don't believe it. Have the two of you become friends?"

"No. But we're no longer enemies."

They stopped in front of the large screen television set which looped a traditional dragon dance for the new year.

"I still don't understand why we didn't do this ourselves."

"We ran out of time, energy and people this year. We decided to put our efforts into George and Ian's fireworks."

"When do they go off?"

"Ten o'clock. We didn't want to wait until midnight. We wanted the kids to enjoy it."

"Did George set it up?"

"No. Boone and his crew did that, with Ian's help. George gets to be the big guy, though, and set them off."

"How'd he get that honor?"

"They flipped for it."

"Have you decided to go with me in April?"

"You're serious about camping? I'm not a camper, Chris."

"Did you even look at the brochure?"

"Sorry. I haven't had time."

"We'll have our own cabin. It's modern, there are nature trails and a large lake. There are row boats, paddle boats. We can even rent wave runners if we want. It's private and pet-friendly."

"I got lost on the word 'modern.' Does that mean we don't have to use an outhouse?"

Chris laughed. He pulled a brochure out of his pocket. "Look. Full bathrooms, equipped with tub and shower. Do you want me to continue?"

"Yes."

"Bedrooms with linens, screened-in porches, outdoor grills, picnic tables, heat and air conditioning. And a fully-equipped kitchen. It says, 'everything but the food.' It will be like a large hotel suite in the middle of nature, with no other rooms in sight. Unless we want to take a walk."

"And the kids can come?"

"All of them."

"Not Honey Bear."

"Please tell me Honey Bear won't be at the Inn much longer."

"Actually, I think he's moving back to the carriage house tomorrow. And in a few weeks, he'll be several blocks away."

"In a house without cat doors, I hope."

"No cat doors. We'll probably only see him when we visit."

Charles Veritone got off the elevator. Until recently, he had never ventured to Chelsea. In the last few months, he had researched the town, its businesses, and many of its well-known citizens. He had time to do that now, since his employment with WQVX was terminated.

He now subscribed to the local newspaper, which had advertised the February block party. His research told him the parties were held on the last calendar day of every other month. The entire town was involved, including schools, businesses, civic groups and government organizations. The primary work was done by a group of business owners and staff on Sunset Avenue.

He also understood the core principles of the parties. Everyone was welcome. No one paid, unless the fee was absolutely affordable and could be waived. In recent times, the only fee that had been charged was for the party one year ago, on leap day.

Someone who received an unwelcome proposal of marriage had to pay to get out of it. If the fee was not paid, the unwelcome weddee need have no fear. The ceremonies were performed by unlicensed individuals. Even if not, one could argue that being chained to a post during the ceremony would amount to duress.

Donation jars and some activities raised funds for an assigned charity, which was different for each party. This month, the charity was St. Jude Children's Research Hospital.

The more he read about the town, the more admiration he had for names he ran across. Pete, the Chief of Police, and his constant companion, Cyril. Chris, the Officer in Charge of the Coast Guard Station, whose exploits during the massive winter storm had been massacred on air by Dan, the onsite reporter.

And, of course, Annie Mack.

He began regretting his part in her denigration several months ago, and he tried to softball Dan Tapper's reporting since that time. After the hatchet job two weeks ago, however, he snapped.

And now, he was unemployed.

A man approached him. Pete, the police chief. "Mr. Veritone?"

"Yes."

"Welcome. This is the first time you've been to a party, right?"

"Yes."

"Is this your first time in Chelsea?"

"No. As a matter of fact, my wife and I came to Bon Vivant on Friday evening."

"That's why I missed you. My friends and I made reservations for Saturday."

"Understandable. We tried to make a Saturday reservation, but it was full. I think we got the last two seats for Friday, and we sat with another couple. There was not an empty seat. As soon as someone left, someone else took their place."

"It was a great place to eat."

"May I ask, why did it close?"

"It was a stretch for Annie and her staff. The restaurant industry is tough, in general. Her staff is consistent, for the most part. One significant staff member moved out of town, and that gave her the opportunity to explore options. They chose to close."

"You say 'they.'"

"She has a talented team. A talented, engaged team."

"It's a loss for the community."

"We hope someone will pick up the slack by the time tourist season is in full swing."

"I'm here for a specific reason. Is Annie around?"

"She is." Pete pointed. "She's on the deck, watching some outside games on the park below."

"Games? In this weather?"

"Here in Chelsea, we're a hearty bunch."

Charles had not met Annie personally, but he had conversed with her via newsfeed on occasion. Those conversations had been adversarial.

Now, their conversations were through their attorneys.

Today, his attorney succeeded in separating his case from the rest of the station. His insurance company, in a surprise move, stated its willingness to offer a settlement for his part in the actions.

Charles approached Annie and her friend, Chris. They stood at the railing of the deck with several other people. Four large dogs, one terrier and cats that were moving too quickly to be counted were there as well. This, he had learned, was typical.

From behind her, he said, "Ms. Mack?"

She turned, stiffened, and softened. Chris stayed behind her, vigilant. She half-turned. "Mr. Veritone, I'd like you to meet my…Chris.

The men murmured greetings. Annie said, "I'm surprised to see you here. Should we be having a conversation?"

"I won't stay. I have permission from my attorney to deliver two items to you. One is a personal check for St. Jude."

He gave her a four figure check. She visibly went through five different emotions, touching down on her noncommittal stance.

"We appreciate this, and the hospital will certainly benefit."

"The other item is this. It's a copy of a letter that will be delivered from my attorney to yours. I understand that your acceptance of this piece of paper doesn't obligate you to anything. I wanted to be the one to give it to you."

Annie opened the envelope, took out a letter and read it, holding her face in the noncommittal stance. She looked up at him while handing the letter behind her to Chris.

"I appreciate the offer, Mr. Veritone. Really, I do. I'm sure my attorney will be in touch."

Charles said, "Good luck to you, Ms. Mack, in every endeavor."

He turned and left the building.

Chris said, "It wasn't a complete success. A non-family member didn't die but gave you hundreds of thousands."

Annie said, "Let's not get over-excited. This could go away for so many reasons. Just in case, though, let's have another dumpling."

Henrie joined them at the table. For the past two weeks, Annie had tried unsuccessfully to put the pain of being shut out behind her. Chris broke the ice.

"Henrie, she said yes."

"To…"

"A vacation in April. We're going camping."

Henrie choked on a spring roll. When he had it under control, he said, "Camping."

Annie looked at him. "You're the one that told me 'you only live once.'"

"I did not realize the living would include camping."

Chris said, "Keep an open mind. Here's the brochure. What do you think?"

Henrie studied the brochure, which included glossy photos of a cabin with polished wood everywhere: floor, walls, ceiling. Large windows and glass sliding doors allowed light to stream in.

Some of the cabins were small; some large; some historic; some modern.

"Which one will you rent?"

"I have a reservation for this one. It has an outdoor hot tub and a fireplace."

Annie said, "You have a reservation? You were pretty presumptuous."

"I had to get it. They go quick. If you had said no, I would have released it."

Henrie said, "This looks large enough for you and all of the children. And it is on the bank of a large lake. Lovely. When in April do you plan to go?"

"In the middle of the month."

"Oh. Well, then, I…"

"Henrie," said Annie. "What is it?"

"Well, I can change my plans."

"What plans?"

"I plan to take someone special home to meet my family."

On Christmas Day, Henrie had told Annie and Chris about his home and family. And his native country. He told no one else. Except, apparently, Felicity.

Annie said, "We'll make arrangements, Henrie. We can cover both of our absences. There are several people who can step up." But she was thinking about the Café. How would she cover it, as well?

"Are you certain?"

"Absolutely. We can put our calendars together this weekend and start talking to people next week."

"I am so very happy to hear you say this. I planned to speak to you this weekend, but it is perfect we have had our chat. Someone special is coming this way. I would like to introduce you."

Annie and Chris turned. A stunning woman, Henrie's height, with Henrie's lean build, and with matching coffee-colored skin, walked toward them.

No. She glided. She was very graceful. A diamond solitaire pendant set in platinum floated in the hollow of her throat.

Henrie stood. Chris stood. Annie couldn't move. "Collette, allow me to introduce Annie and Chris."

"Charmed." With one word, Annie pegged the accent. It was Henrie's.

For the rest of the evening, Annie watched Henrie and Collette work the room. He introduced. She sparkled. When they reached the food station where Felicity worked, she came from behind the table to give Collette a hug.

They were friends. Henrie and Felicity must have shared rides to meet their dates. That was all. She could finally breathe again.

And she could wonder about the man that gave Felicity those dazzlers.

The cats and dogs could barely contain their excitement. Who was that woman with Henrie? Would she be someone new in their lives?

Kali and Ko were so nervous and excited that little mews escaped their mouths. They tumbled off the cushions and paced in front of them.

Henrie turned, looked at them, and took the arm of the woman. He walked her to the cushions. Kali and Ko stood still on tiptoes.

Henrie made introductions. "Children, this is Collette, a very good friend of mine."

In a painfully slow rendition, Henrie introduced first the dogs, by name and breed and the humans they claimed for themselves. He then introduced the neighborhood cats in the same fashion.

Typically, when introducing Annie's cats, he started with the oldest, Tiger Lily, and made his way to the youngest, Mr. Bean. Tonight, he skipped right over Kali and Ko! They looked at one another, amazed. How could he?!

But then, finally, he looked at Collette and said, "If ever my affections should wander, it will be the fault of these two beautiful girls, Kali and Ko. I give you permission to be jealous of them."

Kali evidenced her appreciation by depositing cat hairs on Henrie's trouser legs. Ko beamed. It was very un-Ko-like.

The drizzle was cold enough that Annie had brought her cats in the covered wagon. Annie pulled it and Chris held the umbrella as they walked home, Sis ran ahead, then back, then ahead, then back, then ahead. She stopped and got onto her stomach, pushing her nose under a bush in front of the Inn.

"Do you think she found another body?"

"No. She'd be howling."

"You're right. What, then?"

"Don't know."

Annie got on her knees in front of the bush. From inside, she heard a plaintive "Meow."

She got closer. A cold, wet cat, small, but obviously an adult, crouched in the dirt.

"Come here, kitty," she said.

The cat hesitated only a moment, then rose and walked quickly to Annie, begging to be held.

Annie picked her up and stood. Chris held his umbrella over her as she did. They continued to the porch.

"She's obviously tame."

"It's a she?"

"Yes. I'll bet, when we get her dried off, she has the same dilute calico coloring as Kali and Ko."

"But Mo's long hair."

A gust of wind blew the cat's long, wet hair. Annie sang, *"Away out here, they've got a name for wind and rain and fire."*

Chris finished. *"The rain is Tess, the fire's Joe, and they call the wind Maria."*

"We can spell it with an 'o'."

"We?"

"And we'll add an 'h' at the end, so people know how to pronounce it."

"We?"

"We'll find her a home."

Thank You For Reading!

The family of cats and the author hope you enjoyed reading this book as much as we enjoyed writing it!

About The Author

Kathleen Thompson was raised on a small family farm in Indiana. She has an undergraduate degree in Sociology from Manchester College (now Manchester University) and an MBA from Indiana University South Bend.

In a variety of towns and circumstances, she served as a probation officer, parole agent and juvenile residential counselor before moving into administrative, marketing and fund raising positions in human service organizations. Ms. Thompson took a break from human services for seven years to own and operate a bar and restaurant. Let's be honest; that's another type of human service.

While making plans to return to her rural roots, Kathi and her mother discovered an injured kitten at the family farm. The kitten, whose face was a mass of injuries, decided to make Kathi her guardian. She wrapped herself around an ankle, purred like a V8 engine, and wouldn't let go.

Against the advice of her mother, Kathi took the kitten home and to a veterinarian. The vet diagnosed road burn serious enough to take all the fur from the left side of her face, and the kitten – Tiger Lily – eventually healed and took a huge piece of Kathi's heart.

Tiger Lily was joined by the rest, rescue kitties, all: Little Socks (thank you, Aunt Mary); Kali, Ko and Mo (thank you, Connie); Sassy Pants (thank you, Ant Sherwy); and Mr. Bean (thank you, Pulaski Animal Center). Recent arrivals Speckles (thank you, Tennille) and Moriah (thank you again, Pulaski Animal Center) have joined the cast but will not live at the Inn.

Tiger Lily's Café rattled around in Kathi's brain – there isn't much else up there – for all of the years since, sometimes as an actual café and sometimes as a book. It was less expensive to write the book.

Connect with Kathi and her family of cats at their website: www.tigerlilyscafe.com, or find them on Facebook: www.facebook.com/tigerlilyscafemysteries.

Find us on the web: www.tigerlilyscafe.com

Find us on Facebook: Tiger Lily's Café, A Mystery Series by Kathleen Thompson

Text to join: Emails are sent every two weeks. You can opt out at any time. LILYSCAFE to 22828 (You may also sign up for the emails from the website.)